Rab's voice was muffled by the towel that covered his face. He heard the door open.

There was an audible gasp.

"What's the matter?" Rab asked as he turned toward the door, still rubbing his eyes. He heard a little giggle.

"What the hell?" Rab blurted in shock. Lowering the towel from his face, he wrapped it quickly around his waist.

"You!" she said, recognizing him now that the towel had been pulled from his face.

"You're the woman from the street, aren't you?" Rab said, easily.

"I'm so sorry," Susanna said, backing away from the door. "I was told to come on up, I thought you were expecting me."

Rab paused for a moment, and then unexpectedly, he smiled at Susanna. It wasn't a smile of humor; it was a smile that was malevolent and strangely stirring. She felt a shortening of her breath and diffusing warmth. He began to lower the towel, inching it toward his private parts.

As if mesmerized, Susanna watched the slowly receding towel. She recalled her thoughts back at the lodging house when she found the imprint of his hand on her breast. As then, she felt a warm tingling in her body.

She knew she should turn away, but for the moment, she was powerless to do so.

This title is also available as an eBook

"Come on in."

SUSANNA'S CHOICE

SARA LUCK

POCKET BOOKS
New York London Toronto Sydney New Delhi

Pocket Books
A Division of Simon & Schuster, Inc.
1230 Avenue of the Americas
New York, NY 10020

This book is a work of fiction. Names, characters, places, and incidents either are products of the author's imagination or are used fictitiously. Any resemblance to actual events or locales or persons, living or dead, is entirely coincidental.

First Pocket Books paperback edition January 2012

POCKET and colophon are registered trademarks of Simon & Schuster, Inc.

For information about special discounts for bulk purchases, please contact Simon & Schuster Special Sales at 1-866-506-1949 or business@simonandschuster.com.

The Simon & Schuster Speakers Bureau can bring authors to your live event. For more information or to book an event contact the Simon & Schuster Speakers Bureau at 1-866-248-3049 or visit our website at www.simonspeakers.com.

Designed by Jill Putorti
Cover illustration by Jim Griffin

Manufactured in the United States of America

10 9 8 7 6 5 4 3 2 1

ISBN 978-1-4516-5042-6
ISBN 978-1-4516-5043-3 (ebook)

SUSANNA'S
CHOICE

Prologue

Five-year-old Susanna Ward stood in the middle of the wagon ruts looking at the mound of dirt. Even though the dirt had been pounded down to almost level with the trail, Susanna could see where the hole had been dug. Behind her, she could hear the hushed voices of the women who were preparing supper and the men who were all talking in low, somber tones.

Last night Susanna had been watching her little brother, Caleb, while their mother, Sophia, was helping the other women prepare beans, bacon, and biscuits for the communal supper. Her father, Byron, had been with the men as they smoked their pipes and chewed their tobacco and talked about the condition of the trail ahead—whether the oxen were finding enough forage, or which wheels needed grease.

Her mother wasn't helping cook supper tonight, and her

daddy wasn't with the men. Her little brother wasn't here either. First, it was Caleb, whose skin felt so hot it hurt her hand to touch him. And then, it was her mother. By noon, her father was vomiting, and then all three were dead and wrapped in blankets. Earlier she watched as, one by one, each member of her family was pushed into the single hole.

Now, all the wagons were gathered in a large circle.

All but one.

One wagon had been pulled away from the others, and it sat burning. That was the wagon that had brought Susanna and her family to this place. But now there was no wagon. And there was no Caleb. And there was no Mama. And there was no Daddy.

There was just Susanna.

"What do you mean, leave her on the trail?" Zeke Patterson demanded. Zeke was the guide the members of the wagon train had hired to lead them to California.

"We can't let her stay with us," Eb Johnson said. "She's got the cholera."

"She doesn't have cholera," Zeke said.

"How do you know she don't have it?" Eb challenged. "Last night Byron Ward was standing here talkin' to the rest of us just as fat and sassy as you please. There wasn't nothin' at all wrong with him."

"That's true. He was talking about the farm he was goin' to have once he got to California," Paul Coker added.

"And not only that, his wife was helping all the other women cook supper," Eb continued. "But where are they now? They're dead as doornails, lyin' in that hole out there in the middle of the wagon ruts. Them and their little one, who like as not is the one that caused them to take sick in the first place."

"That's right," Paul said. "I've always heard tell that when someone got took down with the cholera, most usually, why, it was a youngun what give it to 'em."

"Which is why we ain't got no choice but to leave that little girl behind when we start out in the mornin'," Eb said, continuing his argument. "Otherwise, the whole train could come down with the sickness."

"She hasn't shown any signs at all," Zeke said. "Don't you think with her ma and pa and little brother already dead, that she'd have the runs and be throwin' up by now?"

"And I say we can't take the chance," Eb insisted.

Zeke pulled out his pistol.

"Here! What are you planning on doin' with that gun?" Eb asked, holding his hands out in front of him, palms forward, as if pushing Zeke away. Several of the others looked on in shock as well.

Zeke was known to be handy with guns; he had shot an Indian only a week earlier, when he caught him stealing a cow. That was one of the reasons the wagon train had hired him as their guide in the first place.

Zeke turned the pistol around so that he was holding it by the barrel. He held it out, butt-first.

"Here's my gun, Eb. Why don't you just go out there and shoot her?"

"What? Why me?" Eb asked in shock. "I ain't goin' to shoot no five-year-old little girl."

"If we leave her here, she's going to die in a matter of days from starvation, or else be killed by a wolf or a bear, or be snatched by the Pawnees," Zeke said. "So, seeing as how she's going to die anyway, seems to me like the merciful thing to do would be just to kill her now."

"I ain't goin' to do it," Eb said, shaking his head in protest.

"No, but you're ready to leave her here to die."

"That ain't the same thing, and you know it."

"No, it isn't. Because what you folks are proposing is even worse. Any one of you got the guts to do the right thing?" Zeke asked, offering his pistol to all the others.

Nobody stepped forward.

"You are a fine bunch," he said with disgust.

All the men looked down sheepishly.

"Won't any of you take her on your wagon? Tom? You got three young ones with you. Doesn't seem to me like one more little girl would be that much trouble."

"I ain't takin' a chance with her poisonin' my family," Tom Harper answered. "If I was to take her with us, like as not tomorrow or the next day, it might be one of mine that's left all alone, and we'll be talkin' about this same thing all over again. Except for me, that is. I wouldn't be talkin' about it, 'cause I'd be dead."

"Are you people saying that nobody is willing to take the girl?" Zeke asked, his desperation growing.

"Why don't you take her, if you're so all-fired worried about her?" Paul asked.

"I'm the guide, remember? I don't have a wagon. I'm riding a horse and sleeping on the ground at night. And

I don't have a woman. Whoever takes her would need a woman to do for her."

"I'll take her for a thousand dollars," Gus Kirkland said. These were the first words he had offered to the discussion.

"A thousand dollars?" Paul gasped. "Who do you expect to give you a thousand dollars?"

"We've got fifty-nine wagons here, fifty-seven less my two," Kirkland said. "I figure you could sort of divide it up."

"Some of us have more than one wagon in this train," a man named Beechum said. "I got three. Are you planning on charging me for all three, even though they belong to just one man?"

"I figure those who have more than one wagon can afford it better than those that have only one," Kirkland said. "That's why it's only fair to charge by the wagon, rather than by the man."

"Why should we give you a thousand dollars?" Eb asked.

"Because I'm willing to take the chance with my wife and two children."

"He's got a point," Paul said. "And I'd feel a heap better inside knowing that we didn't just leave the girl standing out here. I'm more than willin' to put up my share. What would that come to?"

"Eighteen dollars a wagon ought to do it," Kirkland said.

"All right," Beechum said. "I reckon I'll go along with it, too."

"I can't give but ten dollars," one of the men said. "I barely got enough money to get us there as it is."

"I'll pick up what he can't pay," Beechum offered.

Some of the other more affluent wagon owners made up the shortfall for the ones who couldn't quite handle the whole amount. Within a few moments, the entire one thousand dollars had been raised.

Afterward, Zeke and Kirkland walked to the middle of the wagon tracks where Susanna was sitting by the grave. It was customary to bury the dead not alongside the trail, but in the wheel ruts. Such a practice, it was believed, would protect the bodies from both the Indians and the wolves.

Susanna was clutching a gutta-percha bag to her chest while silent tears streamed down her cheeks.

"Darlin', you will be going with Mr. Kirkland now," Zeke said.

"I won't ever see Mama and Daddy and Caleb again, will I?"

"You'll see them in heaven," Zeke said.

When the wagon train got under way the next morning, Gus Kirkland's wagons were the last two in the long file. His wife, Minnie, sat on a cross board in the family wagon, fanning aside some of the cloud of dust. Kirkland walked alongside, controlling the six lumbering bullocks with occasional flicks of his whip. The family wagon was the last in line.

"Why'd you take such a chance?" Minnie asked Kirkland. "She could give us the cholera and we could all die."

"It's not really that big of a chance," Kirkland said. "If she didn't catch the cholera when her family did, then that means she's got what they call the immunity. And some of that immunity might wear off on us, so that none of us can catch it either. Besides which, I got a thousand dollars for taking her on."

"A thousand dollars?" Minnie gasped.

"Enough to get a store started and then some," Kirkland said as he gestured toward his other wagon, which was driven by a young pioneer who wanted to get to California.

"Mama, how long does that girl have to stay with us?" seven-year-old Alice asked.

"We don't know yet," Minnie replied. "Until we can find some kin that'll take her, I suppose."

"I hope she stays a long time," Jesse said. He jerked on Alice's hair.

"Ow!" Alice complained.

"'Cause if she stays with us, I'll have two little sisters to tease."

"Susanna Ward is not your sister," Minnie said resolutely.

At the back of the wagon, paying no attention whatsoever to the conversation going on up front, Susanna wept silently as she stared at the spot where her mother, father, and little brother lay buried. The grave grew more distant behind them, but she kept her eyes on the spot until she could no longer see it. All the while, she continued to hold on firmly to the small bag.

New Orleans, 1866

There appeared in the New Orleans newspaper the following announcement:

Notice

> I, Pierre Bejeaux, in the firm belief that my cousin Rab Trudeau has brought dishonor to my family by his treasonous and despicable activities during the late War between the States, demand satisfaction from the cad and craven coward on the field of honor, at dawn, Saturday next, October 6, in the year of Our Lord eighteen hundred and sixty-six.

Rab Trudeau stood with his second, David DeLoitte, under the oaks at the foot of Esplanade Street. So many affairs of honor had been settled here that for years the term *meeting under the oaks* was another way to refer to dueling. It was just after dawn, and a blanket of diaphanous fog shrouded the cypress tree knees in the swamp, while the loud staccato tapping of a woodpecker echoed from a distant live oak tree.

"Maybe he won't come," David suggested.

"He'll come," Rab said.

Rab was tall, with black hair, dark eyes, a fine nose, and a strong chin. He was six feet four, with broad shoulders, muscular arms, a flat stomach, and narrow hips. This morning he was wearing fawn-colored riding breeches tucked into calf-high boots, and a white shirt that was open enough to show a patch of hair on his chest. It was also open far enough to reveal the last inch of a twelve-inch scar that made a purple slash from his right shoulder to just below his throat, the remnants of a saber cut from a Yankee officer.

"What makes you so sure that he will? I mean, if he would just stop to think about it, he has to know that he is no match for you, whether you had chosen pistols or swords."

"He'll come because he is a Trudeau."

"He is Bejeaux."

"As much Trudeau blood courses through his veins as does through mine," Rab said.

No sooner had Rab spoken the words than they heard the sound of approaching horses.

Rab's cousin arrived, along with his second, Lucien Thibodaux. There was also a carriage, carrying three young women and a doctor.

Bejeaux was two months older and five inches shorter than Rab. Like Rab, he had gone to war with the First Louisiana Regiment of Cavalry. Like Rab, he had been captured at Mobile, Alabama, and confined at Fort Gaines on Dauphin Island. Unlike Rab, Bejeaux did not escape.

"Why did you bring the women?" Rab asked.

"To humiliate you, of course," Bejeaux replied.

Bejeaux and his second dismounted, then all waited quietly for a moment until Monsieur Andre Garneau, the arbitrator, arrived on horseback. Dismounting, Garneau looked first toward Rab and David, then back at Bejeaux and Thibodeaux.

"Are both parties and their seconds present?"

"We are, sir," Bejeaux replied.

"I beg of both parties now to come to an accommodation, so that this duel need not be fought," Garneau said.

Neither principal nor second responded.

"Who brings the weapons?" Garneau asked.

Bejeaux signaled to his second, and Thibodeaux returned to his horse, where he took a polished walnut case from his saddlebag. Opening the case, he displayed two beautiful dueling pistols, resting in red-felt lining.

"These pistols belong to our mutual grandfather, Toulouse Trudeau. I think it is only fitting that since you deserted the army, you be killed by a pistol belonging to the very man whose name you dishonored."

"I did not desert the army, Pierre. I escaped from a Yankee prison," Rab said.

"To steal a ship and become a blockade runner," Bejeaux responded. "And you think that was the better part of honor?"

"I didn't steal the ship—I liberated it. It was one of Father's own ships that had been captured by the Yankees."

"And you brought shame to our family by using a family ship as a blockade runner to make money off the backs of the suffering South. Choose your pistol, you scoundrel."

Rab nodded toward David, who walked over to the open box being held by Thibodeaux. He picked the pistols up one at a time, then, assuring himself that both were charged with ball and powder, chose one. He brought the weapon back to Rab, who tested its balance, then nodded.

As Rab's second, David, made one final appeal to Pierre Bejeaux. "Monsieur Bejeaux, my principal, Captain Rab Trudeau, wants it well understood that if anyone in the family believes they are dishonored by any act committed by him, it is a matter of misunderstanding. It was not Captain Trudeau's intention to, in any way, dishonor the family Trudeau."

"Is that an apology, sir?" Bejeaux asked.

"It is a statement of fact," David replied.

Bejeaux stood quietly for a moment, motionless except for a little nervous tic in his jaw. Then he looked over toward the arbitrator. "Monsieur Garneau, I want it well understood that this is an affair of honor. If I am slain, I do not wish any legal action to be taken against Captain Trudeau."

Garneau nodded, then looked toward Rab. "And your response, sir?"

"If I am killed, I want no legal action to be taken against my cousin Pierre Bejeaux."

"May I offer a further word for Monsieur Bejeaux's consideration?" David asked the arbitrator.

"You may, sir."

David looked toward Bejeaux, cleared his throat, then continued, "I would like to point out to Monsieur Bejeaux that Captain Trudeau was three times mentioned in the dispatches for bravery and intrepidity under fire, above and beyond the call of duty. He killed four Yankee soldiers, with a pistol, from a distance of fifty yards, thus breaking a charge. And I would remind Monsieur Bejeaux that this duel is being fought from a distance of forty paces."

Bejeaux blanched visibly, then his jaw tightened. "Any heroic action on the part of Captain Trudeau before he deserted the army has no ameliorating effect upon his

later treachery. Does Captain Trudeau now admit that he
is a dishonorable cur, unfit for decent society?"

"I do not, sir!" Rab said in a resonant and commanding voice.

"Then, this affair of honor shall continue until its conclusion," Bejeaux insisted.

"I will now read article thirteen of the code duello,"
Garneau said, holding out a piece of paper.

" 'No dumb shooting or firing in the air is admissible
in any case. The challenger ought not to have challenged
without receiving offense; and the challenged ought,
if he gave offense, to have made an apology before he
came on the ground; therefore, children's play must be
dishonorable on one side or the other and is accordingly
prohibited.'

"Do you understand that and hereby commit yourself
to fight this duel to its conclusion?"

"I do," Bejeaux said.

"I do," Rab responded.

"Captain Trudeau, as you are the challenged, you may
establish the procedure," Garneau said.

Rab nodded at his second, who described the procedure for the duel:

"You will stand forty yards distant from each other.
The arm of the hand which is holding the weapon shall
be bent at the elbow, with the pistol pointing up. I will
drop a handkerchief, at which time you may lower your
pistol and fire."

"I object," Bejeaux said quickly.

"Sir, you can only withdraw the challenge. You cannot object to the procedure as has been outlined," Garneau said.

"I object to Monsieur DeLoitte dropping the handkerchief. How do I know he will not give his principal some sort of signal?"

"Sir, if Captain Trudeau does not kill you, I will," David said in a low and angry voice.

"Monsieur Thibodeaux, count off the distance," Bejeaux said. "Monsieur DeLoitte, sir, the objection is withdrawn with my apologies. You may drop the handkerchief."

Thibodeaux counted off the distance even as, from the swamp, they heard the growl of a cougar.

Garneau walked to a spot halfway between the two men, then stepped aside to be out of the line of fire.

"Assume the ready position!" he called loudly.

Both Rab and Bejeaux presented a side profile, then lifted their weapons to the ready position.

David dropped the handkerchief. Rab and Bejeaux brought their pistols down. Flame patterns erupted from the barrels, and a cloud of smoke wreathed each man. The explosive sounds of two shots rolled out across the swamp water to return in echo.

When the smoke cleared, Rab saw Pierre standing there, looking back across the space that separated the two men. A small, pained smile spread across his face, even as the front of his tunic began to turn a dark crimson.

He fell.

"Pierre!" Rab shouted in an agonized yell. Dropping his pistol, he ran toward his cousin, then knelt beside him. Pierre reached up to grasp Rab's hand in his.

The doctor rushed to the fallen duelist and opened his shirt. A large, ugly, dark red hole was pumping blood from the middle of his chest. The doctor took one look at it, then looked at Rab and shook his head.

"*La blessure est mortelle, Capitaine.*"

"Rab, do you remember when we were boys, how we would play in the cane fields?" Bejeaux asked, his voice weak with pain and from loss of blood.

"I remember," Rab replied in a choked voice.

"I was better at hiding than you were. I would hide, and you could never find me."

"You were much better. And though I tried very hard, I never could find you."

Pierre squeezed Rab's hand hard. "I . . ." Pierre stopped in midsentence and took one last, gasping breath. The pressure on Rab's hand relaxed and Pierre's eyes rolled up in his head.

"Pierre!" Rab shouted.

"He is dead, *Capitaine*," the doctor said.

The women began wailing loudly and Rab looked over at them. "What the hell did you expect to see? A *danse à deux*?" he shouted angrily. Then, with an impatient wave of his hand, he called to Pierre's second, "Lucien, get them out of here."

Thibodeaux nodded, then signaled to the driver of the women's carriage to leave the scene.

Rab stood up and looked down at the still body of his cousin.

"You had no choice, Rab," David said consolingly.

"That doesn't make it any easier," Rab replied.

Port of New Orleans, One Week Later

The ship *Falcon* had been built in the Laird's shipyard at Birkenhead, Liverpool, England. She was a combined steam and sail ship, with a screw that could be raised from the water to turn her into a pure sailing ship if needed. When everything was working well, she could make fifteen knots under a combination of steam and sail power. She lay alongside Pier Three at the Port of New Orleans. Rab, who not only captained the ship but owned it, was standing alongside it on the dock, talking to his younger sister, Emmaline.

"You don't have to leave Louisiana," she said. "It wasn't murder, what you did. It was a duel, and Pierre challenged you. Everyone knows that."

"Emmaline, if I were to walk into Rivière de Joie today, do you think Father would welcome me with open arms?"

Emmaline, who at eighteen was six years younger than Rab, looked at her feet.

"Charles was Father's pride and joy," Rab said. "You know that, in his heart, Father has wished it would have been me who was killed instead of his oldest son. I think it would be best for everyone if I leave."

"Will you write to me? So I can at least know where you are and if you are all right?"

"Do you think Father would let my letters get through to you?"

Emmaline looked dejected for a moment, then she smiled. "I know. Write them to me in care of Father Dupree. He will see to it that I get them."

"Captain!" David called from aboard the *Falcon*. "If we want to catch the tide, we need to weigh anchor."

"I'll write you," Rab promised, pulling his sister to him for a hug. Then, climbing the ladder, he stepped over onto the deck, giving one last wave to his sister. "Mr. De-Loitte, make ready in all respects to get under way."

With the sails reefed, and under steam power only, the *Falcon* pulled out into the Mississippi River and started downstream. In less than three months, Rab Trudeau would be in San Francisco.

1

When the curtain closed at Piper's Opera House on the stage presentation of *Uncle Tom's Cabin*, twenty-four-year-old Susanna Ward, who now called herself Susanna Kirkland, joined the rest of the audience in enthusiastic applause. Susanna, who was working for the *Virginia City Pioneer*, took notes:

> *High praise for Uncle Tom's Cabin performance, as it was not the usual threadbare and ill-played repetition so familiar with audiences over the last several years. Harriet Beecher Stowe's Uncle Tom of this night was a transfiguration. It was as though a new play was presented to the audience, a dramatization of a story read long ago and half-forgotten.*

The five-year-old orphaned child who had been rescued on the trail to California was now a resident of

Virginia City, Nevada. Immediately after the wagon train reached California, Gus Kirkland, the man who had taken Susanna in, opened a store. Even as the other pioneers struggled with prospecting for gold or putting in a crop, the entrepreneurial Gus Kirkland was making money, charging fair prices at his general store. He was so successful that when he realized the Comstock Lode could be richer than the California gold strike, he sold the store at a tremendous profit and moved his family, including Susanna, to Virginia City. Since arriving, his business had flourished.

The Kirklands had treated Susanna well, and as she was growing up, they provided for all her needs, even arranging for her to attend two years of college at the California College for Women. Throughout the entire time she had been with them though, there was never any question as to her status. She was not their daughter; Jesse and Alice were not her siblings. Minnie Kirkland had always been correct with her, even kind to her, but she was never nourishing or loving.

Susanna worked as a printer's devil for the *Virginia City Pioneer*, a newspaper that its publisher and founder, James Loudin, insisted was the best journal in the entire state of Nevada. Her ambition was to be a *collector of news*, a term that would later be changed to *reporter*. That wasn't likely to happen though, as Mr. Loudin did not think the subscribers would accept news that was written by a woman.

Gus Kirkland had been upset when Susanna went to work at the newspaper office. He expected her to work for him at the Kirkland Emporium, but that was not what Susanna wanted.

Monday morning when Susanna got to work, she grabbed the broom and began sweeping. As the printer's devil, this was considered part of her job, but little by little, she was convincing Mr. Loudin that she was capable of doing a lot more. He allowed her to set type, and he now conceded that she was the best typesetter he had ever seen.

B. D. Elliott was the newspaper's ace reporter, and he came in about fifteen minutes after Susanna had arrived.

"Tell me, Susanna, did you enjoy the play last night?" B.D. asked, as he took off his coat and hung it on a free-standing rack.

"Oh, yes, I enjoyed it very much."

"Did you now? Then, you should write a review of it for the paper."

"I did write one."

"Good for you. Show it to James. Perhaps he will print it."

"I asked him about it before I went to the play," Susanna said. "He said he considers play reviews and such to be free advertising, and he won't print something unless somebody pays."

"That sounds like our noble publisher," B.D. said as he sat down to write his daily article. "Black-heart money-grubber that he is."

"If you don't mind, I'm going to throw a few more sticks into the stove." Susanna wrapped her arms around herself and shivered. "I'm a little chilly."

"You'll get no complaint from me."

B.D. had once shared with her his concept of the power of the written word over the spoken word: "Words committed to paper are sacred. There is no telling but that someone, not yet born, will read my humble words fifty—one hundred—one hundred fifty years from now. Those are words of the pen. When I speak, they are but words of the tongue, and words of the tongue have power only until the last echo has silenced."

Susanna picked up one of the stories B.D. had finished and took it back to set the type. As she read the story, she groaned.

"Oh, Jesse," she said, speaking aloud but so quietly that no one could hear her. "When will you grow up?"

Disturbance of the Peace

This morning Messrs. Michael O'Malley and Jesse Kirkland appeared before Justice H. and were found guilty of disturbing the peace. Last week the two men commemorated the win of the horse *Morgan Chief* by a bit of celebratory imbibing. O'Malley fired a pistol through the front window of the Bucket of Blood Saloon. Kirkland, claiming that one bullet hole made but little impression in the glass, hurled a chair through same. Both had a square but expensive drunk, as Justice H. ordered the men to pay all costs as well as a fine, before setting them at liberty.

Susanna could well imagine Jesse behaving in such a manner. He had always been disruptive and rebellious, causing his parents a lot of grief and worry. So far, though, he had never crossed the line into real trouble.

Susanna knew that Jesse was good, at heart. As she composed the article, she smiled, remembering an incident from long ago.

She was eight years old, picking poppies down by the pond. If she could gather enough of them, she would make a bouquet, and maybe Mrs. Kirkland would let her put them in a vase on the sideboard that evening. She had picked ten of them, nice full blooms with long stems, and put them on her sweater.

Then Jesse and two of his friends came along, and as they almost always did, they began teasing her.

"Susanna, do you want a pet mouse?" Jesse asked, holding his hands cupped as if he had one captured.

"No, I don't want a pet mouse. They are nasty."

"How about some worms down your back?" one of the others asked, and he reached toward her as if he were about to carry out his declaration.

"No!" Susanna squealed, twisting away from him.

"Oh, look," the third one said. "See the pretty flowers?" He grabbed the poppies and began pulling them apart."

"Stop it, Darrel!" Susanna said. "That's a bouquet for Mrs. Kirkland!"

"Ha! It's not a bouquet now!" Darrel said as he ripped off the petals and tossed them into the air, allowing them to flutter down like falling leaves.

"Go away!" Susanna shouted. She picked up a dirt clod and threw it at Darrel, hitting him in the chest.

"Don't you throw clods at me, girl! I'll—"

Jesse stepped in between them and said, "Leave my sister alone, Darrel."

"What do you mean, leave your sister alone? You saw what she did. Besides, everybody knows she's not your sister."

"You two go on. I'll catch up later."

"Come on, Adam," Darrel said. "Let's leave Jesse with his *sister,* who isn't really his sister."

Jesse watched as Darrel and Adam walked away, then he turned to Susanna, who, with tears in her eyes, was looking at the destroyed flowers. He handed her his handkerchief. "Wipe your tears, little one."

"Thank you," she said as she began to wipe her eyes.

"Come on. There are lots of poppies in the field. I'll help you. I'll bet we can pick the biggest bouquet that Mama has ever seen."

"You're going to help?" Susanna asked, surprised by the offer.

"Yeah, little one, I'm going to help."

"Thank you, Jesse. But I'm not little anymore."

Jesse ran his hand through her hair. "You'll always be little to me," he joked.

Why didn't that part of Jesse show itself more? Susanna wondered. But she knew that it wasn't only Jesse's reckless behavior that disturbed his parents; it was also that Jesse showed absolutely no interest in the mercantile business. Kirkland Emporium competed with Manning and Duck for the title of the largest and most successful store in Virginia City. Susanna had to admit that Gus Kirkland was an effective merchandiser, and it had been that way from the time she had first gone to live with them.

Susanna filled the type sticks, then fitted them onto the drum.

The three owners of the North Star Mine, Sam Van Cleve, William Burdick, and John Sheehan, were in the billiard room of the Washoe Club. Burdick and Sheehan were at the table playing a game, while Van Cleve was kibitzing.

Van Cleve was from Baltimore, where he had managed a bank, but was discharged when irregularities showed up in the bank's books.

During the late war, Burdick had been a colonel in the Ohio militia, and though his commission had been revoked for incompetence in the first year of the war, he still introduced himself as Colonel Burdick.

John Sheehan was from Missouri. He had a more violent past than the other two, having ridden with Frank and Jesse James. The James brothers expelled him from their group when, during one of their operations, he killed a boy who was no older than sixteen.

Sheehan chalked the end of his cue stick, leaned over, and looked at the lie of the balls on the table. He put the stick in position, then drew it back. "Five ball in the corner pocket," he said.

With a clack, the white ball hit the orange ball, driving it into the corner pocket.

All three men were now living in the Comstock area, Sheehan in Virginia City, while Van Cleve and Burdick lived in Gold Hill. They had come because of the silver mines, and after a few insignificant finds, they pooled their claims to form the North Star Mine.

In the beginning the mine had been doing well, but the silver vein that was the most productive had taken a hard turn to the east, disappearing into the Silver Falcon Mine. They faced the dilemma of how to take advantage of the potentially rich vein that was now no longer on their claim.

"It isn't fair," Burdick said. "We're the ones who discovered that vein." He took a shot at the six ball and missed.

"Hell, they don't even know about it," Sheehan said. He knocked the six ball down, then turned toward the seven and lined up his shot.

"They aren't working it because they don't know it's there. They've got another vein that's just as rich, about five hundred feet above this one. We need to buy the Silver Falcon," Van Cleve said.

Van Cleve, who because of his background in banking was looked to by the others in financial matters, struck a match and held it to the end of his cigar. He took several puffs until the cigar was well lit, and the smoke hovered over the billiard table.

"Buy the Silver Falcon? Are you crazy? It's selling for one hundred thirty-two dollars a share," Burdick said.

Sheehan knocked down the seven ball, but missed the eight.

"That's what it's selling for now," Van Cleve said, smiling around the cigar that protruded from the center of his mouth. "But the value of Silver Falcon stock is about to drop like a lead ball. Pretty soon we'll be able to pick up shares of the stock as if they were no more than scrap paper."

"And just how do you propose we're going to do that?" Sheehan asked.

"I've already put things in motion," Van Cleve said. Looking up, he saw James Loudin step into the billiard room. "Finish your game; we have business to conduct."

San Francisco, California,
Wednesday, May 22, 1878

It had been twelve productive years since Rab Trudeau left New Orleans to start his new life in San Francisco. Now a successful businessman, his company, Sunset Enterprises, had expanded beyond the shipping that got his empire started into several other operations, including a freight-wagon line, a stagecoach line, California real estate, and his biggest money producer, a silver mine in Nevada.

The success of Sunset Enterprises was immediately discernible whether one was walking, on horseback, or riding as a passenger on an omnibus on Mission Street. There, overlooking San Francisco Bay, was a huge four-story brick building that stretched for half a block, designed by Henry Hobson Richardson, one of America's premier architects. Though Richardson was based in New York, Rab had been able to secure his architectural services because at one time the two were neighbors. Richardson was born on the Priestly Plantation, which was adjacent to Rab's family home.

At the moment, Rab was in his office on the fourth floor of the building. The office was large, with a huge oak desk at one end and a seating area, consisting of leather sofas, chairs, footstools, and a library table, at the other end. The windows were open on this warm May morning. Through them, the cry of seagulls competed with the clanging bells of channel-marker buoys and the rattling sound of rigging and stays slapping against mast and arm on the oceangoing ships that were drawn up alongside the piers. Over it all could be heard conversations carried on in the dozen different languages of the foreign seamen on the docks. The breeze coming through the open windows carried on its breath the aroma of salt sea, with an undernote of fish.

Rab was on the telephone with A. F. Coffin, of Coffin, Sanderson and Cook. A.F. was president of the San Francisco Mining Exchange.

"There is no valid reason for the stock to be this low," Rab was saying.

"Mining for precious metals is, at best, a risky operation." Coffin's voice sounded tinny over the phone.

"I know it's a risky operation, I'm in that business. But what is happening with the stock for the Silver Falcon is more than just normal business risk. I believe something sinister is occurring."

"I appreciate your concern," Coffin replied. "But I'm sure you know that we do not police the market."

"Yes, yes, I understand," Rab said, frustrated with the lack of response he was getting from the broker. "But I would think that when there is an anomaly this drastic, the mining exchange would be interested in finding out why."

"As I explained to you, Mr. Trudeau, it is not our business to police the market, or to explain its intricacies. Our business is merely to reflect it."

"Yes, well, thank you for your—help," Rab said, hoping Coffin picked up on his sarcasm.

Putting the receiver back in its cradle, Rab turned his attention to the article he had been reading in today's *Chronicle*.

"Knock, knock," someone called out, opening the door to his office and tapping lightly even as he spoke. "Are you busy?"

Looking toward the door, Rab saw his friend and partner, David DeLoitte, come into the office. David's wife, Lila, and the couple's three little girls, who ranged in age from three to seven, accompanied him. The girls began scurrying around the spacious room.

"Never too busy for you, my friend." Rab stood, and as the very pregnant Lila came into the room, he walked over to embrace her. "And how is my nephew today? I know this one is going to be a boy."

"From your lips to God's ear," David said as he placed his youngest daughter on the richly tufted carpet that covered the office floor.

"Well, now, if it isn't my favorite little people in the entire world," Rab said, smiling as he knelt down to be on eye level with the girls.

"Hello, Uncle Rab," Tina, the oldest, said as she entwined her arms around his neck. Rab wasn't Tina's uncle, of course, but he enjoyed being called that because, out here, David, Lila, and their children were the closest thing to a family he had.

"You look awfully pretty today, Tina," Rab said. "You must be dressed up for your boyfriend."

"Oh, I don't have a boyfriend." Tina laughed at him.

"What? You mean you got yourself looking so pretty just for your uncle Rab? Does that mean I'm your boyfriend?"

"You're so silly." Tina giggled. "You know you are too big for me." She pulled out of his hold and stepped away.

"Ahh, you're just like all the other women I know, as fickle as they come." Rab made a sad face and rubbed his eyes as if crying. Once again he was rewarded with the little girl's laughter.

"Well, this will cheer you," Lila said as she fell into the nearest chair. "David and I have been invited to *the* party of the month—a ball given by Judge Conrad and his wife. Of course Margaret is invited, so that means you'll be going, too."

Rab winced when he heard this news. "Oh, Lila, would it be asking too much for Margaret to check with me before she gets me involved in her societal forays?"

"You know you like Judge Conrad. You will have a good time. So it is settled. You are going. Come, girls, let's get out of here before Uncle Rab has a chance to change his mind." As she rose, she took the hand of her youngest daughter and gave David a peck on the cheek. "Come home as quickly as you can, my dear. You know I can't stand it when we are apart."

"You are a lucky man, David DeLoitte," Rab said.

After Lila and the girls left, the smile on Rab's face was replaced by the grim visage he had displayed earlier while reading the newspaper.

"Did you see this article?" he asked.

"No," David answered. "I haven't read the paper yet."

"Read this." Rab tapped the article with his finger.

David took the paper from Rab, then walked over to sit in a chair near the open window to read it.

Hard Times for the Silver Falcon

(By wire from the Virginia City Pioneer—
B. D. Elliott)

Were one to observe the Silver Falcon Mine from outside, one would get the impression that all is well. Smoke billows from the towering stacks, steam escapes from its mighty engines, and the stamping mill fills the air with its thunder of crushing rock; all indications of a busy and productive mine.

However it would appear that these are mere trappings, perpetrated by the mine owners to make it seem that it is business as usual, and that the production of silver continues. No doubt this stratagem is being played upon the innocent public so that the mine owners, concerned only with their own economic well-being, will be able to salvage some of its loss by artificially inflating worthless stock.

Based upon information learned from an unimpeachable authority, this paper can report that the lead that the Silver Falcon Mine had been working with such success has played out, and the mine is now but a hollow shell of its former grandeur. The mine owners, no doubt reacting to that information, chose the cowardly act of subterfuge, rather than an honest accounting with the shareholders of their mine. We believe it is our obligation to our readers to suggest they sell what shares they hold in the Silver Falcon while there remains some value to the stock. The wise shareholder will do this quickly, for there is no doubt but that the Silver Falcon will soon cease all operations.

"Damn!" David said. "How is it that they can print this? Where did this rumor start?"

"The problem is, this isn't just a rumor," Rab said. "You can deal with a rumor. But this is being printed as fact, and it has been picked up by newspapers all over the country. And words in print tend to give validity even to the most outrageous lies."

"You've got that right. This is the kind of thing that could break us. Lila's 'high-society' family had enough trouble with her marrying a Louisiana Cajun. But at least I was a Cajun with money."

"You are a Cajun with money for now, anyway. But I

just got off the telephone with A.F. He checked for me, and the Silver Falcon stock is trading at one dollar and twenty-five cents."

"Why is the paper doing this?" David asked. "I mean, wouldn't you think that after Mr. McQueen told the editor that the rumors are false, they would have withdrawn this article?"

"There are only two possible answers to that question. The newspaper either thinks that Benton McQueen is telling them that to protect the mine, or the paper knows better but has some other reason to perpetuate the lie."

"Some other reason?"

"I think there is someone behind this and they have enlisted the newspaper in their scheme. Someone is manipulating the stock for their own gain, and I intend to find out who it is."

"It'll be easy enough to have Great Western send a detective over to Virginia City to find out what's going on."

"No need to have Great Western send anyone," Rab replied. "I've made arrangements with Dewey Travertine to let me sign on as a temporary. I'm going myself."

"Don't you think one of his agents might have better luck finding out something? Seems to me like people might be a little hesitant if they thought they were talking to the head man."

"Everything we've done with the mine has gone through Sunset Enterprises. Not that many people know who I am, so when I go to Virginia City, I will just say that I am a detective for Great Western. I need to see for myself what's going on."

"Well, I don't like it. What if you get into trouble and I can't come to your rescue?"

"If you really want to rescue me, tell Margaret I'm not going to Judge Conrad's ball."

"No, no, it's not that easy. You might be fine with upsetting your true love, but I won't let you upset mine. Lila is counting on this party. It will probably be the last time she's out before the new baby gets here."

Rab chuckled. "All right. But I will be going for Lila, not Margaret. And don't call her my true love."

❧ 2 ❧

The gas flames of the dozen crystal chandeliers that hung over the hotel ballroom floor gave off a brilliant light. The men in their tuxedos and the women in their colorful gowns whirled and dipped and glided over the dance floor, the diamonds, rubies, and emeralds at their necks and ears giving off sparkling displays.

Margaret Worthington, of the Nob Hill Worthingtons, was a tall, willowy, pretty blonde. Her father was a prominent stockbroker in San Francisco. Everyone from Isaac Worthington to Margaret to Lila DeLoitte assumed that Rab and Margaret were going to marry. Rab assumed that as well, but he assumed it almost as an obligation. He was not completely opposed to the idea, but neither was he looking forward to it. It was, in his mind, an expected part of life.

Judge Conrad, host of the gala, was moving through the ballroom greeting everyone.

"Rab, m' boy," he said. "The entire city is envious of you for capturing the heart of our fairest young maiden."

Margaret put both hands on Rab's arm and leaned in to him, saying, "Judge, you are too kind."

"Every word of it is true."

"I was wondering"—Margaret smiled up at Rab—"I mean, I haven't even discussed this with Rab yet, but I am sure he will go along. I was wondering if you could find a time in your schedule to perform our marriage ceremony. I would like to be married this August."

"But wouldn't you rather have a church wedding?"

"Oh, but we will have it in a church. I have asked Reverend Bass about it. He knows what a family friend you are, so he has agreed to add his blessings immediately after the ceremony."

"What a wonderful idea," Judge Conrad said. "And since I've known you from the time you were a baby, I would be delighted to perform the wedding." Judge Conrad looked at Rab, who had been shocked into silence by Margaret's announcement, and chuckled. "My dear, you have rendered Rab speechless. I don't think I have ever seen him without something to say. Get used to it, son; once you are married, the women always have their way." The judge patted Rab on the back. "I'd better leave you and greet the rest of my guests."

"What do you think, Rab? I know how highly Judge Conrad regards you. Won't it be wonderful to have him perform our wedding ceremony?"

"Margaret, don't you think we could have spoken about this before you dropped it on me?"

"Dropped it on you?" Margaret replied, obviously hurt and chagrined by his comment. "Is that what you think our wedding will be? Something I'm dropping on you?"

"Margaret, please. I didn't mean that the way it sounded."

"Well, just what did you mean? Are you telling me you don't want to marry me? That's it, isn't it? I mean, you never have actually proposed to me, but we do have an understanding, don't we? At least, I thought we did. Have I erred?"

"It's not that. Well, yes, it is that, sort of. It's just that something like this, I mean, setting the wedding date and making arrangements with whoever is going to marry us, shouldn't that be something we discuss together?"

"We are discussing it."

"Yes, but we are discussing it after the fact."

Margaret laughed. "Rab, my dear, sweet, naive young man. Do you actually think that the groom makes any decisions with regard to the wedding? The only thing the groom ever has to decide on the day of his wedding is what he will have for breakfast that morning. Trust me, that's the way it is. And I'm setting the date for August eighteenth because Lila's baby should be born sometime in July and I want her to be in the wedding. I think it would be great to have her as my matron of honor, and David as your best man, don't you?"

Before Rab could answer, Margaret saw Lila. "Oh, I must tell her that the date is set," she said excitedly, and she hurried across the room.

"Congratulations," David said a few minutes later when he saw Rab standing by the bar, holding a drink in his hand.

"Margaret told you the news, did she?"

"Well, she told us that she had set the date. Of course, Lila and I have known about this for some time now. I haven't mentioned it because I've been waiting for you to say something first."

"It would have been hard for me to mention it, since I didn't know anything about it." Rab took a swallow of his drink.

David chuckled, but it was a troubled chuckle. "Rab, you didn't really expect to be a part of the planning, did you? The women always make the plans."

"Yeah, so I was just told," Rab said drily. He tossed down the rest of his drink.

Rab gazed out across the crowded room, watching as Margaret moved about like a bee going from flower to flower. At every gathering she would say a few words, then the women of the group would break into a smile, and there were hugs all around. At least she had told him before she told everyone else.

Once when Rab was at sea, he saw a storm approaching, a huge black wall to the west, moving inexorably toward his ship. He waited for it because there was nothing else he could do. When the storm hit, it tore away the mizzenmast and swept the decks clean, including the wheel. When at last it had passed, his crew had to jury-rig

a system of ropes to the rudder, and a makeshift tiller—
but they made it back to port.

From the moment Lila had introduced them, Margaret had been moving steadily, inevitably toward this moment, and as in the storm, Rab felt he could do nothing but wait. But was that really the way one was supposed to feel about an upcoming marriage?

Rab refilled his glass. As he turned around, he saw Margaret's father approaching him.

"Well, now, congratulations, Son! I know, I know, it's a little early to be calling you Son, but from the moment you and Margaret met, I knew this was going to happen. I'll have a bourbon, Henry," Isaac Worthington said to the bartender. "I want to propose a toast for my daughter's upcoming wedding to the finest young man in San Francisco."

Isaac Worthington was a polished and dignified-looking man—tall, slender, with silver hair and blue eyes. Isaac had made a great deal of money in his time. He had a silver tongue and was said to be able to talk anyone into anything. A widower, he had been accused by his competitors of using his good looks and considerable charm to entice susceptible, wealthy women into his business ventures.

Isaac got his drink, then held it toward Rab. "To you, Rab, and to the merger of our families and our fortunes."

Rab didn't reply, but he did take a drink with Isaac.

"My boy," Isaac said, "what do you know about electric motors?"

"Electric motors? I know very little about them."

A broad smile spread across Isaac's face. "Don't worry, Son, very few do know anything about them. And that is why electric motors are going to make a fortune for the few people with foresight. I have invested almost every penny I can raise, borrow, or steal into this, and I am going to give you, as my son-in-law, an opportunity to come into this with me."

"I don't know, Mr. Worthington, I've got a lot going on right now, what with the shipping line, the freight company, the stagecoach line, and the silver mine, and as you know, we are pursuing a railroad operation." Almost as an afterthought, Rab added, "And then there is the wedding."

Isaac laughed. "Don't worry about that, my boy; Margaret will take care of all the details, not only for the wedding, but she will be your biggest asset in the rest of your business ventures as well. But, back to the business of electric motors. What could be a better combination than railroad and electric motors? Today all locomotives are steam powered, and that means what? They have to stop to take on coal and water. One day I see all the trains powered by electric motors, and they can go from coast to coast without ever having to stop for fuel, because the electricity will always be there in one continuous current."

"It sounds promising."

"More than promising, my boy, it is absolutely prophetic. Oh, there's Mayor Bryant. I must speak to him and make certain he gets an invitation to the wedding."

Central Pacific Railroad Depot, San Francisco,
Wednesday, May 29, 1878

Throngs of people milled about on the expansive brick platform of the depot. Many were passengers, arriving and departing, but even more were citizens of the town, present to greet or say good-bye to someone. Steel-wheeled baggage carts were rolled here and there, some taking luggage to departing trains, others bringing luggage from arriving trains. The platform was redolent with the aroma of fresh coffee and warm pastries, being enthusiastically promoted by vendors whose voices competed both with the singsong hawking of the newspaperboys and the low, heavy rumble of chugging trains.

David and his entire family came down to the depot to see Rab off. Margaret was there as well.

"Did Sinclair make arrangements for my horse to be shipped?" Rab asked.

"Yes, Rebel will be on the same train. Here is his ticket," David said.

"I'll have to change trains at Reno to take the Virginia and Truckee."

"Trust me, it's all taken care of," David said.

"How long will you be gone, dear?" Margaret asked.

"I don't want to be flippant about it, but I'll be gone as long as it takes."

"I do wish you would let me go with you. I think a trip to a city where gold is being mined would be very exciting."

"There's not much gold, it is silver," Rab said, "and Virginia City is a rough town. Besides, I won't have any time for socializing. I'm going with a very specific purpose in mind."

One of the depot employees stepped out onto the platform, carrying a large megaphone with him. He lifted it to his lips and began calling loudly, "Train for Reno, now loading on track number four. Train for Reno, loading on track number four."

"That's me," Rab said. "I must be going." He reached out to shake David's hand, then said good-bye to Lila and the girls.

"Good-bye, dear," Margaret said, and kissed Rab on the lips.

"Good-bye," Rab said, then returned the kiss.

The kiss seemed rather perfunctory to him. It seemed to him that, if he was going to marry this woman in three months, there should be more to it.

Once on board the train, Rab pulled a letter from his jacket pocket. The envelope was addressed to Father Dupree, St. Patrick's Catholic Church, 724 Camp Street, New Orleans, but it was actually to his sister, Emmaline.

My dear Emmaline,

I am pleased that things are going well at Rivière de Joie with you and Randolph and my two nephews. It gives me great pleasure to hear that my namesake is such a little scamp. Please give them my best. My thoughts and prayers are with you and your family, and with Father, who even in his golden years cannot forgive me. Should you have the opportunity to do so, please tell him that my love for him is unabated.

I have taken pen in hand because I am in need of a woman's advice. I find myself engaged to be married. It is not a condition I sought, but rather one that I blundered into. By that, I mean that I maintained a relationship until such time as it was assumed by all that my intention was matrimony.

It may have been, and, certainly, the relationship has been sustained to a length that, were I to terminate it now, it would bring hurt to the young woman, humiliation to her family, and, I fear, dishonor to myself. Her name is Margaret Worthington, and she is a beautiful and fine woman from one of San Francisco's most prominent families.

I like her very much and for the most part enjoy her company, though she does tend to be more socially active than I find comfortable. But this is my question, Emmaline. How would I know if I am actually in love with her? When I am with her, I feel none of the joie de vivre so extolled by poets. And when we are apart, no longing for her fills my heart.

To further complicate the situation, she is a very good friend of David's wife, Lila, and Lila clearly wants me to marry her. Perhaps, dear sister, this is too big a question and too heavy a burden to place upon your shoulders, but I can think of no other outlet for my questions and concerns. I look forward to your return post.

Your loving brother,
Rab

Holding the letter, Rab put it back in the envelope and sealed it. He would mail it from Reno, when he changed trains.

*   *   *

The first thing Rab noticed when he stepped off the train in Virginia City were the sounds of the town, from the clopping hooves of the six- and eight-mule teams required to pull up to three heavily loaded quartz wagons, to the screech of huge, steam-powered circular saws, to the steady, rhythmic thump of the rock-crushing mills.

The depot was a flurry of activity as newspaperboys competed with each other, a patent-medicine man hawked his potions, and an itinerant preacher made an earnest appeal to save souls from a sure and certain perdition.

Even as Rab was stepping down from the train, Susanna Kirkland was leaving the Chaney House, where she kept her room and took her meals. Waving a cheery good-bye to Mary Beth Chaney, daughter of the owner, she started up Taylor Street on her way to work. The steep incline and the wind forced her to lean forward as she walked to keep her balance. Unbeknownst to Susanna, all along the route, men—draymen, hostlers, store clerks, miners, engineers, carpenters, and blacksmiths—all manner of men planned their mornings to watch the beautiful young woman as she walked to work each day.

Though Susanna had long chestnut hair, she wore it pulled back in a chignon to keep it from getting caught in the printing press. Her eyes were her most prominent feature, big and brown with long eyelashes. Her brows were fuller than she would have liked, and her complexion was an olive gold, typical of her Italian mother's side of the family. At five feet eight inches tall, Susanna had a defined figure, but she was not overly endowed. She eschewed the bustles and flounces that were so in style, choosing instead to dress conservatively, the straight lines of her dress, more suited for work, also having the unintended effect of showing off her figure.

Rab's first stop would be the Silver Falcon Mine, so after Rebel was off-loaded from the train and saddled, Rab started toward the mountain. When he passed by Morrison's Shoe Store though, he realized that, while he had brought the proper clothes for the task he had set for himself, he had not brought the right shoes. He needed a pair of work boots, so he dismounted in front of the shoe store.

As Susanna turned onto C Street, she noticed a man tying off his horse at the hitching rail across the street. He was big, clearly taller than any other man she knew. A red flannel shirt stretching across broad shoulders was tucked into denim trousers that molded to the musculature of his legs. He was dressed like any other miner, but with one notable exception. He was wearing a pistol, the tooled-leather holster tied down and hanging low from its own belt.

Something about the way he moved, with a graceful economy of motion, made her think he was not a miner.

His hair was black, perhaps a bit too long, and he looked as if he needed a shave.

"I could cut that, and I could give him a shave, although that stubble—it looks pretty good," Susanna said aloud. Then self-consciously she looked around to make certain no one was within hearing distance.

What was she doing? She didn't ogle men, but this stranger definitely caught her attention. Uncharacteristically, she altered her course, walking across the street directly in front of him.

Her friend Annie Biggs would be proud of her boldness.

Out of the corner of his eye, Rab had caught the tall, slender woman staring at him. As he knew she would, she started across the street. For years, girls—women—had been throwing themselves at him. But he was never sure if it was because they were really attracted to him or if it was because they knew he had money.

Her olive, almost golden, skin reminded him of some of the beautiful quadroons he had known in New Orleans. Guilty delights to be sure, but they had established for him a bar of sexual pleasure that would be difficult to meet.

Suddenly a runaway team of horses came pounding up Union, pulling a light delivery wagon. Because the horses were coming up behind her, the young woman could not see them.

The driver was standing in the wagon, calling to his horses, trying to stop them.

"Whoa! Hold up there!" he was shouting. The team turned right, heading directly for the young woman.

"Look out!" Rab shouted.

Running out into the street, he scooped Susanna up and carried her under his arm, almost as if she were a sack of flour. At first, Susanna let out a cry of alarm, but then the team and wagon swept by them, so close that she could feel the dirt being tossed up by the horses' hooves.

Rab held her as he stepped onto the boardwalk in front of the Brass Rail Saloon. "Are you all right, miss?" He set her down, but did not let go of her. Holding her, he found himself staring into a most expressive pair of brown eyes.

"Oh!" Susanna said as she began to squirm in his arms. "Let me go!"

Rab released her and, as he did so, noticed a large smudge of dirt on the bodice of her dress. Instinctively, he tried to brush it off, but his fingers trailed across the woman's breast. Immediately, he realized his mistake and was truly embarrassed. Thankfully, the woman turned her attention elsewhere.

"My dress, this is—couldn't you have simply shouted a warning to me?"

"I beg your pardon, ma'am. I saw a woman in what I thought could be danger and I just reacted."

"I—I must go home and change my clothes."

"You're welcome," Rab said, touching the brim of his hat before he turned to start back toward his horse.

Susanna watched him, then realized that she had been anything but grateful to him for saving her from being trampled by the horses.

"Wait!"

Rab stopped, then turned toward her.

"I'm sorry. It's just that I was frightened. You saved me from certain injury, and for that I am very grateful. Please forgive my rudeness."

Again Rab touched the brim of his hat and, without comment, he continued on across the street. Farther north, on C Street, the driver finally got the runaway team under control.

When Susanna returned to the lodging house, Annie Biggs was sitting in the parlor with Mary Beth Chaney, who along with her mother ran the place where both Annie and Susanna lived. There could not possibly have been a greater contrast between the two women. Mary Beth was wearing a plain gray dress with a pinafore and a lace cap. Annie Biggs was wearing a bright yellow dress, cut so low that the tops of her breasts almost seemed to spill out. Each woman was having a cup of coffee; one was drinking it before beginning her daily routine of cleaning, the other was drinking it before going to bed for some much-needed rest.

A smeared slash of crimson lip color highlighted Annie's lips, with smudged red circles of rouge dotting her cheeks. Even though Annie was a prostitute, she, Mary Beth, and Susanna were good friends. Both women looked up in surprise when Susanna came back to the house.

"Susanna, what are you doing back? You just left," Mary Beth said.

"I had an . . . *incident.*"

"Oh, my! I daresay that you did," Annie said, as a big smile formed on her face. She was looking directly at Susanna's chest.

"What's wrong?"

"Have you looked at yourself?" Annie asked, and both Annie and Mary Beth began to snicker.

Susanna stepped to the hall tree and looked into the mirror. She gasped at what she saw. The smudge on her bodice was more than just a dirt stain. The perfect impression of a large hand covered her breast.

"The beast!"

"What happened?" Mary Beth asked.

Susanna told the story of the runaway team and wagon, and how a man had dashed out into the street, scooped her up, and carried her to safety.

"Well, I would hardly call him a beast," Mary Beth said. "I would call him a hero."

"Yes," Susanna said as she tried to brush the handprint off her dress, "I guess he was. And I guess he really couldn't help where he put his hand when he grabbed me. But it is humiliating to think about it. I wonder, who else saw this?"

As Susanna changed her dress upstairs, she thought again of the incident. Was it humiliating? Or was it exciting? After all, doesn't every woman dream of a hero to sweep her off her feet?

Susanna chuckled. This hero actually did sweep her off her feet.

She put her hand on her breast, where his had been, and now as she thought about it, she felt an incredible warmth. How would it feel if he had not grabbed her in an emergency, but had put his hand there, not on the dress, but on her flesh, in a moment of tenderness?

Susanna became aware of a strange feeling inside her body, and she reached out to grab the corner of the clothespress until that feeling passed.

❊ 3 ❊

Leaving the shoe store, Rab rode up to Stewart Street, where the more affluent had their homes. Here, Benton McQueen, the superintendent of the Silver Falcon, lived rent free in a large, two-storey brick house that had been built and furnished by Sunset Enterprises. He drove a fine pair of horses that were a present from the company, and his salary was the princely sum of twelve thousand dollars a year.

Stepping up onto the broad front porch, Rab turned the crank to operate the doorbell. The door was opened by a servant, a Chinese man who was wearing a red-and-gold jacket and black trousers.

"I am here to see Mr. McQueen," Rab said.

"Who is your name?" the Chinese butler asked.

"The name is Trudeau."

"That's all right, Kahn," McQueen said, coming into the room, wearing a broad smile. "Show the gentleman in."

Kahn stepped out of the way and Rab went inside, met almost immediately by McQueen's extended hand.

"Rab, what a pleasant surprise," McQueen said.

"Has there been any change in the reports?" Rab asked. "Are we still proving out well?"

McQueen's smile faded to a frown. "On second thought, it isn't that much of a surprise. I thought either David or you might come, given the newspaper reports that have been going out."

"What about the reports? Are they true?"

"No, sir, they are not true. I've just been going over the latest assay reports. They are as good as, maybe even better than, any assay report on any other mine on the Comstock."

"Then, why are there such negative articles in the paper?" Rab asked. "Where are they coming from?"

"I'll tell you the truth, I don't have an idea in hell where they came from. As I said, the mine is in full production and doing very well."

"And yet the newspaper is reporting that the Silver Falcon is playing out."

"That's what the paper says. At least the *Pioneer* is saying that."

"What about the *Enterprise*? Is it disputing the reports?"

"No, DeQuille isn't saying anything about it, one way or the other."

"Who's the publisher of the *Pioneer*?"

"His name is Loudin. James Loudin."

"Have you spoken to this Loudin, to see where he's getting his information? Or rather, misinformation?"

"I've tried to, but the son of a bitch won't tell me. He says that to compromise his source might make it more difficult for him to get closely guarded information in the future. I told him it was false, but he doesn't believe me. He says that I have a vested interest in seeing that people think the mine is producing, and he would rather use information he has gathered independently of anyone connected with the mine."

"So he is going with his secret source," Rab said. It was a comment, not a question.

"Yes, sir. You want my opinion?"

"Of course."

"If you ask me, whoever is feeding him that information is doing it for his own purpose. I don't know what that purpose might be, but I think this whole misinformation thing is deliberate. At least, that's what I think."

"I think you're right," Rab said. "Someone is trying to deliberately sabotage the Silver Falcon."

"What do you want me to do?"

"Nothing, yet. Oh, except keep it quiet as to who I actually am. I'm going to be passing myself off as a detective for the Great Western Detective Agency. I think people might be a little more open around me if they thought I was a detective than they would if they knew I was an owner of the Silver Falcon."

"Yes, sir, I think you might be right," McQueen said. "Oh, and while you're looking around, you will stay here, of course. I have a great guest room, thanks to you."

"I don't think I had better do that," Rab said. "I don't

want anybody connecting me with the Silver Falcon, and if I stay here, that's what they'll do. I think I'll ride down to Gold Hill and find a place there. That's probably where I'll start my investigation."

"Would you like a suggestion?"

"Sure, I'm always open to suggestions."

"Before you actually tell anyone that you're a detective, you might want to poke around a bit."

"That's probably a pretty good idea. What do you think I should do that wouldn't raise too much attention?"

"I would suggest you start by going through the tailings. Lots of folks do that, going through the discards to see if there's any silver left over. None of them get rich, but quite a few can and do make a living at it. And since everyone is used to seeing that, you probably won't raise much attention."

"Good idea," Rab said. "That's exactly where I'll start."

Because Susanna had gone back to change clothes, it took her another half hour before she stepped into the office of the *Pioneer*. The smell of liquor was overpowering, and she saw B. D. Elliott sitting at his desk trying—not too successfully—to drink whiskey straight from the bottle. Some of it was dribbling down his chin.

"Oh, Mr. Elliott," she said, speaking to the reporter for the newspaper. She didn't have to say anything else; the tone of her voice and the expression on her face showed her disappointment.

"Susanna, don't be so hard on an old man," Elliott

said. "I know I told you I would quit drinking, and I did, too. But the demons won't let me be."

"What was it this time? Cards, or horses, or what?"

"Ha! Those are the good sins. No, I'm afraid it was the mining stocks that have taken me down. I bought ten shares of the Knickerbocker Mine when it reached fifty dollars. I was sure it was going to a hundred. It's gone the other way. It's a dollar a share now."

B. D. Elliott was short with a paunch, a cherubic face, and a head that was bald on top, but wreathed with gray hair. He topped off his discourse by draining the last of the whiskey, then let the bottle fall to the floor. He wiped the back of his hand across his lips.

"There is something evil about the mines," he said. "It is as if the devil himself has taken up residence there." He tried to pick up the empty bottle but stumbled, keeping himself from falling only by grabbing the edge of his desk. He sat down clumsily.

"You can't keep doing this," Susanna said as she picked up the empty bottle and put it back on his desk. "Do you have your stories ready for today's issue?"

"They're here, but I confess to you, girly, that they are going to need a bit of a rewrite. But you're the girl that can do it. I do have a quaint that you can set, though. This one gives even me a bit of a chuckle."

B.D. was, as were Mark Twain and Dan DeQuille before him, good at writing fictitious short stories in such a way as to lend an air of credibility to them. Such stories left the reader not quite sure whether what he had just read was truth or fiction. These stories were referred to as quaints.

The Baptism

In a pious group there was a Miss Wilson who wanted to be a Baptist, and she presented herself for baptism. Now Miss Wilson weighed two hundred pounds, including her cork leg, which was a full-length leg and modeled in due proportion.

She made an attempt to reach the officiating clergyman breast deep in the water, but her cork leg was seized with unwanted activity. Miss Wilson knew nothing of the law of specific gravity and was not to blame.

She was suddenly reversed in the water. The minister, feelingly, righted her up and, observing the grinning of the spectators at the solemn scene, asked Miss Wilson to please not do that again.

He was innocently ignorant of the cause of the disturbance of her equilibrium. He gently led the maiden out, when, with a shriek, she fell backward, and again, her lively leg shot out of the water.

The minister made half a dozen efforts, but could not keep the convert right end up long enough to baptize her. At length she told him of her trouble, and he called for a weight to ballast her.

The spectators fled precipitately to give vent to their feelings. Miss Wilson flip-flopped ashore in indignation and amazement and went and joined the Presbyterians.

Susanna read the quaint, then laughed. "Very good."

"The rest of my—stories—will, as I said, require a bit of rewrite," B.D. said.

"All right, let me see what you have. And if I were you, I would leave before Mr. Loudin gets here. It would not do for him to see you like this. I'll tell him you are out on a story."

Elliott got up from his desk and laboriously tried to put on his jacket.

"Let me help you." Susanna guided his arm into the sleeve.

"Ah, what a fine girl you are." He staggered toward the door, leaving the bottle on his desk.

"Mr. Elliott?" Susanna called after him.

Elliott stopped, then looked back.

"Don't forget this." Susanna pointed to the empty bottle.

"Now, why would I want to be carrying an empty bottle with me? I ask you."

"If Mr. Loudin sees it on your desk, don't you think he might figure out why you're not here?"

Elliott scratched his cheek for a moment, as if trying to understand what Susanna was saying. Then realization hit him, and he smiled and raised his finger in salute, then came back for the bottle. "You're a smart one all right. If ever I wanted to hide some misdeed, you would be the one I would turn to."

"You already have," Susanna replied, though it was obvious that either Elliott didn't hear her or didn't choose to understand.

He grabbed the empty bottle and, with a parting wave, left the newspaper office.

Susanna watched him lurch and stumble out onto the boardwalk, anxious that he might fall, but somehow he righted himself. She picked up his notes and started toward the composing table.

Susanna liked, admired, and respected B.D. She thought B.D. was every bit as talented as his friend Samuel Clemens, who now went by the nom de plume Mark Twain. Mark Twain was now recognized as one of the premier writers in America, but at one time he and B.D. and their friend Dan DeQuille had worked together on the *Territorial Enterprise*. B.D. had written a book as well, but it went nowhere, and, disappointed, perhaps even a little jealous of Twain's success, B.D. found solace in a bottle.

Susanna looked over the material he had left for her. More and more often now, she found herself being pressed into service to complete the articles B.D. had started but was unable to finish. She didn't really mind all that much. She loved writing, and she loved to see people react to her stories, even though nobody knew that she was the author.

As she examined the notes that Elliott had said would need just a "bit of a rewrite," she wasn't surprised to see that the stories would require much more. Nothing was here but a few notes, some names, and one or two disjointed sentences.

She set up the printing bed, preparing to write the story as she composed the type. It was not difficult for her to write that way because she had learned to read the type as easily backward as she could forward.

"Is B.D. drunk again?" Loudin asked when he came into the office and saw B.D.'s empty desk.

"I believe he is covering a story," Susanna replied, not directly answering him.

"More than likely he's covering a story about the best watering holes in Virginia City," Loudin said, scoffing. "I'm meeting Theodore Manning at the Red Men Club this afternoon to get some advertising. If you could talk Kirkland into increasing advertising for the Emporium, I know I could get Manning and Duck to match it."

"I don't think Mr. Kirkland would go along with that. He complains now that he has more advertising than he needs."

"Why do you always call him Mr. Kirkland? Most adopted children call the parents Father and Mother."

"Because I'm not adopted."

"You must be. You call yourself Kirkland."

"I'm not adopted."

"But they raised you," Loudin said. "Everybody in town knows that."

"Yes, I was raised by them."

Raised, but never accepted as one of them, never loved as parents love a child.

Susanna's mother had been loving. She could remember that, even though it had been nineteen years since she had last felt her mother's arms around her. Those memories were helped by the diary Sophia Ward had kept. The diary, her father's letters, and a small, gold, jewel-encrusted crucifix were the only tangible things Susanna had from her life before the Kirklands.

On that terrible day when the Wards' wagon was pushed away from the others and set ablaze, Susanna had plucked a gutta-percha bag from it, in which her mother had kept what had now become Susanna's most prized possessions. She had shed many tears over her mother's last entries.

> *Caleb is sick. The fever come on him before sunrise. By breakfast he was so sick that he couldn't sit up. We dassn't tell the others. They would make us pull our wagon away from the train and leave us behind.*

> *Since what I wrote this morning, we have learned that it is the cholera and now Byron and I have it, too. I only pray that my sweet little Susanna . . .*

Susanna was never to learn what the prayer for her was, because that was the last entry in her mother's diary.

Two weeks later, Alice and her husband came by the newspaper office. Alice was married to Harold Ponder, who had worked at the Emporium for Kirkland ever since he opened the Virginia City store. Alice was a plain woman who had always been quiet and withdrawn, the complete opposite to the pretty and outgoing Susanna. As girls, and as women, the two had always gotten along well, though Alice, like her mother, was relatively aloof, so never, at any time in their relationship, had Susanna thought of Alice as her sister.

Alice had once confided in Susanna that she was afraid she would never get married. "I'm not pretty the way you are. Boys don't ever look at me the way they look at you."

But Alice's fears were misplaced, because she was married and Susanna was not. Susanna was glad for Alice, even though Susanna strongly suspected that Harold had married Alice just to better his own position.

Alice and Harold had a beautiful child. Everyone loved six-year-old Betsy, especially Susanna.

"Harold and I must go to Reno today," Alice said, "and we were wondering if you would watch Betsy for us."

"I don't mind at all," Susanna replied. "If you don't mind that she stays with me here, in the newspaper office."

"I see no difference in her staying here, with you, than her staying in the store."

Susanna smiled at Betsy. "Then, we will have a fine time, won't we?"

"Oh, that is a beautiful bouquet, Betsy," Susanna said much later that day. "What are you going to do with it?"

"I'm going to give it to Granny."

"What a wonderful idea. That will make a fine gift. I'm sure your grandmother has never gotten a more beautiful bouquet."

Betsy's staying in the newspaper office had not been an imposition. The little girl was especially well behaved and was sitting on the floor in the composing room, off to one side so as not to be in the way. Earlier, Betsy had stepped out through the back door to gather some of the wildflowers that grew in colorful profusion along the back alley.

B.D. had suggested that she make a bouquet, and he even provided her with a vase.

"I like red," Betsy said. "What color do you like, Miss Susanna?"

"Oh, I like red, too." Susanna wished the little girl would call her Aunt Susanna, but the Kirklands had been specific in explaining to Betsy that Susanna was not her aunt.

"Not me," B.D. said. "I like yellow. Do you have any yellow?"

"I have lots of yellow." Betsy continued to work on the flower arrangement. "Miss Susanna, look!" Betsy pointed to her finished bouquet. It had no pattern, no shape or formation, just several flowers stuck down into the vase, but the broad smile on Betsy's face showed her pride in it.

"Oh," Susanna said. "It's beautiful, Betsy. It is absolutely beautiful."

"When can we take it to Granny?"

"I heard the train arriving a few moments ago," Susanna said. "I'll just bet your mama and daddy are back home. Why don't we walk down to the store and see? We'll take it and you can give it to Mrs. Kirkland."

"Do you think she'll like it?" Betsy asked anxiously.

"Oh, I'm sure she will," Susanna replied reassuringly.

"Did you enjoy your time with Betsy today?" Mary Beth asked. She was two years younger than Susanna, and the two women were great friends.

Mary Beth helped run the lodging house, and even now as they were talking, she was setting the table for the evening meal that was provided to the boarders.

"Oh, I enjoyed it very much. She is such a well-behaved little girl, and so smart."

"You should get married so you can have a child of your own. You would like to have a child, wouldn't you?"

"Yes, if it could be a child like Betsy."

"But not a husband like Harold."

Susanna laughed. "Oh, you're awful. You're right, but awful."

On the other hand, she thought, though she didn't speak her thought, if she could marry someone like the handsome man who had clutched her from the jaws of death a couple of weeks ago, she would be fine with it.

She blushed at the thought and was thankful that Mary Beth didn't notice.

4

Rab had been working the tailings for two weeks and had actually brought out almost fifty dollars in silver. That established his presence, and it gave him an excuse to spend some time in the Gold Hill Miners' Union Hall. There, he introduced himself as a private detective.

"What is it you're detecting?" one of the miners asked. A few minutes earlier, the man had introduced himself as Taggart.

"I'm sure you are aware that there have been some wide swings in the value of the mine shares lately," Rab said.

"Ha! That always happens."

"Why?"

"Why? I don't know why. I just know that it always happens. What difference does it make, anyway? I mean, as long as the mines are still here."

"It makes a difference, because the mine stock is traded

all over the country," Rab said. "All over the world, actually. And if traders can't have confidence in the value of the stock, they may quit trading altogether."

"That's mostly for rich people anyway," Taggart said. "Me, I just go down into the mines, knock down some rock, and collect my four dollars a day."

"You think that's good pay?"

"Mister, in my last job I froze to death in the winter, roasted in the summer, and punched cows for twenty dollars a month and found. Four dollars a day is six times as much money. Yeah, I think it's damned good pay."

"The mine owners get their operating capital by selling stock. If they can't raise enough money, they go out of business. If they go out of business, you lose your job. That's why you should care."

"Oh," Taggart said. "Yeah, well, I don't reckon I thought about it like that."

"Well, somebody else has, and that's why I'm here."

Two days later, Rab was sitting on a boulder on the side of Mount Davidson with his binoculars. He looked down toward the hoisting works of the Sierra Nevada, Belcher, Ophir, and Caledonia Mines. All four hoisting works were busy. Then he turned his attention to the stamping mill for the Ophir. He watched as cars loaded with ore were pushed over an iron track to one of the chutes that led down through the roof of the mill and into the huge ore bin below.

Even from here he could hear the steady thump,

thump, thump of the rock being crushed by the eight-hundred-pound stamps.

"You want to tell us what you're doing here, mister?" a gruff, angry voice suddenly called out.

Looking toward the sound of the voice, Rab saw three armed men standing there.

"Who are you?" Rab asked.

"We work for a group of mine owners," the biggest of the three men said. "And I'll be asking the questions. Now I'm going to ask you again, what are you doing here?"

"I'm just having a look around."

"Yeah? Well, if you're lookin' around to see whether or not you can steal somethin', I'm tellin' you now, you're wasting your time. There ain't never nobody got away with stealin' from any of my mines. And as long as I'm workin' here, there ain't never goin' to be anybody do it either."

"There's no need for us to be enemies," Rab said. "We have the same job, so to speak."

"What do you mean, we have the same job?"

"I work for the Great Western Detective Agency. I've been hired to look out for the miners' interest."

"Who hired you?"

"I don't see that you need to know that."

"Is that a fact? Well, mister, as far as I'm concerned, you got no business pokin' around out here. So if I was you, I'd be gettin' on my way now."

All three men were holding their rifles low, and Rab doubted if any of the rifles even had a round in the chamber. He was sure that if he wanted to, he could draw his pistol faster than they could cock and raise their rifles.

If he thought they would give up as soon as they saw he had the drop on them, he might have done it. But one of them might push it, and he would be forced to shoot to defend himself. That he did not want to do. As far as he could tell, these were just men doing the job for which they had been hired.

"All right, I'll be going," Rab said. "But you fellas had better get used to seeing me because, like you, I've been hired to do a job, and I plan to do it."

Van Cleve, Burdick, and Sheehan were in the mine office of the North Star.

"I've got to hand it to you, Sam, that idea you had about spreadin' the rumor of poor pickin's in the Silver Falcon to run the price down was a good idea," Burdick said. "We've got more than thirty percent of the stock right now."

"Twenty-eight percent," Van Cleve corrected.

"We won't ever have controlling interest in it, will we? I mean, Sunset Enterprises has more than fifty percent, don't they?"

"As long as we can keep the share value down, we can continue to buy up everything they don't control, and if a company like Sunset Enterprises decides the mine is a losing proposition, they'll be glad enough to get rid of it."

"Yeah, well, how are we going to buy much more of

the stock?" Sheehan asked. "We've got over three hundred miners working for us at four dollars a day, and we hardly have enough money left to pay them for one more month."

"We're going to sell some of our stock to get money to buy stock in the Silver Falcon," Burdick said.

"Did you see this morning's quote on our stock? It was ten and a quarter."

"We're going to buy at least a thousand shares of our own stock; then we're going to drive the price up and sell when it's high. We'll use that money to buy the Silver Falcon."

"And just how do you propose we do that?" Sheehan asked.

Before Van Cleve could answer, there was a knock on the door to the small office building, and Sheehan pulled it open. It was Lawrence Sims, the head of the security detail that the mine owners had hired.

"Mr. Sims," Van Cleve said. "What can we do for you?"

"Mr. Van Cleve, did you hire a private detective to go around after us and make sure we're doing our job?"

"No, why would you ask that?"

"Because we've been watchin' a fella that's been snoopin' around here for the last couple of weeks. He claims he's a private detective. Only when we asked the fancy-talkin' son of a bitch who he's workin' for, he won't tell us. He says he's lookin' out for the miners, but we don't believe it. We figure he's workin' for some owner, but so far, we've checked at the Sierra Nevada, the Mexican, the Ophir, the Silver Falcon, the California, the Consolidated Virginia, and a whole bunch more, and they ain't none of 'em owned up to hirin' no private detective. You're the last one we've come to, so that's why I'm thinkin' the North Star is the one that did it."

"I assure you, Mr. Sims, we have not hired a private detective," Van Cleve said. "Do you know anything about him?"

"Well, we did find out his name. It's supposed to be Rab Trudeau, if he's tellin' the truth."

Van Cleve shook his head. "It's not a name I recognize. What's he supposed to be looking for, do you know?"

"Turns out he's been talkin' to some of the fellas over at the Gold Hill Miners' Union Hall. He's tellin' 'em he's looking for reasons why the mine stocks keep goin' up and down."

"Ha," Van Cleve said. "Perhaps someone should tell him that's the nature of the business."

"Yes, sir, that's pretty much the way I see it," Sims said. "If you didn't hire 'im, we'll be gettin' on out o' here."

"All right," Van Cleve said, "and thanks, boys, for telling us about this."

The three men waited until Sims left.

"You know what I'm thinking?" Burdick asked.

"You're thinking the Silver Falcon is behind this," Van Cleve said.

"That's exactly what I'm thinking," Burdick said.

"And I'm thinking we may want to keep an eye on this Mr. Rab Trudeau," Van Cleve said.

"What if he finds out we're the ones who caused the collapse of Silver Falcon share prices?" Sheehan asked.

"Then, we may have to take action," Van Cleve said.

"Yeah," Sheehan said with a big smile. "And if we do,

then you fellows can leave that up to me. That's the kind of thing I do best."

"Oh, Mr. Sheehan, we fully expect you to take care of it," Van Cleve said.

"Where is B.D.?" Loudin asked when he came into the newspaper office.

"He stepped out a little while ago," Susanna said.

"Drunk or sober?"

"He may have been drinking a little." Susanna was uncomfortable lying, but neither did she want to get B.D. in trouble.

"Well, no matter. You're probably the one I need to talk to anyway. I just found out that there is a detective in town. Someone has gone to the trouble of hiring a private detective to investigate the good people of our mines. Now what, I ask you, could that possibly do but cause unrest and suspicion?"

"What's he supposed to be investigating?" Susanna asked.

"That's just it. No one seems to know. Why don't you try and find out?"

"Me?" Susanna replied, pleased that Loudin had asked her. "Are you sure you want me to do it? Shouldn't B.D. be doing that?"

"Do you mean should I take a chance on catching B.D. when he isn't drunk, and then hope he will stay sober long enough to get the job done?"

Susanna didn't answer.

"Susanna, you and I both know that you will probably end up writing the story anyway. How many stories have you written for him, now? Half of them? Three-quarters? All of them?"

"Oh, I wouldn't say that."

"No, you wouldn't say that because you aren't the kind of person who would betray a trust. But the stories have been well written, and I'm receiving a lot of compliments from readers. And although B.D. is a fine writer—in fact, one of the best writers I've ever known—he is seldom sober enough to do anything right now, let alone write what you would call a good story. On the other hand, you're doing a fine job."

"Thank you," Susanna said, beaming under the praise.

"That's why I want you to do the story on this detective and whatever it is he is investigating. And that's also why I want you to write the story under B.D.'s byline. I know you'll do a better job than he would, and I know you won't betray the trust."

Susanna's smile faded.

"Susanna, you didn't think I intended for you to write this story under your own byline, did you?"

"I—I suppose I hoped as much," Susanna said, her tone suggesting her disappointment.

Loudin shook his head. "That would be impossible. A story about mines, possible corruption, and an investigation? Why, if the public thought that a woman was writing such a story, it would lose all credibility. They'd think it was a quaint. I know it isn't right, but it's true. Believe me, I published newspapers in Kansas, Nebraska, and

California before I came here, and if there's one thing I understand, it's the mind of the reading public. The only stories they'll accept written by women are stories about women's doings."

"I think you are wrong."

Loudin looked directly at Susanna. "I'll tell you what I'll do. I'll give you your own column that you can write every day, and you can use your own byline. You can write about church socials and women's meetings, or maybe new dresses or cotillions and such. Those are the types of things that interest women. You'd like that, wouldn't you?"

"Yes." Although it wasn't what she really wanted, it was definitely a step up from being a printer's devil. "What's his name?"

"I beg your pardon?" Loudin asked, confused by the sudden swing in the subject.

"The detective I am to interview. What is his name?"

"Oh, it's, uh, some French-sounding name. Wait, I wrote it down." Loudin took a piece of paper from his vest pocket and consulted it. "It's Trudeau. Rab Trudeau. And if I were you, I would start over at Gold Hill, at the Miners' Union Hall. I understand he has been there several times."

Back at the Chaney House, Annie Biggs had just received a message suggesting that she might do some business at the McAuliffe House, so she took special pains to get ready. The dress she chose was a deep green and cut low in front. The dress, and her artful use of makeup, highlighted her emerald eyes and red hair. The makeup she used was not the harsh, almost harlequin paint of the typical prostitute, but more like that applied by the actresses when they were onstage at the opera house.

Because over 80 percent of the men who worked the mines were unmarried, Virginia City and Gold Hill had large contingents of prostitutes. Most of these women plied the saloons and brothels in a part of the town known as the Barbary Coast. The Barbary Coast was an unseemly, lawless area, as dangerous for the unsuspecting pedestrian after darkness as was the Divide, as the area that separated the two cities was called.

Annie Biggs was a "lady of the evening," and she made no bones about it. But she didn't work the bars, the cribs, or the streets. Her beauty, sparkling personality, and stunning figure put her at the top of the echelon. She was well educated, a graduate of Kansas State, and she had, at one time, been a schoolmarm.

Because schoolteachers were always maiden ladies, Annie lost her position when she married Keith Biggs, an engineer who helped build the Virginia and Truckee Railroad. They had a happy marriage and were making plans to move to Fort Worth, Texas, where Keith would be helping to build another railroad. But Annie's husband was killed in an accident, and Annie suddenly found herself without any means of support. Hoping to get her old job back, she applied to the school board, but they refused to rehire her. So she became a "soiled dove."

Since entering the profession, she was now in better financial shape than she had ever before been in her life. She was a favorite of the mine owners, supervisors, lawyers, and other professional people, especially visiting dignitaries. She had once been the consort of a governor, though she was much too discreet to disclose who it might have been.

Mary Beth was polishing the furniture when Annie came downstairs. "You're going out early today, aren't you?"

"I have an appointment," Annie said.

"In the middle of the day? Isn't that a little unusual?"

"It's Mr. Holloway again. The stockbroker. He could afford any hotel in town, but he's staying at the McAuliffe. He thinks there's less of a chance that someone from San Francisco will see him in his assignation," Annie said with a chuckle.

"Will he give you some tips on what stocks to buy?"

"He always does." Annie sighed. "If I would just pay attention to him and not try and figure stocks out on my own, I would have quite a nice portfolio by now. But, no, I always think I have some hot tip, that this time is going to make me rich, and I play it. Then, it's almost always the wrong thing to do."

Mary Beth laughed. "Annie, you wouldn't have it any other way, and you know it."

Rab had spent the last two weeks moving between Carson City and Silver City, then on to Dayton and Gold Hill. Half the time, he camped out on Mount Davidson, and the rest of the time he took a room in a miners' shelter in Gold Hill. But because Gold Hill and Virginia City were as linked as conjoined twins, he knew that sooner or later his investigation would have to extend to Virginia City as well.

As he was leaving Gold Hill, he saw passengers disembarking from the omnibus that made the regular runs across "the divide" between Gold Hill and Virginia City. One in particular caught his eye. An exceptionally pretty woman, she had chestnut hair, dark eyes, and a golden complexion. She looked familiar, and then he remembered.

This was the woman he had rescued from the runaway wagon. He recalled the feel of her soft body as he carried her from the street, and he particularly thought about the feel of her breast in his hand. He felt a little twinge in his groin, and he stared at her until she looked toward him. The contact between them was immediate, as tangible as if she had spoken to him. He smiled at her and touched the brim of his hat.

Susanna felt his eyes burning into her before she looked around. When she did, she lost herself in the intensity of his gaze. She recognized him immediately, and she remembered the warm tingling she had experienced at the feel of his hard body against hers on that day. When he touched the brim of his hat in a salute to her, she nodded, almost imperceptibly, then turned away. She had business to take care of. When she looked back a moment later, she saw that he was already riding away.

*   *   *

The first thing Rab did in Virginia City was to make arrangements to board Rebel. That done, he draped his saddlebags over his shoulder and walked down the boardwalk, the loose boards rattling with every step. He saw the International Hotel and considered staying there. It was the best hotel in town, and the only times he had come to Virginia City before, he had stayed there. But he decided against it this time because he didn't want to run the risk of seeing anyone who might recognize him. Also, he didn't think staying at the best hotel would be the image a Great Western detective would project. He saw three or four hotels on C Street and arbitrarily chose the McAuliffe for no other reason than that he had served in the First Louisiana Cavalry with a Captain McAuliffe.

When Rab stepped into the hotel, he saw a floral carpet on a painted wood floor, a settee, and a couple of chairs nearby. A potted lemon tree sat in front of a window. He thought that was a good sign. The miners' shelter he had been staying in at Gold Hill had single pine beds and feed sacks stitched together for walls. He had accepted that, but he didn't want to rough it any more than he had to.

Rab approached the front desk, dropping his saddlebags on the floor beside him. The desk clerk raised an eyebrow, but said nothing.

For just a moment Rab wondered why he was receiving such a look. "Sorry, I didn't mean to make so much noise."

The hotel clerk cleared his throat, still not saying anything.

"This is a hotel, isn't it?"

"It is, but we expect our guests to be civilized," the clerk said.

"And you think I'm not?"

Then Rab thought about the time he had been spending in the mountains, poking around the mines, descending the shafts and examining the winzes to question the hard-rock diggers and the mining engineers. That and the Gold Hill miners' lodge had left him with a scruffy, down-at-the-heels look.

"It's just that, at two dollars per night, you may find the McAuliffe a bit pricier than you expected," the clerk said. "On the other hand, you can get a bed at the Miners' Shelter for a bit a night. It's over on Union Street."

"I appreciate the information, and if I see anyone in need of a ten-cent bed, I'll be sure to tell them where they can find such a place. Does your hotel have a bathing room?"

"No, sir, we do not. The International is the only hotel in town with bathing rooms."

Having stayed at the International on his previous visit, Rab knew that. He didn't know that other hotels did not offer such facilities.

Rab took out a twenty-dollar gold piece and put it on the desk. Seeing the double eagle, the expression on the clerk's face changed from one of patronizing disdain to obsequious respect. "We have no bathing rooms, but we can bring a tub and hot water to your room, if you wish."

"Yes, please do that."

The hotel clerk produced a registration book. "Yes, sir, I'll see to it right away, Mr. . . ." He waited until Rab signed the book, then turning it around read, "Trudeau." The clerk took down a key and handed it to Rab. "You will be in room 204."

Rab picked up the saddlebags and draped them over his shoulder again. "Where can I get these clothes washed?"

"We don't have a laundry here in the hotel, but we have an arrangement with Wo Fan to do the laundry for our guests. That is, if you don't mind doing business with the Chinese."

"Does he get the clothes clean?"

"Yes, sir, and he is the quickest in Virginia City."

"Then, I don't mind doing business with him. Send him up," Rab said. "Oh, and I have a trunk that will be delivered. Will you see to it that it reaches my room?

"Hello, Mr. Hume," a woman's voice called from the door. Turning toward the sound of the voice, Rab saw an attractive woman with bright red hair and a most revealing green dress.

"Hello, Annie," the hotel clerk replied. "Your—uh—gentleman friend is in room 203."

"Thank you." Annie turned her attention to Rab. "I don't think I have had the pleasure"—she drew out the word as long as she could—"of meeting you. I'm Annie Biggs. My, my, you are one big boy, aren't you? I'm busy now, but you can be sure that I'll know where you are." She hurried up the stairs.

Rab turned back to the clerk. "Tell me, Mr. Hume, is

that what makes this a civilized place? If it is, it won't be the first whorehouse I've ever inhabited."

"We are most certainly not a brothel, sir," Hume said with as much effrontery as he could muster.

"Really? Are you telling me Miss Biggs is a chambermaid?"

"No, she is not a maid."

"She's a whore, isn't she?"

"We prefer to call them working women," Hume explained. "Look, if our guests make some sort of arrangement—we don't interfere. That is, as long as they are discreet and don't bother anyone else."

"I'll keep that in mind," Rab said. "Don't forget to send up my trunk when it arrives, but get a tub and bathwater right away. And send the man for my clothes."

"I'll take care of it right away, sir."

As Rab reached the top of the stairs, he saw Annie Biggs standing outside the door to room 203. When she saw Rab, she winked at him, then mouthed a kiss in his direction. When the door opened, she embraced a short, chubby man and planted a kiss on top of his bald head. The man ushered her into the room, but not before she had one more chance to wave to Rab.

5

Once inside his room, Rab walked over to the window and looked down onto C Street, which was the main commercial street in Virginia City. He saw a wagon and team running pell-mell, causing pedestrians to scurry for the boardwalks. That reminded him of the woman he had seen over in Gold Hill earlier today, and he thought about his reaction to seeing her, this long after the incident.

She was pretty, yes, but he had been around many pretty—even beautiful—women. He had held her tightly as he carried her across the street, and though at the time his primary intent was to get her to safety, now he found himself thinking about holding her body against his.

Maybe it was the way she had been looking at him before she stepped out into the street, and then again when they had made eye contact this morning in Gold Hill. Her eyes were big and brown, but what he remembered about them now was a vulnerability. It was as if he could see through them into her very soul.

She was just another woman, and it was a brief occurrence. By a set of unusual circumstances, it was a little more intimate than the average incidental meeting, yes, but in the end it was just another chance encounter. Why, then, did the soft feel of her body linger on so?

Did she live in Gold Hill or did she live in Virginia City? Because she had been stepping down from the omnibus when he saw her in Gold Hill, he thought she probably lived in Virginia City. Rab smiled. Maybe in a town this size, he might just have another chance encounter.

There was a knock on the door, and when Rab walked over to open it, two young Chinese boys brought in a large tub. Over the next few minutes, they filled it with hot water.

Susanna wondered about the man she had seen this morning. She knew he had recognized her, not only because of the way he stared at her, but also because of the salute. That is what bothered her, the arrogance—no, the insolence of that salute. It was as if he was telling her, *I know where my hand has been.*

Yet, despite the insolence, despite the haughtiness of his behavior, she could not get her mind off the power of his gaze. It was as if tiny bolts of lightning had leaped from his eyes to hers.

Susanna shook her head to clear her mind of the disturbing thoughts. She had come to do a job, and she intended to do it. She wasn't intimidated that Mr. Loudin had sent her to Gold Hill because she had often been over the Divide.

The Divide was the ridge that separated Virginia City from Gold Hill, though *joined* would be a better word, for it formed the suburbs of both towns, creating a rather large metropolis from the eighteen thousand citizens of Virginia City and the ten thousand who called Gold Hill home. At night, the Divide was a dangerous place to be because villains, referred to as footpads by the residents, loitered in the darkness to relieve unsuspecting victims of their purses, and sometimes their lives. By day, however, omnibuses ran scheduled routes safely between the two towns.

Susanna started her search by going to the Gold Hill Miners' Union Hall. She had been there many times before because the main fund-raiser for the GHMU was the lottery, and they had a drawing every day. Loudin never missed a chance to gamble—he bet on shooting contests, horse races, dog and cock fights, any kind of card game, and of course, the lotteries, both in Gold Hill and Virginia City. And if Loudin was too busy, he would send Susanna with his money for the lottery.

Because of her previous visits, Hiram Felker, the union clerk, recognized her as soon as she came into the hall. "Good morning, Miss Susanna. We've got a big pot today. How much is James in for?"

"Mr. Loudin will be in himself, later on," Susanna said. "Today, I am here for a different reason. I need some information, if you don't mind."

"If I know, I'll be glad to help you out."

"I'm looking for Rab Trudeau."

Felker squinted his eyes as if thinking about it, then he shook his head. "No, I don't think that's a name I recognize. What do you need him for?"

"Mr. Loudin wants me to find him. We think he is a detective, and he may be doing some investigating up at the mines."

"Oh, well, why didn't you say so? I didn't recognize his name, but I know who you're talking about. He's been in here a few times. And I think he's been poking around out at the mines, too. They say he's looking into the trading, and his investigation has gotten everybody all discombobulated."

"Why?"

"Miss Kirkland, you know how this works. If it weren't for trading stocks, we'd all be out of business. That is, unless you want every shareholder, big or small, payin' huge assessments."

"But what if someone is really doing something wrong? Don't we need to know that?"

"Sometimes we all have to look the other way—why, if someone's manipulating a little bit one way or the other, no harm's done. But if some big shot is trying to find out what's going on here, it can't be good. Nobody seems to know who hired this fella. Do you know?"

"No, I don't, but that's one of the things I'd like to find out," Susanna said.

"His name is Rab Trudeau, you say?"

"Yes. Do you have any idea where I might find him?"

"I don't have any idea. But as I said, he's been in here several times, and I expect he'll be back. He doesn't seem to do any gambling, though. He just talks to a few of the miners. You might try Alf Doten, down at the *Gold Hill News*. If anyone knows anything about this fella you're looking for, I expect it would be Doten. He pretty well keeps up on things."

"Thanks," Susanna said. "I'll give that a try."

Athough the *Gold Hill News* and the *Territorial Enterprise* were competitive papers with the *Virginia City Pioneer*, the competition was generally friendly, and Susanna was a welcome visitor. Doten, the owner and editor of the *News*, was working on the recently acquired steam engine that ran his press.

The tall, thin-faced, bearded man looked around toward Susanna as she came into the office.

"Hello, Susanna. Get tired of working for Loudin, and that amateurish rag he puts out, did you? So you want to come work for a real newspaper?"

Susanna smiled at Doten's joke. "No, sir. I've come to ask you for a little information."

"Information, is it? Loudin sent you here because he knows that I have a weakness for a pretty face, didn't he? And it would not be beyond that brigand to take advantage of that just to scoop me."

"Nobody in the history of newspapers has ever scooped Alf Doten. . . . Oh, by the way, how is your new baby doing?" Susanna asked about his newborn son to defuse what was obviously a flirtation on his part.

"We call him the 'extra' edition. But he is doing well,

thanks. So is his mother. Now, tell me what information you need."

"I'm trying to locate a man named Rab Trudeau. I understand that he has been here in Gold Hill for the last couple of weeks."

"He was here off and on. But I happened to have breakfast with him this morning, and he said he was going to be prospecting in Virginia City from now on—seems like everything's on the up-and-up in Gold Hill." Alf rolled his eyes and looked charmingly toward Susanna.

"What is he investigating?"

Doten smiled. "Sorry, darlin', you're going to have to find that out for yourself, or else read about it in the *News*. All I can tell you is that he's taken his investigation to Virginia City. If I were you, I'd start making the rounds of the lodging houses and hotels over there."

"Thanks," Susanna said. That was exactly what she planned to do, and she would take the next omnibus back.

When Susanna returned to Virginia City, she wondered which she should start checking first—hotels or lodging houses. She decided on the hotels because there weren't nearly as many, so she could check them more quickly. Also, if his stay was temporary, a hotel was likely where he would be.

Susanna checked the International, the Comstock House, the Depot Hotel, and the Arcade without success. As she was going into the McAuliffe, she met Annie Biggs coming across the lobby.

"Susanna, what are you doing here? You're not trying

to take some of my business, are you?" Annie asked as the two women greeted each another with an embrace.

"If I want to see you, is this where I have to come?" Susanna asked.

Annie and Susanna both lived at the Chaney House. In normal times, Harriet Chaney would not have allowed a woman in Annie's profession to board with her, but times were tough. Harriet had been widowed over a year ago when her husband had been killed in a cave-in at one of the mines, and while the Miners' Union had paid for the funeral, that was all they had paid.

Harriet was left with no source of income, so she turned her home into a lodging house and accepted any-one who could be a paying resident. She was glad that she had. Despite Annie's profession, she, Susanna, and Harriet's daughter, Mary Beth, had become fast friends.

"Well, I'm just surprised to see you here," Annie said.

"I'm doing something for Mr. Loudin. It's always 'Susanna do this, Susanna do that.' "

"I could get you a lot more money doing something else . . . ," Annie teased.

"Annie, Annie, Annie, what am I going to do with you? Can you imagine what Mrs. Kirkland would say if I took up the trade?"

"Go on, do what you have to do," Annie said with a laugh as she moved out of the doorway.

Ernest Hume was too far away from the two women to hear what they were saying, but from the smiles and the way they were acting toward each other, they were obviously friends. Hume didn't recognize the woman who had just come in, but he assumed that she, like Annie Biggs, who was a regular at the hotel, was a prostitute. She was certainly pretty enough, but Hume wondered about the clothes she was wearing. She was almost dowdy-looking in her gray serge skirt and high-necked white blouse. She should take lessons from Annie on how to dress and make up her face. It was a wonder that this girl, as pretty as she was, got any business at all.

"Can I help you, miss?" the hotel clerk asked.

"I'm looking for Mr. Rab Trudeau."

Hume smiled. "I'll say this about him; he doesn't let any grass grow under his feet."

"I beg your pardon?" Susanna replied, confused by the clerk's strange response to her inquiry.

"He's in room 204. Just go on up. It will be the second door on the right."

"Go on up?" Susanna asked, surprised by the remark.

"Yes, he's expecting you."

"Thank you."

As Susanna approached the stairs, she was frowning. Mr. Loudin must have made the arrangements, but if that was true, that meant he knew all along where Trudeau was staying. Why, then, didn't he just give her that information, instead of sending her to Gold Hill to look for the man?

She felt somewhat uneasy about going upstairs to visit a strange man in his hotel room, but she was sure that if B.D. had been given this story, he would have had absolutely no hesitancy about doing it. She did want to be a reporter, after all.

With the dirt washed off, Rab felt like a new man. The water had been too hot, but when he got out, the air cooled his warm body. He stepped over to the washbasin that sat on the dry sink, then worked up a generous lather in his shaving cup and liberally applied it to his face—too liberally, it seemed, because he got some of the soap in his eyes.

"Damn!" he said, closing his eyes and reaching for a towel.

There was a light knock on the door, and he figured that the laundryman had chosen that exact moment to come for his dirty clothes.

"Come on in!" he called, his voice muffled by the towel that covered his face. He turned toward the door.

Susanna gasped audibly. Except for the towel over his face, the man she had come to see was totally naked! She couldn't help but stare at his perfectly proportioned body. Obviously just from his bath, he had little drops of water clinging to his chest, shoulders, and muscular arms. An invasive purple scar ran from below his right shoulder, then curved up, like a fishhook, just before it reached his neck.

As she stood there staring at him, her gaze trailed down

from the wide expanse of his chest, across the lean, flat stomach, to a large, fascinating, and rather mysterious appendage that hung from a nest of black hair at the junction of his legs.

"What's the matter?" Rab asked, still rubbing his eyes. "Am I that different from a naked Chinese man?"

He heard a little giggle. "I don't know," a woman's voice replied. "I've never seen a naked Chinese man."

"What the hell?" Rab blurted in shock. Lowering the towel from his face, he wrapped it quickly around his waist, restoring what he hoped was some modesty, but little dignity, to the scene.

"You!" she said, recognizing him now that the towel had been pulled from his face.

"You're the woman from the street, aren't you?" Rab said easily. "I saw you this morning, too. Are you following me?"

"I'm so sorry," Susanna said, backing away from the door. "I was told to come on up, I thought you were expecting me."

"Well, I hadn't made any—what did Hume call them—arrangements? But since you are here, I'm sure we can work something out."

"Work something out?"

"Yes. We don't need to let an embarrassing moment stand in the way. Besides, in a few more minutes we'll both be naked anyway, so it really doesn't make any difference that I'm a little ahead of you."

"Mr. Trudeau! What are you talking about?" Susanna asked in a high-pitched, shocked voice.

"I'm pretty sure you aren't here to pick up laundry for

Wo Fan, so I figured—you know, that perhaps you were a—uh . . ."

Suddenly Susanna realized what he was saying. "A prostitute? Is that what you think? How dare you think such a thing! I assure you, Mr. Trudeau, I am not a prostitute."

Susanna lowered her head and started to leave the room, clearly disturbed by the turn of the conversation.

"No, wait," Rab called out. "If you aren't here for the laundry, or to warm my bed, may I ask just what the hell you *are* doing here?"

"I work for the *Pioneer*," Susanna stammered. "Mr. Loudin would like an interview with you."

"An interview? With me? Why?"

"He knows that you are a detective working for Great Western, and you're here to investigate what's going on at the mines. Since this city, and for that matter most of Nevada, is about one hundred percent dependent upon the mining operations, you can see why our readers might like to know what it is you are investigating."

"Tell your publisher, tell your Mr. Loudin," Rab said, drawing out the name with a derisive sneer, "that I am not interested in doing any interview, and definitely not with the *Pioneer*."

"What's wrong with the *Pioneer*?"

"That rag isn't worthy of being called a newspaper. It is too loose with its facts."

"We are not!" Susanna said defensively.

"No interview."

"But surely you can understand the concerns people

have? Isn't there anything we could do to convince you to grant us an interview?"

Rab paused for a moment; then, unexpectedly, he smiled at Susanna. It wasn't a smile of humor; the smile was both malevolent and strangely stirring. She felt a shortening of her breath and a diffusing warmth.

"Now that you mention it, I'm sure we could work something out," Rab said. "If you are really that insistent." Once again, he began to lower the towel, inching it toward his private parts.

As if mesmerized, Susanna watched the slowly receding towel. Her breath came in short, quick intakes, making her feel light-headed. She recalled her thoughts back at the lodging house when she had found the imprint of his hand on her breast. As then, she felt a warm tingling in her body. She knew she should turn away, but for the moment she was powerless to do so.

Rab stopped the towel short of any further exposure. "Shall I drop it, madam?" he asked in a raspy voice.

His words brought Susanna to her senses. She turned and began to run down the hall to the stairs as quickly as possible, chased away by Rab's laughter.

"That may be the fastest engagement I've ever seen," Ernest Hume called out to her, and he began to guffaw, while Susanna raced out the door.

"Did you get the interview?" Loudin asked when Susanna returned to the newspaper office.

"No." Susanna stared at Loudin with her eyes flashing anger. "Did you set that up?"

"Did I set what up?"

"That—that encounter with that disgusting man," Susanna sputtered.

"Look, Susanna, I sent you to get that interview. If you can't do it, I'll send B.D. You say you want to be a reporter—well, prove it to me. Now, don't let me down."

6

As Susanna lay in bed that night, she let her mind pass over the events of the day. First there had been her encounter with Rab Trudeau when she saw him in Gold Hill.

Then, there was this afternoon.

This afternoon in the hotel room, she had seen him totally naked. It had been a fleeting glimpse to be sure, but she had verified with her own eyes the man's commanding physique. That sight had burned into her, where it remained like a bed of glowing coals in the pit of her stomach. Even now she could feel the arousal of the nipples of her breasts as the brushing of the silk fabric of her nightgown caused them to harden.

Why could she not put that incident out of her mind? Was it just because he was the first man she had ever seen naked? Well, that wasn't entirely correct. She had seen Jesse and some of his friends when the boys were swimming naked in a pond near where they had lived at the time. But that was a long time ago—before the Kirklands had moved to Nevada.

They were but boys then, only fifteen years of age, and she was a young girl of nine. Susanna had been mesmerized by the sight of the male bodies as she hid in the bushes to watch as they cavorted in the water. She knew she should not have been doing that, and she had withdrawn with embarrassment, never to tell anyone what she had seen.

Susanna was without experience, but not without imagination. She had read the forbidden Ouida novels, those that were supposedly unfit for an unmarried woman, but now, unbidden, her mind played out a scenario with Rab Trudeau that set her entire body aflame. She tossed and turned in her bed, and despite the rather cool night, she found that she had to push the quilt aside just to rid her body of this powerful and disquieting heat.

Finally, and only by counting backward from one hundred, she was able to clear her mind of its corporeal thoughts.

The next morning, as would happen every morning and every afternoon during the workweek, a telegrapher hired by the Virginia City accounting firm of Barry, Patmore, and Daigh received the reports from the San Francisco Mining Exchange. As quickly as the reports were received, the telegrapher would call out the quotes, and one of the accountants would record them on a large blackboard in the front window of the office building.

Nearly everyone in the city dabbled in the mining stocks, some more deeply than others. As a result, when the stocks were volatile, either rising or falling rapidly, the morning and afternoon postings of the latest numbers would always gather a crowd. Store clerks from Kirkland, or Manning and Duck, sometimes with yardstick in hand, would leave their stores to check the postings. Barkeepers with garters around their sleeves, butchers with bloodstained aprons, blacksmiths with hammer in hand, bakers, cobblers, tinkers, and miners would join the crowd. Women were there as well, from the soiled doves to the seamstresses to the respectable homemakers. All would gather to exult in joy or moan in despair at the rise and fall of the numbers that would mean bonanza or borasca for them.

Jesse Kirkland was thirty years old and unmarried. Uninterested in working in his father's mercantile, he earned his living by trading in mine stocks. More than a mere dabbler, his situation would vary widely from day to day so that he would often have holdings worth thousands of dollars, and almost as often, he would be completely broke.

When Gus Kirkland built the store, he built it on the east side of C Street. The town of Virginia City being laid out on an incline, the front of the store was two stories high, while the back was three stories. Gus made one-half of that bottom floor his stockroom, and he had intended to make the other half of that floor available as office space for a doctor or lawyer. Instead, Jesse lived there, paying ten dollars a month rent. The ten dollars included board, and either his mother or his sister would provide meals for him, generally bringing the meal to his room and leaving it on a table under a cloth to keep the flies away.

Jesse was just short of six feet tall, with hair the color of wheat and eyes that were more gray than blue. He was, most women agreed, a handsome man, though something about him, like a tiny imperfection in a stem of crystal, was ultimately off-putting. Perhaps it was the rather sardonic curl of his lips, as if he alone knew a joke, or the glint in his eyes that was both appealing and frightening.

This morning Jesse got up before anyone had arrived at the store. Lifting the cloth on his table, he grabbed a biscuit and a pork chop left over from last night's supper, then left quietly, not wanting to deal with his father in case he was already at work.

Jesse was a constant worry to his parents. It wasn't just his unwillingness, or perhaps inability, to settle down that caused the problems. This morning he started for the Divide, where there would be cockfights. Jesse had just bought a fighting rooster named King George. It seemed like a good investment because King George had been in six previous fights and won every one.

Several others were already present when Jesse got there, many with their own fighting roosters. Burt Mc-

Kinney, the man Jesse had bought King George from, was there as well, and he was about to introduce a new fighting rooster, which he called General Lee.

"Hello, Jesse," Michael O'Malley called. "Your pa let you off the leash this morning, did he?"

"I didn't ask, I just left. Let's get these chickens to fightin'."

"How about putting King George up against General Lee?" McKinney asked.

"I'll do that, and I've got twenty dollars to bet on King George. Who wants some of the action?"

"I'll bet against him," O'Malley said.

"You are betting against me?" Jesse asked, surprised at the bet. "Michael, you've seen King George fight before. You know nobody can beat him."

"I'm thinkin' maybe McKinney knows somethin' the rest of us don't know. Otherwise, he never would have sold him."

"Yeah? Well, I know roosters, and I'm saying there's not one here that can beat ol' King George."

"Do you like chicken and dumplin's, Jesse?" Burt asked. "Because after this fight, about the only thing King George is going to be good for is if you can get your mama to cook him up for you in a pot of dumplin's."

"We'll see," Jesse said. "Ol' King George here is goin' to be mad at you for sellin' him in the first place. He's goin' to rip General Lee apart."

The two men teased the roosters against each other, then dropped them on the ground. The roosters immediately attacked with flapping wings, beak thrusts, and slashing talons. Feathers flew, then blood, until finally King George lay dying on the ground.

"What was wrong with King George?" one of the on-lookers asked. "I've never seen him act like that. He didn't have hardly no fight in him at all."

"You did something to him," Jesse charged angrily. "You did something to him before you sold him to me."

"You accusin' me of cheatin'?" McKinney asked.

"Yes, I'm accusing you of cheating."

Gus Kirkland and his daughter, Alice, were laying out merchandise on the sale table, while Kirkland's son-in-law, Harold Ponder, stood by to attend to any customers. Kirkland was a master at conducting special sales, using them to get rid of the last few items of a particular product. A month before a product was slated to be moved out, he would raise the price. Then, when he put the product on sale, he would lower the price to just above what it had been originally, while advertising as "On Sale." Invariably the merchandise would sell quickly, with few ever noticing that it was higher than it had been for most of the time it had been on the store shelves.

"I don't know why this calico didn't sell," Alice said as she affixed the price to the bolt of cloth. "It is such a pretty print."

"Women don't want pretty—they want good, service-able linen or wool or serge," Harold said.

A small, ringing bell that was affixed to the front door signaled that someone had just entered the store.

"Mr. Kirkland?" someone called.

Looking up from his work, Kirkland saw Officer Billy Swain of the Virginia City Police.

"Yes, Officer, I'm back here. Is there something I can show you?" Kirkland asked, always the consummate salesperson.

"No, sir. It's about Jesse."

Kirkland felt a sinking sensation in his stomach. Had Jesse's tomfoolery gotten him killed? "What—what about Jesse?"

"We have him in jail."

Kirkland's first reaction was relief that Jesse was in jail and not dead. But his second reaction was concern that this time it might be something serious.

"What did he do now?"

"He was up on the Divide this morning, wagering on the chickens. Jesse accused Burt McKinney of cheatin' and Burt didn't take to that. They got into a little scuffle, and the next thing you know, Jesse laid Burt's head open with an ax handle. If McKinney didn't have such a hard head, he'd like as not be dead."

"What happens now?" Kirkland asked.

"Chief Ferrell said if McKinney doesn't press charges, he'll let Jesse go."

"Well, is he going to?"

"Now, that all just depends," the deputy said.

Kirkland knew exactly what Officer Swain was talking about when he said it "just depends."

"How much?" Kirkland asked.

"Fifty dollars ought to take care of it this time."

Kirkland walked over to the cash drawer, opened it, and pulled out five ten-dollar notes. "Will you see to it that Mr. McKinney receives this money?"

"Yes, sir, I will. And, uh, Mr. Kirkland, I don't mean no offense or nothin', but I've seen fellas like Jesse before. They just keep gettin' into trouble, one little thing after another until, first thing you know, they done got themselves into more trouble than you can buy them out of. Even someone with your money."

"Thank you, Officer," Kirkland said, not responding directly to the policeman's comment.

Ten minutes later a sheepish Jesse Kirkland came into the store. He didn't say anything to anyone, but picked up a broom and started sweeping. After he swept the floor and hauled out the trash, he began straightening merchandise on some of the shelves.

Gus Kirkland had been with customers when Jesse came in, but when the activity lulled, he walked over to talk to his son.

"You cost me fifty dollars this morning."

"I'm sorry."

"You cost me seventy-five dollars when you broke out the window in the Bucket of Blood Saloon."

"I paid that money back."

"Son, when are you going to grow up?"

"I have to go. I'm supposed to meet some friends. Uh, Pop, can I borrow a hundred dollars?"

"Borrow? As if you intend to pay it back?"

"I'll pay it back. I have some stock I'm going to cash in."

Kirkland stared at his son for a long moment, then he went over to the cash drawer and pulled out five twenty-dollar gold pieces. "The only reason I'm doing this is because I don't want you becoming a footpad out on the Divide tonight, stealing from some innocent person."

"I've never been a bandit, Pop, and I never would become one," Jesse said resolutely. "And I don't know how you could even suggest that I would do something like that."

"You have to admit, Son, your life is such that you don't instill much confidence."

"I've done well buying and selling mine shares. Right now I have over a thousand dollars' worth of stock."

"No, right now you have mine shares that are worth a thousand dollars if—and that is a big if—you can find a buyer."

"I'm going to visit some friends," Jesse mumbled, hurrying out of the store.

"Where is he going?" Minnie asked when Kirkland came over to join his wife and daughter.

"He said he was going to visit some friends. Alice, did you talk to him?"

"I talked to him, Papa. I tried to get through to him, but he just waved me off. He said I was worrying too much and that I should just take care of Betsy and not try and be his mother."

"What are we going to do with him, Gus?" Minnie asked. "Like Officer Swain said, one of these days he's going to wind up in jail and we won't be able to get him out."

"Or worse," Kirkland said.

"Gus, we have to do something."

"I know. I've been thinking about it, and I might have an idea."

"What?"

"I'm not ready to talk about it just yet. First I have to see if it is feasible."

The Improved Order of Red Men Club, Paiute Tribe Number One, had nothing to do with the Paiutes, or even with Indians. It was instead a collection of fifty men, stockbrokers and professional men mostly, who were part of the national and respected fraternal organization.

In Virginia City, however, several of the members of the Paiute Tribe Number One had formed their own little group within that noble organization, and they called themselves the Comstock Betterment Association.

James Loudin was not only a member of the Order of Red Men, he was also part of the Comstock Betterment Association, and as soon as he walked into the club building, he spotted Van Cleve, Burdick, and Sheehan sitting at their "special" table in the back of the dining room. He hurried over to join them.

"You sent word that you wanted to see me," Loudin said. "What's it about?"

"We are putting the North Star Mine on shutdown today," Van Cleve said.

"Really?" Loudin replied excitedly. "So you finally hit it, huh? A new silver vein?"

It had become routine over the last few years that when a new, rich vein of silver ore was discovered, the owners of the mine would shut it down, preventing anyone from entering as well as locking all the miners inside for several days. The idea was to prevent knowledge of the new discovery from getting out, so that those who were in the know would be able to buy stock cheaply. Once all the cheap stock was bought up, the mine would be opened again, and knowledge that a new vein had been discovered would be made public. Invariably, the result was an increase in the value of that mine's stock.

"Now, Mr. Loudin, you know we are not at liberty to say anything like that," Burdick said.

Loudin drummed his fingers as he looked at the others who were seated around the table. "You know, do you not, that once news of the shutdown gets into the paper, people will think that a new vein of silver ore has been discovered, and the price of North Star stock will rise precipitously? I'm not sure I should print such a story without further verification."

"Perhaps if you knew the content of a paper we have drawn up, it would provide you some incentive to publish the article," Van Cleve suggested.

"Oh?"

Van Cleve looked toward Burdick, and Burdick pulled

out an envelope and handed it to Van Cleve. Van Cleve removed a paper from the envelope and showed it to Loudin.

> *Know Ye by These Presents*
> *This document, when signed by all parties, transfers, and is a good and honest deed, to a claim of fifty feet of the North Star Mine, such claim representing, in real property, two and one-half percent of the mine.*

Picking up the paper, Loudin saw that it was signed by all three owners of the North Star, thus making it a legitimate transfer of property.

"I hope you aren't making this available to me in expectation of my writing a newspaper article that I know is false. Because, I could not accept that."

"Oh, no, sir, nothing of the kind," Van Cleve said. "The only thing we are asking you to print is the fact that we have shut down the mine. And, as that is true, you will not be in violation of any of your ethics."

"I see." Loudin held up the paper. "There is no quid pro quo attached to this?"

"Not at all," Van Cleve said. "I prefer to think of it as a token of gratitude for the support your newspaper has always given, not just to the North Star Mine, but to the entire silver industry of Washoe Valley."

"I see."

"And of course, given your history of editorial support and favorable mention, I'm sure we can count on similar articles in the future."

Loudin smiled, then nodded. "I am nothing if not a supporter of the silver industry."

"I look forward to this evening's news," Burdick said.

As James Loudin was meeting with Van Cleve, Burdick, and Sheehan, Jesse Kirkland was playing cards in the Brass Rail Saloon. He had enjoyed a run of good luck, and now the one hundred dollars he had received from his father was well over five hundred dollars. He had just dragged in his third successive pot when one of the other players challenged him.

"Mister, there ain't no one as lucky as you are this morning," the big man said. He had a bald head that looked like a cannonball balanced between his left and right shoulder.

"Take it easy, Hank," one of the other players said.

"I ain't goin' to take it easy when this slick-dealin' son of a bitch takes away my hard-earned money."

"Mister, if you can't afford to lose money, you have no business playing poker," Jesse said calmly. "Sometimes you win and sometimes you lose. That's the way the game is."

"Yeah? Well, you ain't lost yet. And that tells me somethin' ain't right about this game."

"Hank, I've seen Jesse lose a lot of times," one of the other players said. "You're gettin' out of hand here. Like he said, if you can't afford to lose, don't be playin' the game."

"I'll be askin' for my money back, now," Hank said.

Jesse looked across the table at him for a moment, then reached down and put his finger on a silver dollar.

He slid the dollar across the table. "Go have lunch and a drink on me."

Hank looked at the silver dollar, lying alone and gleaming against the green felt covering. "You took more'n a hundred dollars from me this morning and you think you can just pass it off by givin' me a dollar?"

"I didn't take it, I won it, fair and square."

Suddenly Hank let out a deep, guttural yell. He picked up his chair and tried to bring it crashing down on Jesse's head, but at the last possible moment Jesse threw himself onto the floor, avoiding the blow. Before Hank could raise the chair for a second attack, Jesse pulled his gun and shot Hank just below the kneecap. With a shout of rage and pain, Hank went down, clutching his leg.

The sound of the gunfire was loud and unexpected, and everyone else in the saloon jumped up from his table or hurried away from the bar out of the way. They stood against the walls, leaving the middle of the saloon to the two players in this drama.

Jesse put his pistol back in its holster and scooped up his winnings, except for the silver dollar. Then he picked up the coin and dropped it on the floor in front of Hank.

"Like I said, have lunch and a drink on me," Jesse said, just before he turned to walk out of the saloon.

Over at the *Pioneer,* Susanna heard the gunshot and, wondering what it was, stepped out onto the walk in front of the newspaper office to look up and down the street. She stood there for a moment, but, not seeing any frenzied activity anywhere, decided it must not have been anything of significance. Perhaps it was just a firecracker, she thought as she turned to go back into the office.

Right now B. D. Elliott was in an argument with the owner and publisher of the newspaper. Their heated discussion was taking place in the small, glass-enclosed office of James Loudin, and even though Susanna tried not to eavesdrop, their voices were so loud she could not avoid overhearing.

"And if you don't mind my asking, just where are we getting the information that there's been a bonanza at the North Star?" B.D. asked.

"What does it matter where I got the information?" Loudin replied. "I don't need you to be questioning me. All I need for you to do is to write the article."

"But a story like this is going to be causing the stock to go zooming up, and you know it. I'm not all that comfortable writing stories about 'facts' when I know nothing about those facts."

"Ha! Are you telling me that you never amplify your stories? That you don't, to use your own words, 'spice them up with the crushed red pepper of satire, and the garlic of embellishment'?"

"Perhaps from time to time I dip the pen in a bit of the blarney ink," B.D. admitted. "But in the quaints I pen, everybody knows they're fiction. They just fill up column inches with amusement. Nobody gets hurt by the embellishment. If we are saying that the mine is being shut down for a few days, all the readers will be thinking that a new vein has been struck."

"We are making no such assertion. We are merely reporting what is actually happening. The North Star is being shut down. That is the truth, and that is news."

"But if the story is misunderstood, then it's real people that will lose their shirts. And there is no doubt in my mind but that unscrupulous people know this and will be taking advantage of it. I don't like this, James."

"Either you write this story for me or you drag your carcass back to the *Enterprise*. Maybe DeQuille will work with you again. But I grow weary of your defiance."

"There is no need for you to be doing that," B.D. said. "Coward that I am, I will write the story just the way you want it."

"I thought you might see it my way," Loudin said condescendingly. He left the little room, then turned his attention to Susanna. "B.D. has a story to write. It is imperative that it be in today's paper, and I'll expect you to see to it that he gets it done and that you get it set."

"Yes, sir," Susanna said.

"I'm going down to the Red Men Club. By the time I get back, I want the paper put to bed."

"Worry not, James Loudin. We'll get your damned paper out," B.D. said.

"Good. By the way, B.D., how is it that you are sober this morning?" Loudin asked as he moved toward the front door of the *Pioneer* office.

"I had little choice, I'm afraid. I ran out of whiskey last night, and that's the sad fate of it."

Loudin chuckled at the response, then left the office.

*   *   *

Like her foster brother, Jesse, and her friends Mary Beth and Annie, as well as her fellow workers B.D. and James Loudin, Susanna had investments in mining stocks. Just about everyone she knew except Gus and Minnie Kirkland, and Alice and her husband, was invested in the mines. But unlike many of the other speculators, Susanna was unconcerned about the huge swings in value, for her investments were modest and had already earned back her initial outlay. That money, plus a healthy profit, she had already cashed out and deposited in the bank. Now, as she continued with her investments, she was, as she had once heard B.D. describe it, "playing on the mine owners' money."

Because her investments were modest and well planned, she saw no reason to react to the news of the shutdown of North Star Mine.

When Loudin returned to the newspaper shop later that same morning, he saw Susanna taking the type sticks off the press roller drum, then extracting the individual letters of type, dipping them in a small vat of kerosene before returning them to the proper cubicles.

"Did B.D. write the story the way I told him to?" Loudin asked.

"Here is the paper, all printed, and ready for this afternoon's distribution as soon as Mickey gets here to deliver them."

Loudin took his reading glasses from his pocket and put them on, carefully hooking the earpieces over one ear at a time; then, using his index finger, he slid them up his nose. He found B.D.'s story and began to read:

North Star Silver Mine on Shutdown
None of Its Employees Allowed on Surface

It was reliably learned by this newspaper that the North Star Silver Mine has closed all access and egress apertures to its operations in order to prevent any of the miners currently inside from leaving, and to bar any outsider from entering.

Although no specific purpose was given for the shutdown, which operation the mine is attempting to keep quiet, it is well-known by mining engineers and investment speculators, as well as the general public, that such a procedure is normally used to prevent information of new and rich discoveries from reaching the public.

As a guardian of the freedom of the press, as well as the protector of the people's right to be informed, this paper is undertaking to publish this information as a service to its readership. And though we cannot report with unreserved and absolute validity that a new silver vein has been struck, we can speculate to that end, and that we do without hesitation or discomforting thought.

"Good, good, this is very good," Loudin said after he finished reading the article. "B.D. can turn a fine phrase when he is sober."

"Yes, he is a wonderful writer," Susanna agreed.

"By the way, I just saw Kirkland down at the post office. He asked me to tell you that he wants you to meet him at the Silver Dollar for lunch."

"What? Are you sure he said lunch? It's not like Mr. Kirkland to take off work in the middle of the day."

"Lunch is what he said. Oh, and while you are with him, don't forget to ask him to increase his advertising."

7

Leaving the McAuliffe House, Rab Trudeau walked up the incline on Sutton Street and then turned toward the Miners' Union Hall. The union hall was a two-story brick building with a balcony that extended out over the boardwalk. A couple of men were standing on the balcony, smoking cigars and talking animatedly. They paid no attention to Rab as he stepped through the front door.

People in the meeting hall were gathered in half a dozen conversational clusters. Rab picked up a newspaper and found a chair near one group of men. He pretended to be reading, but was listening.

"We're assaying out at three thousand dollars a ton," one of them said.

"What level?"

"Yes, well, that's the thing. We're near three thousand feet down now."

"Ha, that's nothing. We're already lower than the Sutro Tunnel," one of the others said. "But our assay is holding out."

"Did you hear, they've got the North Star on shutdown. Nobody in or out."

"The North Star was three dollars a share last week. It'll be climbin' higher than a cat's back now. If I was you, I'd be buyin' some stock."

"How is it goin' to climb if nobody knows about it?"

"It'll be in this evening's *Pioneer.*"

"How do you know?"

"Trust me, the story will be in this evening's *Pioneer.*"

"I hear they're goin' to be puttin' out some bad news on the Silver Falcon and the Ophir again."

"I don't understand that. I know for a fact both of 'em are producin' just real good right now."

"Ha! Just think about it, Rufus. It's the same reason they said the North Star was played out a couple weeks ago. Somebody wants to run the stock down, so they can buy it at the bottom. Then when it starts its run up, sell it when it's high again."

"You ever think about the real folks who get taken on this?"

"Nah. If they don't know what they're doin', they got no business in buyin' into it in the first place. Now me, I bought some Chollar stock when it was down. Made a couple thousand out of it."

"Who's behind all this manipulation?" Rab asked.

The four men who had been talking looked over toward Rab.

"Who wants to know?" one of them asked.

"The name is Trudeau. Rab Trudeau."

"Are you a miner?"

"Just a minute, I've heard of you," one of the other men said. "You're the detective fella that's been over in Gold Hill pokin' around out at the mines, aren't you?"

"I've been looking around, yes."

"What are you lookin' for?"

"Evidence," Rab said.

The four men looked at each other as if they didn't quite understand the answer.

"Evidence? What do you mean by that? Evidence of what?"

"Evidence of fraud and corruption in operation of the mines," Rab said. "In fact, evidence of the very kind of thing you gentlemen were just discussing."

"There ain't no fraud or corruption that I know of. All the mine owners are bein' well served by the managers; the local investors here in town are makin' money; and miners are makin' four dollars a day. Everybody's happy, which is damn good."

"Who you doing the investigatin' for?" one large and muscular man asked. "There's nobody complainin' that I know of."

"Excuse me, sir," another man said, coming over to address Rab. This wasn't a miner, but one of the employees of the hall. "This Union Hall is for miners only. Are you in the mining business?"

"Hell no, he ain't in the mining business. He's a damn

detective, here to put all of the rest of us out of business," one of the four men said.

Rab had a letter that would authorize his presence, but he decided this was not the time to show it. For the time being he would rather maintain his separation.

"I'll be on my way," Rab said as he started toward the door.

"Mr. Detective," the big, muscular man called toward him. "My name is Arnie Slade, and I'm second-level foreman at the Yellow Jacket. I want you to remember my name, because if you come pokin' around out at my mine, you're going to have to deal with me."

Rab stopped, turned, and looked coolly at the challenger. "Will I?" he asked in a cold, calm voice. "I'll tell you what, Mr. Slade. Suppose I just deal with you now?"

Slade was used to intimidating people just because of his size and strength. When he saw that Rab was not intimidated, it made him a little uneasy, and he hesitated before he responded.

"You just mind what I say," the big man said, though with considerably less bluster and bravado than before.

As Rab left the Miners' Union Hall, the smell of cooking was coming from the Silver Dollar restaurant. It was nearly noon, and he was hungry, so he walked across the street to have his lunch.

Specifically selecting a table that placed his back to the wall, Rab ordered oysters on the half shell as an appetizer, and steak and potatoes for his entrée. His appetizer was delivered, and he was just opening the first oyster when he saw her enter. This was the fourth time he had seen this same woman: the day he had rescued her, when she had gotten off the omnibus in Gold Hill, and, yesterday—oh, yes, yesterday. He couldn't forget yesterday, when she had waltzed into his hotel room to find him naked. Rab smiled thinking of her interesting, but definitely interested, reaction. And now here was another chance encounter.

When Susanna stepped into the Silver Dollar at noon, she looked around for Mr. Kirkland. She didn't see Kirkland, but she did see Rab Trudeau. Sitting all alone at a table that was backed up against the wall, he was eating raw oysters, skillfully popping open the shells. He was much more dressed than he was the last time she had seen him, or at least she assumed he was wearing something more than the white, collarless shirt and the black vest that she could see.

He was incredibly handsome—why did he have to be such a jerk?

As the image of him naked popped up in her mind, Susanna's face began to burn with embarrassment. She turned to leave, but then she saw Mr. Kirkland at another table, with his head buried behind a newspaper. How would she get past Rab Trudeau? Taking a deep breath, drawing up to her full height, she would pass directly in front of him. Just as she approached his table, he dropped his knife in her path, forcing her to stop.

"Excuse me, madam," he said as he retrieved the utensil. His eyes never left hers. "It was entirely my fault, and I am sincerely apologetic."

"Apology accepted," Susanna said as she maintained steady eye contact for a moment. Then she hurried on to Mr. Kirkland's table.

Typically, Kirkland did not rise for her when she arrived, but he did put his paper down as she pulled out a chair to join him.

"I suppose it is absolutely necessary to write a story about Jesse every time he has some sort of trouble," Kirkland said.

Susanna thought the way Mr. Kirkland had worded his opening comment was strange. It was neither query nor declarative, but somewhere in between.

"Mr. Kirkland, everyone in the saloon saw what happened, and we could not very well print a story about Mr. O'Malley and not include Jesse's name, since he was involved in the same incident," Susanna replied.

"I suppose not. And now there has been another incident. Two more incidents, actually."

"Oh, my, what was it this time?"

"I may as well tell you. It'll wind up in the news anyway," Kirkland said. "It seems Jesse got into a fight with Burt McKinney, and after he hit McKinney in the head with an ax handle, he was put in jail. Officer Swain said it's a miracle that McKinney wasn't killed."

"Jesse's in jail now?"

"No. I took care of it."

"I'm glad he's not there, but I fear the time may well come when you won't be able to get him out."

"Officer Swain said the same thing," Kirkland said.

"You said there were two incidents?"

"Yes, but from what I can gather, the second one really wasn't his fault. He got into a fracas at the Brass Rail a couple of hours ago, and he wound up shooting someone."

"Oh! I heard a shot this morning. What happened?"

"An argument over a card game. Someone tried to bash Jesse's head in with a chair, and Jesse shot him in the leg."

"Oh, thank God he didn't kill him. I guess Jesse didn't have a choice."

"Yes, he did have a choice," Kirkland said. "He made the choice when he went into the saloon to play poker in the first place. If he would just work for me like I want him to, these situations wouldn't come up."

"Was Jesse arrested over the shooting?"

"No, not this time, because he had witnesses to back up his claim. But he certainly has the attention of the police now. They'll be watching him like a hawk."

"It seems to me like maybe he already had their attention," Susanna suggested.

Before Kirkland could answer, a waiter came to their table, and after Kirkland ordered a bowl of vegetable soup, Susanna ordered a half dozen raw oysters.

"Raw oysters? I've never seen you eat those before. I suppose that's something your harlot friend has introduced you to," Kirkland said.

"I thought I might like to try them."

Why did she order oysters? Was it because *he* was eating them? Looking into the mirror on the wall behind Mr. Kirkland, she realized that she could see Trudeau.

Mr. Kirkland returned to his newspaper, and they sat in silence for a few minutes. Then, as the waiter returned with their order, the picture of Trudeau standing naked before her flashed into her mind again, and she smiled. *I've seen you naked.* She thought of the offer he had made, bargaining for the interview, and she blushed. She wasn't blushing over the offer as much as she was over her reaction to it. A small voice, somewhere deep inside her—a voice that she could not squelch—wondered what it would have been like if she had accepted.

She felt her cheeks burning.

"Are you all right?" Kirkland asked as he lifted a spoonful of soup to his lips.

"Yes, of course. Why do you ask?"

"Your face suddenly flushed."

"Did it? I don't know why." Susanna lifted her hand to her face.

"It must have been a reflection."

"Yes, I'm sure it was." Susanna turned her attention back to the oysters on her plate.

When the busboy came to clear his table, Rab got his attention. "The young lady over there, sitting with the older gentleman. Do you know her name?"

"That is Susanna Kirkland," the busboy said. "The gentleman with her is Mr. Gus Kirkland. He owns a big store in Virginia City—the Kirkland Emporium. I'm sure you have seen it."

"Yes, I have seen it. And is he her husband?"

"No, sir, he is her father."

Rab smiled. "Thank you."

"Did you have a particular reason why you wanted me to have lunch with you? Or did you just want to talk about Jesse's problems?" Susanna asked Kirkland as she worked on the raw oysters. She didn't like them and couldn't eat them without a lot of horseradish, but she had made such a big thing of ordering them, she felt she could not leave them on her plate.

"Yes, I want to talk about Jesse's problems."

"Mr. Kirkland, you must know that I don't have any say as to what stories go into the paper. For that, you would have to talk to Mr. Loudin."

"I know that. I also know that if I would increase my advertising with him, I could probably convince him to keep the stories out. But that doesn't address the real problem. I am very concerned about Jesse. I am worried that the time may come, and very soon, when Jesse's escapades will go beyond rowdiness and evolve into something major and very dangerous. I do not want to see him wind up in prison, or worse. But I know he is heading that way if we do not intervene."

"Yes, I fear the same thing." For some time, Susanna had been thinking this, but she had been hesitant to suggest it to either Mr. or Mrs. Kirkland.

"Then, you do care for him?"

"Of course I care for him. How could I not? We were raised together, and he is a part of my youth. Why would you even ask such a thing?"

"I know that Jesse made things difficult for both you and Alice as you were growing up."

Despite herself, Susanna smiled. "You mean like the time he dropped a frog down my back while we were at school? Or the time he cut Alice's hair while she was sleeping?"

Kirkland smiled as well. "Yes, that and a lot of other things. He was such a . . ." Kirkland paused, as if looking for a word.

"Pain in the rear," Susanna said, but that she was still smiling ameliorated her comment.

"First Corinthians 13:11 says, 'When I was a child, I spake as a child, I understood as a child, I thought as a child: but when I became a man, I put away childish things.' Evidently that is a part of the Bible that Jesse has never read. Or, if he read it, he does not heed it."

"I am sure you have tried to reason with him," Susanna said.

"My dear, I have had scores, perhaps hundreds, of talks with him, and this goes all the way back to when he was but a boy. My talks did no good for the boy, and they are even less effective for the man."

Susanna listened, wondering where this conversation was going. Neither of the Kirklands had ever discussed Jesse's behavior with her before.

"Why won't he work in the store?" Kirkland asked. "It

is an honest profession and I have proven by my success that it can be a most profitable one."

"Maybe Jesse is just looking for something."

"What do you mean, looking for something?"

"I think he doesn't want to work in the store because he wants to prove to himself that he is capable of doing something on his own," Susanna said.

"You mean by investing in the silver-mine stock?"

"It's his way of independence."

"You call it independence, I call it a lack of responsibility," Kirkland said. "But maybe if a young person, very nearly his own age, were to talk to him—show some interest in him—he might respond."

"You may be right. Has Alice spoken to him?"

"She has, and it did no good. That's why I'm coming to you. Susanna, I want you to go to him. Speak to him with all your heart and with all your soul. Make Jesse understand just what is at stake here."

"Well, of course, Mr. Kirkland, I would be glad to. But if Jesse refused to listen to Alice, what makes you think I would have a chance of getting through to him? She is his natural sister; I am not." Susanna thought to add, *As Mrs. Kirkland has told me many times,* but she held her tongue.

"It is precisely because you *aren't* his sister that you can do something Alice cannot."

"I don't understand."

Susanna was confused by the direction the conversation was going, and she had a somewhat uncomfortable, queasy feeling. "What could I possibly do for Jesse that Alice cannot do?"

Gus Kirkland looked down at the table for a few moments, then raised his head and stared at Susanna with an ominous expression. "Alice cannot marry him, but you can."

"What?" Susanna dropped her fork, making a clatter on her plate. She shouted the word so loudly that the dining room grew quiet as everyone strained to hear what had caused the outburst.

"I said," Kirkland repeated, leaning across the table and speaking so quietly that only she could hear, "you can marry him. No, let's make that, you *will* marry him. You owe me that, my dear. In fact, you owe it to our entire family. May I remind you, Susanna Ward, that if I had not agreed to take you into our wagon that terrible day so long ago, your bones would even now be bleaching out there on the trail?"

Susanna felt her insides turn to mush. Not since the day that she watched as her entire family was put in blankets, rolled into that hole, then covered with dirt, had she felt such an intense grab of emotion.

"I know this is asking an awful lot of you," Kirkland said, his words less demanding now and more pleading. "But I also know that, deep down, Jesse is a good and honest man. Like I said, all he needs is a good woman to straighten him out. And I believe you are that woman, Susanna. After all, you are twenty-four years old, and unmarried. You are practically on the way to spinsterhood yourself. I would think you would welcome this opportunity."

Susanna did not reply.

Kirkland smiled. "Look at it this way. If you marry Jesse, you truly will be a part of our family. And when I pass, and it becomes time for my worldly possessions to be divided, why, you will inherit an equal share, just as will Jesse and Alice. Now, of course, you know you are not included in my will."

"Nor should I be. It is as you said; my very existence is due to your generosity and that of others who contributed money. But it was you who took me in so long ago, when nobody else would." She took a deep breath, then held it, both to force back a sob and to muster the courage to say what she was about to say. "But it is because I owe my life to you, and not for any future inheritance, that I will consider marrying Jesse."

"You will not consider it—you will do it. Of course, Jesse knows nothing of this, so you must convince him." Kirkland reached into his jacket pocket and pulled out a piece of paper. "And tell Loudin that he may run this advertisement in his newspaper."

"Thank you," Susanna said, afraid to say anything more as she snatched the paper from his hand. Did this man not realize what he had just done to her? Whatever future she could ever have was forever tied directly to the Kirkland family, and all he could think about was business—advertising. She rose from the table and hurried out of the restaurant, passing in front of Rab Trudeau. She did not even glance in the man's direction, for if she had, tears would surely have streamed from her eyes.

When Susanna returned to the newspaper after lunch, the building was locked. She had a key, so she let herself in and was glad no one was in the office. She went to B.D.'s desk and began rummaging through it. Surely he had a bottle of whiskey somewhere, but when she found one, it was empty. She threw the bottle against the brick wall with all the strength she could muster, listening to the tinkling of the broken glass as it shattered. Next, she wadded up Kirkland's ad and stamped her foot on it, trying to obliterate the odious piece of paper. She was fuming mad, and at that very moment the door opened and in walked B.D. He looked around the room, then picked up the broom and began to sweep up the mess. Thankfully he said nothing, and Susanna went to her stool and sat down.

"You seem to have dropped this," B.D. said as he handed Kirkland's crumpled ad to Susanna. "The *Pioneer* needs every penny it can get, no matter where it comes from."

"Thanks, B.D."

"I'll not be asking what's troubling you. But if you have need for a soft shoulder and a willing ear, it's here for you."

"I'll be all right."

Susanna began to set the ad Kirkland had given her. The routine of the typesetting calmed her emotions, and as the ad was rather large—at least twenty-four column inches—Mr. Loudin would be pleased.

Kirkland Emporium

Attractions Extraordinary

EVERYTHING NEW AND NOBBY!

New Lot—New Patterns!

At last the ad was finished, but it was too late for to-day's newspaper. It would have to run tomorrow.

Susanna sat down and began to think about her reaction to Mr. Kirkland's request. For her entire life she had been told many times that she owed her life to Gus Kirkland. Had it not been for his exposing his entire family to the risk of cholera, she would have been left to die. And so now Kirkland had decided to collect his due by asking—no, he'd made it clear, he wasn't asking—*demanding* that she marry his son.

Up until this very moment, she had not thought much about marriage. She had been too busy with her career, and she had not met anyone in Virginia City who appealed to her.

At those rare times when she had let her mind wander ahead to consider such things as husband and family, she'd always imagined a handsome prince on a white horse who dashed forth to clutch her from the jaws of a dragon.

Or, perhaps, a runaway wagon.

Susanna gasped, then giggled, as she glanced toward where B.D. would be sitting, but he had already slipped out. She was alone again.

She was well aware that in many cultures marriages were arranged by the parents. Maybe even in Italy, the country where her mother was born. But she wasn't aware of any such culture in America. Even in those cultures where the parents did arrange the marriages, at least both sets of parents were involved. In this case, only Jesse's parents had made the decision.

The irony was that, like her, Jesse had no input into this decision, and according to Mr. Kirkland, Jesse didn't even know about it. Susanna was not only going to have to marry him, she was going to have to convince him that it was something she wanted to do . . . and she was going to have to win him over.

Susanna did not like it, but if this marriage was what it would take to repay the Kirklands for her life, she would accept her lot. She resigned herself to the situation. She did care for Jesse, though not in a romantic way of course, but then she wasn't really sure what the words *romantic way* even meant. She had never had romantic feelings for anyone, had she?

She wondered about the feelings she was having toward Rab Trudeau. She had experienced a strange and somewhat unsettling reaction to him every time she had seen him. Why? Were those romantic feelings? Whatever they were, she knew she would have to set them aside now because they could play no role in her life. She was going to have to marry Jesse Kirkland.

Could she bring herself to do this? She did know that she cared enough for him that she did not want to see him wind up in prison, or worse, lying dead up on the Divide. Maybe Mr. Kirkland was right. Maybe marrying Jesse would save his life.

She was tidying up from having set the type for Kirkland's ad when she heard the tinkling of the little bell that was attached to the front door.

Susanna thought it was probably B.D. returning, and she needed to thank him—for cleaning up after her tirade and also for not asking any questions. She poured a little kerosene over her hands to clean off the ink, then wiped her hands dry and walked out into the front of the shop to talk to B.D.

But it wasn't B.D.

It was Rab Trudeau.

Susanna hesitated and drew in a quick breath of apprehension. When she did so, she caught the strong smell of coal oil and she dropped her hands along her side, sticking them into the folds of her skirt.

"What are you doing here?" she asked.

"I came to apologize."

"You already apologized." Susanna turned to go back to the press.

"Susanna."

Susanna turned around quickly. "How did you know my name?"

"Well, I *am* a detective."

"What?" Susanna replied sharply. "You are investigating me?"

"Not exactly. I just asked the busboy at the Silver Dollar who the beautiful young woman was, and he told me."

"I'm not sure I like having you ask around town about me."

"It's not exactly like I was going door-to-door. I only asked one person."

"All right, you asked, and now you know." Again Susanna started toward the back of the office.

"Susanna wait, please."

Susanna stopped, but she didn't turn around. *Why did he say "please"?* Susanna thought. Why couldn't he just stay the jerk she thought he was?

"Please?" Rab said again.

Susanna turned toward him. "What do you want?"

"I would like for us to start over. We got off on the wrong foot the day we met. Well, I got off on the wrong foot anyway. You weren't even on your feet as I recall. You might say I swept you off your feet."

Susanna smiled.

Rab couldn't help but notice that the smile was not only radiant, but genuine, in stark contrast to the artificial smiles so often seen on the faces of the women of San Francisco's society.

"I behaved badly then," Susanna said. "If it had not

been for you, I could have been seriously injured, or maybe even killed. I apologize for my intemperate remarks."

"No need for that. You already apologized. Now it's my time to apologize for whatever misunderstanding there might have been between us when you were in my—bedroom." He set the word *bedroom* apart from the rest of the sentence, calling attention to it in a soft, almost seductive way.

It did not escape Susanna's attention that he used *bedroom* when he could have used *hotel room*. "I am curious. Just what made you think I was a prostitute?"

"When I arrived at the hotel, I saw a, I'll just call her a working woman, go into one of the rooms. Not too long afterward, you came into my room unannounced, so . . ."

"It wasn't exactly unannounced. I knocked on the door."

"Yes, and I thought you were coming to pick up my laundry. Then, when I saw that you weren't, I thought . . ."

"I know what you thought. But even after I told you I was with the newspaper . . ."

"I agree. After you corrected my misinterpretation I did behave inappropriately, yes. I was quite rude, and that is why I came here to apologize, and also, perhaps, to make it up to you."

"And just how do you intend to do that?"

"By taking you to dinner tonight," Rab said.

"Let me understand. You have insulted me, but now you would make it up to me by having me go to dinner with you?"

"Yes. Men and women do that all the time."

"Men and women who have been properly introduced," Susanna replied. "We don't even know each other. I'm afraid that wouldn't be proper."

"Why not? You do eat, don't you? Though, as light as you are, apparently you don't eat much. And I do know how light you are. I can understand, of course, if you feel no sense of obligation to me for saving you from certain injury. Perhaps you would have preferred to be run over by a wild team of horses and a heavy wagon, so I apologize for grasping you from the certain jaws of death."

Susanna laughed. "You do have a way of making your point, don't you, Mr. Trudeau? But, really, to be seen in public with you—a perfect stranger? It would be most inappropriate."

"First of all, I may be a stranger, but I'm not perfect," Rab said with a self-deprecating smile. "And I don't understand how you think it would be incorrect to dine in a public place with me as you are getting your interview, but you had no compunctions about being alone with me in my hotel room to achieve the same end."

The smile lacked any sarcasm, and she found herself drawn both to the smile and to the gleam in his eyes, which she could only describe as sensual.

"Interview? Mr. Trudeau, are you saying that if I have dinner with you, then you will grant me an interview?"

"Yes, I am saying that. I think I owe you that as recompense for what can only be described as my boorish behavior."

"All right, Mr. Trudeau, if you put it that way, I will have dinner with you."

"Wonderful! Where shall I call for you?"

"That won't be necessary. You tell me where you plan to take your dinner, and I will meet you there."

"All right. Let's say we'll meet at the Washoe Club at seven," Rab suggested.

"The Washoe Club?"

"Yes. Would you rather not go there? I have heard that the food is quite good. And I'm told it is a very nice place."

"Yes, it is very nice, but it's for members only. Surely, Mr. Trudeau, you aren't a member of the Washoe Club?"

"Not exactly. The detective agency I work for has made arrangements for me. After all, if I am going to be thorough with my investigation, I need to rub elbows with the bigwigs, and the Washoe Club is where I will likely find most of them."

"I guess that makes sense."

"Then, you will meet me there at seven?"

The Washoe Club was primarily for men, with a library, a reading room, and a billiard room. However, it also had a dining room to which women, if accompanied by a member, would be admitted. Susanna had never been inside the club, and she had always been curious about the place.

"Yes, I'll be there at seven," Susanna promised.

8

"Don't set a plate for me tonight, Harriet," Susanna said when she returned to the lodging house.

"Very well," Harriet replied.

"Did Mickey deliver today's paper to you all right? I talked with him when he came in and told him that he's forgotten you a couple of times."

"Oh, yes, he delivered it. I've already read it, and I think I'm going to buy some stock in North Star tomorrow if I can get down there before the price starts skyrocketing."

Susanna remembered the conversation she had overheard between Mr. Loudin and B. D. Elliott this morning. "Oh, Harriet, I wouldn't be so quick to do that, if I were you."

"Oh? Why not? Mr. Elliott's article said that the mine has been shut down." Harriet picked up the paper and

began to read: "'. . . it is well known by mining engineers and investment speculators, as well as the general
public, that such a procedure is normally used to prevent
information of new and rich discoveries from reaching
the public.'"

"That's what the article says, but the shutdown might
be because their vein has run out of silver. If that's so,
they might want to unload their own stock before anyone
else finds out about it," Susanna said. "We both know
the North Star claim has never been one of the bigger
producers."

"Oh. Oh, my, I hadn't even thought about that. Perhaps you're right. I think I'll just wait a while and see
what happens."

"I think that would be wise."

"Why aren't you going to be here tonight?" Mary Beth
asked.

"Because," Susanna said, trying to keep a smile off her
face.

"Because why?" Mary Beth prodded.

"I have a dinner engagement tonight."

"What, you? And just who would you be dining with
that makes you as smug as a cat?" Mary Beth asked.

"It's with Mr. Trudeau."

"A man?"

Susanna chuckled. "The word *mister* implies that. Yes,
he is a man."

"Oh, do tell all about it," Mary Beth entreated excitedly. She was two years younger than Susanna and looked
up to her as one would an older sister.

"There's nothing to tell."

"Nothing to tell about what?" Annie Biggs asked as she was just coming down the stairs, already made up and dressed for an evening of activity.

"Susanna has a dinner engagement with a gentleman friend," Mary Beth said.

"I do not."

"But you just said—"

"I said I have a dinner engagement, but he is not a friend. Mr. Loudin has asked me to interview Rab Trudeau and find out what his investigation is all about. He is a detective and his presence is causing quite a stir, so that makes him a subject for a news story."

"Rab Trudeau? He'll cause a stir all right—a stir for Susanna Kirkland if she's not careful. He is a handsome one, he is," Annie said.

"Have you—uh—met him?" Susanna asked.

As close friends as she and Annie were, Susanna did not want to think that Annie had done business with Rab Trudeau. But why not? What was he to her? Why would it matter whom he slept with?

"I haven't exactly met him," Annie said. "But according to Mr. Hume, that is the name of the man I saw at the McAuliffe yesterday when I was there on"—she halted out of deference to Harriet—"when I was busy."

Harriet was well aware of what Annie's business was, but by an unspoken agreement, it was never directly mentioned in the lodging house.

"Oh! Then, that's why he thought . . ." Susanna started, but she halted in midsentence.

"That's why he thought what?"

"Nothing, it was just something Mr. Trudeau said."

"Hmm, something he said? You say that as if you have shared intimate conversation with him, and yet your dinner with him is only for business?"

Intimate? Susanna thought. She smiled. She had seen him naked in his—bedroom. How much more intimate could it get?

"Strictly business," Susanna replied.

"If you say so, honey," Annie said. "Enjoy your dinner with Mr. Trudeau, even if it is 'strictly' business."

As she went up the stairs to her room, Susanna thought of her insistence that this was strictly business. Was it? If so, then why was she so looking forward to it? Was this a romantic encounter? She knew that romances began with social occasions such as this.

But even as the thoughts of a possible romance played in her head, she was aware of the commitment she had made to Mr. Kirkland. She was going to marry Jesse. There was no longer any room for romance in her life. Her dinner with Rab Trudeau would have to be just as she had explained to Mary Beth and Annie—business.

Once in her room Susanna went through her wardrobe trying to decide what she should wear. She took out a dress and laid it on her bed to examine it with a critical eye. She had bought the beautiful dress on a whim last year from one of Mr. Kirkland's competitors, actually getting it at a real bargain price, not the "bargain prices" advertised for the Kirkland Emporium.

She tried on the dress. The crimson fabric clung to her natural curves and, because of the scoop neck, displayed the tops of her breasts. She twisted and turned, examining herself in the full-length mirror, pleased that this style did not include a bustle. She had to admit that the straight lines of the dress, made popular by the Princess of Wales, looked chic on her, and she wondered how Rab Trudeau would react when he saw her in it.

Wait a minute! What was she doing? She definitely could not wear this dress! Were she to do so, Mr. Trudeau would surely get the wrong idea.

She took one last look at herself in the mirror, almost convincing herself to wear it just to observe his reaction, but knew that she should not and could not. Reluctantly, she took off the red dress and put on a conservative navy-blue serge suit with a tight-fitting bolero jacket that Harriet had sewn for her. It was copied from a picture of an outfit made by the popular London tailors Redfern and Co. She chose a high-necked white waist to wear with it. This time when she looked in the mirror, she saw the professional woman she wanted to portray—the woman who could get an interview without help from anyone. But something was missing. She chose a brightly colored jabot and added that to her blouse, the pleats falling casually down upon her chest.

Susanna picked up her mantle as she was leaving her room. When she slipped into the cloak, she noticed that a few errant strands of her hair were hanging loose. She was about to coax them back into her chignon, but in an impetuous move, she undid the knot and shook her head, letting the dark hair fall free to her shoulders.

When Rab returned to his hotel after making the dinner engagement, he was thinking about Susanna Kirkland. Something about her fascinated him, something that stirred his curiosity.

Why? What about her so intrigued him? She was pretty, yes, even striking. But Rab had known women who were even more attractive, from the Creole beauties of New Orleans to the exotic lovelies of the Orient to the stunningly attractive debutants, even including Margaret, of San Francisco society. Yet, none—not one—affected him quite the way this woman did.

He was thinking about the upcoming dinner as he took the steps, two at a time, up to the second floor and his room. Fishing the key from his pocket, he pushed open the door. It wasn't quite dark yet, but the shadows were long, so for the moment he had only the wedge of light from the single, wall-mounted gas lamp in the hall-way to guide him to the bedside lamp. He lit the wick, then adjusted it until a bright yellow light filled the room.

Not until he turned to go back and close the door did he see a piece of paper on the floor. It had not been inadvertently dropped, for it was lying folded in half, having been pushed under the door. Curious as to what it might be, he picked it up and sat on the edge of the bed where he had enough light to read.

Trudeau

 We don't need any detectives looking around in Virginia City. Be on the next train out of town. If you stay, you will be hurt real bad.

Wadding the paper into a little ball, Rab tossed it into the trash, then began dressing for dinner.

He was looking forward to it.

It was six blocks from the lodging house to the Washoe Club, and Susanna walked as quickly as she could up the slanting incline of the street, wishing she had chosen her sensible shoes instead of her fashionable boots with the spool heels. The sun had set long ago, as Virginia City stood on the eastern face of Mount Davidson, making it quite cool at the 6,205-foot altitude of C Street, even though it was late June. Susanna wrapped her mantle tightly around herself as the almost-always-present breeze blew briskly. She passed many people along the way, either leaving their places of business for the day or entering their places of entertainment for the evening.

Rab Trudeau was standing in front of the Washoe Club when she arrived, and she was surprised to see that he was wearing a black jacket, gray wool trousers, a gold-colored vest, and a crimson cravat, certainly not the kinds of clothes she had seen him in before. She laughed as she added to her thought—when she had actually seen him in clothes.

Despite the fashionable attire he was wearing, or perhaps because of it, she was even more aware of his rugged handsomeness. She stopped for just a moment, feeling a strong and rather frightening awareness of this man. He smiled, then came toward her.

She compared how elegantly he was dressed with her own attire, something that might have been better suited for work than for a fine evening dining experience, and for just a brief moment Susanna regretted having passed on the crimson dress.

"You came," he said, taking her hand in his. "I wasn't certain you would."

She was surprised by the feel of his hand against her own. It was big and strong and comforting—not soft, but not calloused either. A hand that she knew would keep you safe, a hand that could fondle a breast.

She immediately withdrew her hand from his grasp, not wanting to allow any more wanton thoughts about this man.

"Of course I came," she replied, much more brusquely than she had intended. "I want the interview."

The smile altered slightly, from one of unrestrained delight to one of somewhat more measured pleasure. "Ah, yes. The interview."

"I hope, sir, that you did not think there was any other reason for my accepting your invitation?"

"Of course not." Rab offered his arm. "Shall we go in?"

Susanna reluctantly accepted his arm, knowing what it would do to her senses, but knowing she could not pointedly refuse the offer without being rude. Even this benign social contact made her very much aware of his masculinity—and his nearness, the slight citrusy aroma of his aftershave lotion. She tried to take her mind off the strange sensations she was experiencing by paying close attention to the decor of the Washoe Club.

Inside the building the hardwood floor glistened under a large Axminster carpet. The carpet was lawn green with wine-colored, nine-point starbursts in attractive patterns throughout. The walls were richly paneled cherry with carved camphor-wood insets that Susanna knew must have been imported from China. The chairs around the white-linen-covered tables were elegantly upholstered in a green-and-white bargello-needlework tapestry, and the dining room was liberally festooned with oil paintings, mostly of majestic animals and landscapes. Susanna recognized the work of Albert Bierstadt, a German-born artist who had spent some time in Virginia City. She loved his work, especially those paintings depicting the Sierra Nevada and the area around Lake Tahoe.

"Good evening, Mr. Trudeau," the maître d' said.

"Hello, Maurice."

Susanna wondered, without asking, how Trudeau and the maître d' knew each other.

The maître d' snapped his fingers and a host appeared to show Rab and Susanna to a table that sat not under one of the many glistening crystal chandeliers, but in a more shadowed corner of the dining room.

"Oh," Susanna said as she looked at the menu.

"Would you trust me to order for us?" Rab asked.

"I'm afraid I'm going to have to. I don't know French," Susanna said, lowering her menu.

When the waiter came, Rab gave the order. *"Nous allons commencer avec pain grillé avec des huîtres fumées. Pour le plat principal, un gigot d'agneau aux petits pois la menthe, suivie d'une salade verte. Et pour le dessert, nous aurons un gâteau au chocolat,"* Rab said, *"et une bonne bouteille de Cabernet Beringer."*

"Très bon, monsieur," the waiter answered.

"That was very well done, sir, but I think you know more than just a few words," Susanna said.

"I ordered smoked oysters, leg of lamb with minted peas, a green salad, and for dessert, chocolate cake," Rab said. "I also took the liberty of ordering wine. I hope that meets with your approval."

"It sounds delicious. But I'm very impressed."

Rab's laugh was spontaneous, and warm. "You might not be so impressed if you knew I was Cajun."

"On the contrary. My mother was Italian, and she was teaching me the language. But unfortunately she died when I was very young, and I have retained very little of it."

"Se sarà solo lo parlano, la lingua tornerà a voi."

"Yes, I do need to speak it for it to come back to me," Susanna said, surprised to hear him speak Italian. *"Tu parlano anche l'italiano?"*

"I speak just enough to shamelessly try to make you think I know more than I do," Rab answered, again with a rich laugh. "In a previous life I was a sailor, so I have visited a few ports in my day."

"There is no need for you to try and make fancy with me, Mr. Trudeau," Susanna said, a flash of humor crossing her face.

"Foolish vanity on my part."

How fascinating this man was. She had never met anyone quite like him, sophisticated but not self-centered, one who laughed easily, and one who made her feel as if he genuinely enjoyed her company. What if he had come into her life earlier? Could there have been more to this relationship?

"You say your mother died when you were young?"

"Yes, my parents and my little brother all died on the wagon train on our way out West. They were cholera victims."

Rab looked perplexed. "Both of your parents died? But Gus Kirkland?"

"My name is actually Susanna Ward. The Kirklands took me in and provided a home for me when I was only five years old, but they never adopted me. I am very grateful to them."

"I would think he would want you to work in his store instead of at the newspaper."

"He does want me to work there. In fact, he is probably sorry he ever sent me to school. Mr. Kirkland desperately wanted his son to get an education—he had it in his mind that Jesse would be either a lawyer or a doctor—but that wasn't what Jesse wanted, so he sent me to college for two years in hopes that his son would get jealous and want to go as well."

"Well, did it work?"

"No," Susanna said, not wanting to say anything more about Jesse. "And I guess his plan failed with me, too. I wanted to use my education for something other than selling broadcloth or women's shoes, so I went to work at the *Pioneer*."

"Are you enjoying working for the paper?"

"Yes, and no. I enjoy working there, but I would like to be writing. I guess you could say that is my passion."

"You aren't writing for Loudin?"

A bemused smile spread across Susanna's lips. "You are very clever, Mr. Trudeau."

"Clever in what way?"

"You have been asking all the questions. I thought the purpose of this dinner tonight was for me to interview you."

"I did say that, didn't I?"

"Well, then, I'll ask the questions. You said you used to be a sailor. How many countries have you visited?"

"Oh, let me think. At least twenty, I would say."

"What's your favorite?"

Rab smiled. "That's an easy one, the United States."

"That's not fair. You know what I meant."

At that moment the waiter brought the food.

"Ah, this looks and smells delicious," Rab said as the plates were set before them. The waiter uncorked the bottle of wine, then poured some into a glass. Rab took it and held the glass over the white tablecloth to examine the rich, red color of the wine. Twirling the liquid slightly to release its essence, he held it to his nose and inhaled the aroma. Then he took a mouthful and, before swallowing, let it rest on his tongue to gauge its taste.

He looked up at the waiter and nodded. "Excellent," Rab said, taking the bottle from the waiter.

Rab reached for Susanna's glass, poured the cabernet,

then returned it to her before pouring his own. Holding his goblet out over the table, he said, "Here is to a hope that this relationship proves to be more positive than its rather inauspicious beginning."

"I will drink to that." Susanna touched her goblet to his. What was she doing? What relationship? There was no relationship, and there wasn't going to be one, other than that of an interview.

Susanna realized that she was enjoying Rab's company much more than she had expected.

"About this interview," she started, trying to refocus her attention on the purpose for this evening's get-together.

"Surely you would not want to discuss business over a dinner like this," Rab challenged.

"Are we to sit here silently as we consume the food like pigs at a trough?"

Quite unexpectedly, Rab threw back his head and let out a guffaw of unrestrained laughter, and even Susanna had to cover her mouth as she giggled.

"Well put, Susanna, well put."

He couldn't help but compare her to Margaret. Susanna's reaction was spontaneous and honest, whereas Margaret would never allow herself such spontaneity or honesty.

Rab felt a slight twinge of guilt. He was engaged to be married, yet here he was with one of the most intriguing and genuine women he had ever met. He was playing with fire, he knew that, but he could not resist the temptation to spend this time with her, to learn more about her, to bask in her charm and beauty.

"Very well, we will engage in a back-and-forth, spirited discussion. But, nothing about business until after our meal. Agreed?" Rab asked.

"All right."

"What do you like to do? Do you enjoy art? Reading? The theater?"

"Yes, to all three. Mr. Trudeau, again you are turning things around. You have asked all the questions. Please, allow me to ask a few."

"Be my guest. But if you would call me Rab, you might find a more willing subject for your interview."

The air of authority about him seemed incongruous with his position as a private detective. He had the self-confidence of one used to giving orders and having them obeyed.

"Where do you live?" She couldn't help but notice the suggestion of gray at his temples. She wondered what it would feel like to run her fingers through his hair.

"In San Francisco."

"Are you married?" Susanna suddenly looked horror-struck, and she gasped and clasped her hand across her mouth. "Oh, please forgive me! I had no right to ask such a personal question!"

Rab smiled back at her, his grin irresistibly devastating. "It's not at all an intrusive question. And it is certainly appropriate under the circumstances. After all, we are getting to know each other over a friendly meal, in what I hope might become a long and valued friendship. And the answer to your question is no, I am not married."

Susanna stared at her plate for a moment, still embarrassed by her question.

"How do you like San Francisco?" she finally asked, thinking that would be a safe question.

"It is a beautiful city. You'll have to visit someday."

"Oh, but I've been to San Francisco. Mr. Kirkland's first store was there, and the family lived there until we came to Virginia City. Then when I went away to school it was to California College for Women."

"Ahh, a very fine women's institution. But you haven't been to San Francisco with me. I can show you places you haven't seen."

"And what would those be?"

"Have you been to Grant Street in Chinatown, listening to the musical lilt of ten thousand Chinese conversations, wrapped in the spicy aromas of mu shu pork and feasting your eyes on the gabled roofs that cover the buildings of red and gold?

"Or to Mission Dolores, where the city first began? Or Fisherman's Wharf, where merchant and customer haggle over fish that spent the night in San Francisco Bay?"

He was talking about a city, but an underlying sensuality in his description made Susanna feel as if she were there—actually standing on Grant Street with him at this very moment.

Don't sit here like a ninny, melting in front of this man, she scolded herself. *Say something.*

"You describe San Francisco so beautifully." *What a weak response,* she thought.

"Oh, but I show it much better. The invitation to come to San Francisco is genuine."

"We'll have to see about that." With every ounce of her being, Susanna wanted to say, *Let us go, now. Let us go down to the depot, board the train, and leave.*

But she didn't say that. Instead, finishing her dessert, she pushed the plate away. "Our meal is over. The interview?"

"There are other things in life besides business, you know. Are you sure you want to do this interview?"

Rab asked the question not challengingly, but with an expression of bemusement, as if he was offering her a better way to spend this time with him. She almost found herself wanting those possible alternatives, but she regained her composure and answered his question.

"Yes, of course I want to do the interview. That was the purpose of our getting together, wasn't it?"

His smile broadened, and his eyes, which seemed to burn her skin, had a flirtatious sparkle "About our—getting together." He let the words *getting together* slide out of his mouth as if they were laden with a meaning she hadn't intended. "Is it too much to suggest that the meal was to provide an opportunity to enjoy each other's company?"

"Is that what this was for you? Enjoyment?"

"Yes, I enjoyed it immensely. And you can't tell me that you haven't enjoyed it, too."

"No, I'm not going to say that. I've had a wonderful evening."

"Well, then, no matter what happens, you will have a pleasant meal to remember."

"What do you mean, 'no matter what happens'?" she asked, confused by the odd statement.

"I mean that if you insist upon doing this interview, you may not like the answers I give to your questions." Rab leaned back in his chair and folded his arms across his chest, almost as if closing himself off from her.

"Will your answers be truthful?"

"They will be truthful."

"Then, how can I not like them? I am seeking the truth, after all."

"Are you?" The easy smile left Rab's face, to be replaced by an uncompromising, almost harsh look. He brought his arms down from his chest, leaned forward, and placed his hands on the edge of the table. "Then, why has your paper printed so many unfounded rumors, innuendos, half-truths, and, in some cases, outright lies?"

The challenging words, spoken in a tone so different from the dulcet sound of his conversation until then, startled her, and involuntarily she jerked back in her chair, as if retreating from him.

"What?" Susanna gasped. "Why would you say such a thing?"

"What was the paper's lead story today?"

"I'm not sure what you mean. To me, the most important story was the one about the Central Pacific making an offer to buy the Virginia and Truckee Railroad."

"Come on, Susanna, you know the story I'm talking about."

"Could it be the story about the North Star going on shutdown?"

"Good guess. And tell me, why did the owners put the mine on shutdown?"

"I don't know for sure, but I assume—"

"Ahh," Rab said, holding up his finger. "You assume?" He reached inside his jacket pocket, then pulled out an article he had torn from the paper. "Let me give you an example of what happens when you assume. This story ran in today's paper. Reading here, I quote, 'It is well-known by mining engineers and investment speculators, as well as the general public, that such a procedure is normally used to prevent information of new and rich discoveries from reaching the public.' And here, reading again: 'And though we cannot report with unreserved and absolute validity that a new silver vein has been struck, we can speculate to that end, and that we do without hesitation or discomforting thought.'" He returned the article to his inside jacket pocket. "Do you have any idea what an article like this is going to do to a market as volatile as the silver market?"

"I ass—" She was about to say the word *assume,* but she caught herself. "I am sure that such articles are not without effect," she said, recalling the conversation between B.D. and James Loudin.

"Not without effect, you say? Susanna, hundreds of thousands of dollars will be invested on the strength of that one, nonsubstantiated article. And I'm not just talking about thousands of dollars from wealthy speculators; I'm talking about a hundred dollars here, twenty dollars there, ten dollars somewhere else, from store clerks to stagecoach drivers to farmers to widows who are trying to make their meager resources do more. If there really hasn't been a new strike, they will all lose their money—money they cannot afford to lose."

Susanna had heard B.D. making much the same argument to Mr. Loudin, and she felt ill at ease defending the paper against such an accusation, but under the circumstances, she felt she had no choice.

"That raises the question, why do such people as you describe invest if they can't afford to lose their money?" But her defense sounded weak even to her own ears. She expected a sharp retort from Rab, but he merely asked another question, this one in a more gentle tone.

"Do you have any stock in silver mines?"

"Yes."

"When you heard that the North Star had shut down, did you buy North Star stock?"

"No."

"Why not? You were right there at the newspaper; you probably even set the story. That means you knew about this before anyone else, and yet you didn't buy North Star when you could have gotten in on the ground floor. Tell me, Susanna, is there something you know that wasn't in the article?"

Susanna thought about Harriet Chaney. Harriet had quoted the same passage from the newspaper and had said that she was going to buy stock, only to have Susanna caution her against it.

"I don't know why I didn't buy it. I guess I just didn't have a good feeling about it."

"That was a smart thing," Rab said, softening his tone. "Unfortunately your newspaper gave no such cautionary advice."

"It is the job of a newspaper to print the news. We aren't to play governess to our readers, nor are we to give them financial advice. We must assume . . ." She paused in midsentence. Aware that she had used that word again, she cleared her throat. "We must *assume*"—this time she came down hard on the word—"that our readers are rational adults who can make their own decisions."

"All right, I will grant you that as a reasonable assumption. What is your next question?"

"I haven't asked the first question yet," an exasperated Susanna replied. "Again, you have adroitly managed to turn it around so that you were asking me questions."

"I'm sorry. What is your first question, then?"

"Do you believe that the volatility of the silver market is something that is purposely created?"

"Yes."

"To what end?"

"Surely you are aware that a great deal of money can be made if one is adroit at manipulating the market. And I believe that is exactly what is being done here."

"You aren't in this business, Mr. Trudeau, so you don't understand how it works. You are a detective, and therefore your natural tendency is to suspect evildoing around every corner. But the truth is, it is very expensive to operate a mine, much more expensive than the average person can even begin to comprehend. And until the silver is producing, the only source of income for the owners is that provided to them through selling stock, and of course the assessments that may be levied to the shareholders."

"Investment from people like you," Rab said.

"Yes, from people like me."

"Then, I rest my case. My investigation is to determine if there actually is corruption going on. I'm not accusing every mine owner of being corrupt, but until I find out which ones are, the onus is on everyone."

"What you are saying is that you presume that everyone is guilty until they are proven innocent."

"Let's look at that from a different perspective. I should think that the mine owners, superintendents, foremen, indeed everyone who works in the mines, would welcome my investigation, for when I find the guilty parties, it will establish the innocence of everyone else."

"I suppose if you put it like that, I would have to agree with you."

Rab smiled back at her with no trace of his earlier challenge. "Good. Then, that's all there is to it. Except, perhaps, for the dance."

"The dance? What dance?"

Rab chuckled. "Don't you read your own paper? It was the story between the one about the Central Pacific making a bid on the Virginia and Truckee and the one about the North Star being put on shutdown. There's going to be a big dance held at the Miners' Union Hall on the Fourth of July. Come to the dance with me. You'll be able to observe me among the miners and mine owners. That might give you an angle for your story."

"Mr. Trudeau, let me get this straight. Are you asking me to go to a dance with you?"

"Yes, not as a social engagement, you understand, but strictly business."

Strictly business. Susanna forced back a smile because that was exactly how she had described this engagement to Mary Beth and Annie.

"You are smiling," Rab said. "Does that mean you'll go with me?"

Susanna hesitated before she answered. She would love to go to the dance with him. More than anything else in the world, she wanted to say yes right now. But, fighting down that almost irresistible urge, she made the only response she could make, under the circumstances.

"No, I don't think so."

"Too bad, I think you might enjoy it."

"No, it is quite impossible, I'm afraid."

Rab pulled out his pocket watch to examine it. Was it gold? How could an ordinary detective afford a gold watch? Ordinary? No, that word did not fit this man. He was anything but ordinary.

"Well, it's getting late," Rab said. "I'll walk you home."

"Oh, thank you, but that won't be necessary. I can walk home."

"You don't understand. I will either walk with you or I will walk five paces behind you. But I have no intention of letting you walk home alone. After all, it's because of me that you're out this late."

In truth, Susanna welcomed the offer. She didn't mind the walk as long as she was on C Street, because even at this hour, there would be enough people about that she wouldn't feel apprehensive. But once she turned onto Taylor Street, it would be more deserted—and much darker as well, because only C Street had gas lanterns at the corners to provide illumination.

They spoke in general terms during the long stroll down C Street, passing under the streetlamps and in and out of the bubbles of light that spilled out onto the boardwalk. They could hear pieces of conversation.

"I said to Johnny, I said, 'Johnny, looks to me like that mule ain't goin' nowhere 'less you get out and push!' "

The pronouncement was followed with an outburst of laughter that was drowned out by the sounds of a piano as they passed the next saloon.

When they reached the fire station, they turned left onto Taylor and ventured on into the dark. Though they walked but five blocks, the tone and tint had changed so drastically that it was almost as if they had left the town of Virginia City behind them. Here it was quiet, and they could hear the sounds of the night creatures.

They passed St. Paul's Episcopal Church, then crossed G Street. "There it is—Harriet Chaney's lodging house." Susanna pointed to a rather large, two-storey white house with a mansard roof and dormer windows. "This is where I live."

Rab turned toward her and stared at her for a long moment, seeming to hold her captive with his bold gaze. Then, putting his finger under her chin, he leaned forward to close the distance between them. He kissed her, not hard and demanding, but as soft as the brush of a butterfly's wing. It was but a brief moment, then he pulled away, continuing to stare at her. It was too dark to see his eyes, but she didn't need to see them; she could feel the heat of them burning on her skin.

Susanna was surprised by the kiss, but she was even more shocked by her own reaction to it. She felt a tingling in her lips that spread throughout her body and warmed her blood. Reaching up, she touched her lips and held her fingers there for a long moment.

"What made you think you could do that?" Susanna asked in a bare whisper.

"I meant nothing more than to express my appreciation for a most engaging evening," Rab said easily. "Good night, Miss Ward."

❋ 9 ❋

As Susanna lay in bed that night, she tried to deal with the tumultuous feelings that were tumbling through her. The feel of his lips on hers, the intoxicating musk of his body, the thought of his rugged good looks, caused her to feel a trembling inside that was almost euphoric.

In her mind, she took the kiss further and thought of his hands on her body, first through her clothes, then her imagination took wing and his hands were not on her clothes, they were caressing her naked skin. She could feel the palms of his hands on her breasts, then her stomach, then between her legs, where she imagined his fingers would tease her, igniting a burning fire.

Not merely feeling his hands and his fingers against her skin, she felt the hard musculature of his legs on her own. She recalled the sight of him naked in all his male glory, and she incorporated that sight into the erotic fantasies that were playing through her mind.

"Rab," she said quietly, just wanting to hear his name on her tongue.

Then, in a sudden thought that took the breath from her and erased all the euphoria, another name leapt to her mind.

Jesse.

As the doors to the lobby of the McAuliffe House closed behind him, Rab heard the night clerk call out from behind the desk, "Mr. Trudeau?"

"Yes?"

"I have a letter for you, sir. I picked it up at the post office this afternoon."

"Are you talking about the one I found that was slid under my door?"

"Slid under your door, sir? No, I don't know anything about that. As far as I know, I still have a letter for you."

The clerk turned to a cabinet of small, square cubicles on the wall to the right of his desk. He withdrew an envelope from a pigeonhole that was marked with the number 204.

"Yes, I thought so, it's still here," he said, handing the letter across the counter.

"Thank you," Rab said, taking the envelope. As he climbed the stairs, he glanced at the neat and clearly legible penmanship. He recognized it immediately.

Opening the door to his room, he stepped over to the bedside lamp, lit it, then opened the letter and began to read.

My dearest Rab,

How time does drag in your absence. I have asked Mr. DeLoitte to tell me when he thinks you might return, but he has been unable to do so. As you occupy yourself with the business that has taken you away from me, so too have I occupied myself with the business at hand, that of planning our wedding. I find some solace in realizing that each day you are gone is but one day closer to that wonderful moment when we will be married.

I don't know what you are doing there, darling, for Mr. DeLoitte has not told me. But I do hope it is not something that is tawdry, and beneath your station. Everyone says that this wedding will be the most important social event of the year.

Return to me soon, my prince.

Most fondly, your
Margaret

"Margaret," Rab said as he finished reading the letter. "Damn."

Rab stood up, then walked over to look through the window. The moon was full and Mount Davidson stood out in black and silver. The mills were working, and the escaping steam was so white that it was almost luminescent against the black-velvet and star-bejeweled sky. He had literally forgotten all about Margaret. He hadn't literally forgotten her, but he had done a good job of putting the upcoming wedding out of his mind.

He wondered if his sister, Emmaline, had received his letter yet.

When he went to bed that night, he thought of the strange twists and turns one's life could take. Growing up, he thought his life was all planned out. His older brother, Charles, would be master of Rivière de Joie, the Trudeau plantation, and Rab would manage his father's shipping company. But the war came, and since that time, nothing had gone as planned. Here he was more than a thousand miles away from his ancestral home and family.

The battle was a cacophonous roar: thundering cannon, booming muskets, shrieking shells, screams of rage, curses of defiance, fear, and pain, the whole enshrouded in a thick, opaque cloud of noxious gun smoke. Charles was the company commander, and Rab was his lieutenant. As the lieutenant, Rab was on one side of the battle line and Charles on the other.

The Yankees had charged their lines fifteen minutes earlier, but they had been beaten back, in part because of Rab's accurate shooting.

"Come on, men! We have them on the run!" Charles called, and leaping up from the ditch where they had taken shelter, Charles charged across the open ground toward the enemy lines. The rest of the company, Rab included, charged with him.

The Yankees met the Confederate charge with devastating

*firepower, including grape and canister from their cannon.
Charles went down.*

*"No!" Rab yelled. He ran to the side of his brother but
could see as soon as he got there that he could do nothing.
Charles had been hit by canister shot, and his gray tunic had
been dyed red by the half dozen wounds in his chest. Charles
lived long enough to see his brother come to his side, and
when Rab took his hand, Charles squeezed it and smiled
at him.*

"Don't die, Charles, don't die!" Rab pleaded.

*Despite Rab's pleas and prayers, he saw the light of life
dim in Charles's eyes.*

*After they stopped the Confederate charge, the Yankees
mounted a countercharge. Rab stood his ground, firing the
last three rounds in his pistol. With his pistol empty, he tried
to draw his saber, but before he could pull it from its sheath, a
Yankee cavalry officer galloped by with his own sword drawn.
He made a slash toward Rab, trying to decapitate him. Rab
twisted away enough to avoid a killing blow, but the saber
slashed him deeply from his shoulder, across his chest, and just
to the base of his neck.*

*After that a cannon shell exploded beside him, knocking
him out. When he came to, he had no idea how much later
it was, a patch was on his wound, and he was a prisoner of
the Yankees. He heard the screech of a . . .*

Mill whistle! Waking from his dream, Rab heard not
one but several of the mill whistles, calling the miners
to work. It was Sunday, but that didn't matter, the mines

operated twenty-four hours a day, seven days a week. Rab lay in bed for a moment longer, his body drenched in perspiration, as he let the last vestiges of the dream slip away. It had been nearly a year since the last time he had experienced what he now thought of as "the dream." He was thankful for that. For the first few years after the war, he was haunted by "the dream" at least once a month, and sometimes more often.

Rab rolled out of bed, then began to dress. To get the memories of not only "the dream" but the actual battle out of his mind, Rab thought about the previous evening. He had been to dinner with more women than he could count, but he could not think of one who had made a more enjoyable dinner companion than Susanna Ward.

"Susanna." He spoke the word aloud, listening to the musical lilt of it. It was a beautiful name, for a beautiful woman.

She had asked if he was married, and then was embarrassed by the question. She wouldn't have asked such a question unless she was feeling about him the way he was feeling about her. She had pretended annoyance over being kissed, but he knew it was pretending only. He had felt her lips respond to his, and he knew that if he had pulled her body against his, she would have been totally compliant.

He thought of David DeLoitte and what a wonderful marriage he and Lila enjoyed. Rab had always been happy for them and sometimes even envied David, but he had never actually considered himself in such a situation. That was because he had never met a woman who he believed could be more than a temporary and pleasant diversion.

Until now.

He knew it was crazy, he had only known Susanna for such a short time. But never had any woman affected him so.

As he finished dressing, he glanced over toward the lamp table. There, shining white in the morning sun that was streaming in through the hotel window, was the envelope with Margaret's letter.

Rab picked the envelope up, held it for a moment, then put it back down and walked over to the window to look out onto the early-morning traffic: the ore and freight wagons, a carriage now and then, the pedestrians, the goats and the burros wandering about, belonging to no one yet belonging to all. He recalled the conversation he had had with Margaret the night of Judge Conrad's party, shortly after she had made public their engagement.

"I can hardly wait to get married. Everyone I know is going to be green with envy. Why, our wedding will be the social event of the summer," Margaret said.

"Margaret, what would you think about having a quiet wedding, with just a few people, then we get on a ship and sail away?"

"What? What are you talking about? Sail away to where?"

"I don't know, anywhere, wherever the ship may take us. Maybe someplace like Pago Pago."

"Pago Pago? What in heaven's name is Pago Pago?"

"It's a port of call on Tutuila Island in the South Pacific. It's a beautiful island, with a wonderful climate, and delightful people. Just think, coconut trees, sandy beaches, balmy breezes—it would be an island paradise."

"And just how long would we be doing this?"

"I don't know, a month, a year, five years, maybe. After we stay at Pago Pago for a while, we could sail on to somewhere else, the Philippines, Australia, Egypt, Spain, France, England, maybe. We could see the world."

"And just how would you make a living while we are seeing the world?"

"Oh, that is the beauty of it. I have enough money that we could be gone indefinitely. And David can take care of things here. We could be gypsies of the sea. We would live in the wind."

"Live in the wind?" Margaret laughed out loud. "Darling, for a moment there I thought you were serious. Ha, I can just imagine us being away from San Francisco where there would be no more parties, no more balls, no more theatrical performances, and away from all our friends and family? Please tell me you were just teasing me."

Rab took a long moment before he answered.

"I was just teasing you," he said without further pursuit of the question.

Margaret laughed again. "You are just too funny. I suppose that once we are married, I'll just have to get used to your rather bizarre sense of humor."

*   *   *

When we get married, Rab thought as he stood at the hotel window. He looked back at the envelope. He was already committed to a woman. He had said that he would marry Margaret. Or at least he hadn't told her that he wouldn't marry her, and in his mind that was practically the same thing. What right did he have to even think about Susanna?

Five blocks away, Susanna was asleep in her room at the Chaney House when the sounds of the city began to intrude, from the thunder of mining machinery to the rumble of huge ore wagons coming up Taylor Street. The ore wagons were formed into a train of three connected wagons, drawn by teams of sixteen mules. Jangling bells attached to the harness of each of the mules filled the city streets with music. In addition to the rumble of the heavy wagons and the ringing of the bells, she could also hear the clatter and clomp of the horses as they pulled the omnibuses, hurrying on their appointed rounds. Adding to the morning cacophony was the chugging sound of the steam locomotive as it approached the Virginia and Truckee Railroad depot.

Susanna lay in bed for a few moments longer, thinking about her evening with Rab, playing it over in her mind. Rab Trudeau was the most handsome man she had ever seen. His powerful shoulders filled the jacket he had worn last night. He exuded masculinity, yet he had a polished veneer about him that made her believe he would not be out of place in the depths of a mine or the ballroom of a king's palace.

When he had scooped her up from the street to carry her to safety, she was very aware of his undeniable strength. Yet, she thought of the touch of his finger under her chin last night. It had been as light as a feather, yes, but she had felt so much heat from it that she could almost think that she had a scar there this morning. And it was funny, because the heat was not painful. On the contrary, it caused the most pleasurable sensations to course through her body that she had ever experienced. Not until he kissed her had she known she could feel even more pleasure.

Perhaps she should have accepted his invitation to the dance. She had wanted to accept it more than she had ever wanted anything else, but she had turned him down because she was frightened. For the first time in her life, a man had awakened a feeling within her, a stirring— something that was previously unknown to her. Could he be the . . . ? Suddenly, as it had last night, another name pushed its way through her thoughts.

Jesse.

"No!" she said, picking up the pillow and screaming into it. "No, no, no!"

She realized that no matter the promise of bliss that a relationship with Rab might foretell, it could never be, for with one comment, one request from Mr. Kirkland, any thought of pursuing any man but Jesse had been taken away from her.

She had to marry Jesse.

By now tears were streaming uncontrollably down her cheeks, and she wept aloud, using the pillow to muffle the sound. It was so unlike her to lose control like this. She had to think in a rational manner.

Mary Beth had already been in bed when Susanna came home last night. She was anxiously waiting for Susanna to come down.

"Well?" Mary Beth said, a huge smile on her face. Mary Beth was not someone a person would describe as beautiful, but she was attractive, with blond hair, big blue eyes, and a light dusting of freckles across her nose.

"Well what?" Susanna replied.

"You know 'well what'," Mary Beth said, laughing nervously. "The dinner. You must tell me about the dinner last night. Did you enjoy it?"

"It was a pleasant evening," Susanna replied without showing too much emotion.

"Is he just devastatingly handsome, like Annie said?"

"Yes, I suppose you could say that, though I would describe him as more rugged than handsome."

"Handsome and rugged." Mary Beth wrapped her arms around herself and twisted back and forth as if embracing herself. "Now that's my kind of man."

Susanna chuckled. "Your kind of man?"

"Yes. Well, I mean if I had one. Did he kiss you?" The question came out of the blue.

"Mary Beth!" Susanna gasped. "Whatever would make

you ask such a thing?" Susanna could feel the flame in her cheeks, and she hoped that Mary Beth didn't notice.

"Ha! He did! Susanna, you are blushing! He did kiss you, didn't he?"

"I—all right, yes, he did. But it wasn't what you would call a real kiss. It was nothing more than a chaste peck after he walked me home last night."

"A chaste peck where? On your forehead? On your cheek? On your lips?"

"It—it doesn't matter."

"It was on your lips! Wasn't it?"

Susanna laughed again. "Mary Beth, you are impossible."

"Are you going to see him again?"

"I—I don't know. I suppose I will. I still have to get the interview from him."

"What? You mean you didn't get the interview last night?"

"No."

"Then, what did you do?"

"We talked."

"You talked, but you didn't get an interview. What did you talk about?"

By that time Annie came in. "What are you two talking about?" she asked as she stepped over to the hutch and poured herself a cup of coffee.

"We're talking about Susanna and her evening of sparking," Mary Beth said.

"It wasn't an evening of sparking!"

"Oh? You said you were kissing," Mary Beth said.

"Kissing, were you?" Annie offered. "Oh, Susanna, do tell. You must tell everything!"

"There is nothing to tell. Nothing happened. As I said, we merely had dinner together, then I came home."

"You said he walked you home."

"He did, yes, but only because it was the gentlemanly thing for him to do."

"And you said he kissed you. Was that also the gentlemanly thing to do?"

Involuntarily, Susanna put her fingers to her lips.

"You are thinking about it now, aren't you?" Mary Beth said.

Susanna laughed. "Mary Beth, you do have a wonderful imagination."

"If you see him again today, you will let me know, won't you?"

"I won't see him today. It's Sunday. I visit the Kirklands on Sunday, remember? And Betsy."

The Kirkland house was on A Street, right behind the store. It was quite large, so Alice's family lived there as well. Because it was a climb of over two hundred feet from G Street to A Street, Susanna paused for breath before she walked up to the house. Standing in front of the house, she could literally look down on the roofs of the houses and businesses of the town and, from this elevation, quite easily see all of Virginia City.

Once she regained her breath, she walked up to the front door and pulled on the bell cord.

Maria Sanchez, the Kirklands' hired girl, opened the door and smiled broadly at Susanna. "Senorita Susanna. Betsy has been waiting for you."

"Hi, Maria."

"Miss Susanna!" Betsy called as she ran to meet her. "Come with me, you're invited to my tea party!"

"A tea party? Oh, how wonderful!"

Betsy had her dolls seated around a little table, with a small chair for Susanna as well. She loved the time she spent with Betsy and never grew tired of any imaginative play that Betsy might ask her to join.

While Susanna was occupied with Betsy, she could hear quite clearly the conversation in the parlor.

"I had hoped that Jesse would come today," Mrs. Kirkland said.

"I hate to say this," Harold said, "but you may as well give up on him. He's never going to amount to anything."

"Harold, how can you say such a thing about my own brother?" Alice scolded.

"I'm sorry," Harold said. "But you know I am speaking the truth."

"I don't know," Gus Kirkland said. "You never can tell. Jesse may change."

"What makes you think he will ever change?" Harold asked.

"I think that when he marries a good woman, he will settle down," Gus said.

Susanna knew that Gus was alluding to the ultimatum he had given her. Placing her imaginary cup of tea on the table, she drew Betsy into her arms, hoping to draw comfort from the child's unconditional love for her. She knew she would soon have to join the adults.

"Well, Susanna, how was your tea party?" Minnie Kirkland asked a few minutes later when both Susanna and Betsy joined them.

"We had a wonderful time, didn't we, Betsy?" Susanna replied.

"Oh, yes, it was a wonderful party."

"Susanna, dear, do have a piece of cake and join us," Minnie invited.

Susanna cut a piece of cake for Betsy, then another for herself.

"Jesse is never going to get married," Alice said.

"What makes you say that?" Gus asked.

"Papa, why would you even have to ask me that? Tell me one redeeming quality he has that a woman might find appealing."

"Courage," Susanna said as she took a bite of her cake.

Everyone else in the room looked at her with surprise on their faces.

"Jesse has courage?" Harold said. "What a strange thing for you to say."

"You do remember the fire three years ago, don't you?" Susanna replied.

"How can anyone forget it? Half the town burned down."

"You may also remember that he saved the lives of three women."

"You are talking about the Barbary Coast, and the three women were harlots," Harold said. "The only reason he was there to save them is because he was already there when the fire started."

"There were other men there as well, but Jesse was the only one who went back inside to find the women and bring them out."

"Susanna is right," Gus Kirkland said. "That did take courage. And it takes a good heart for someone to recognize it."

Later that day as Susanna was leaving, Gus Kirkland walked to the front door with her.

"I appreciate you taking up for Jesse as you did," he said.

"I was just telling the truth."

"It is more than just telling the truth. It shows that not only do you have a good heart, but you will also be a good wife to him. I presume you have spoken to him about marriage."

"No, not yet."

"Why not?"

"Mr. Kirkland, this is not something you rush into. I'm sure that this whole idea is going to be as big a surprise to Jesse as it was for me."

"It is not something that can be put off indefinitely. The problem that I spoke to you about still exists, and I do not see it getting better anytime soon."

"I know."

"And the only solution to that problem is for you to marry him. So don't draw this out. Get it done, and get it done soon."

❊ 10 ❊

The next morning, as Susanna was on her way to work, she saw a crowd standing in front of the Barry, Patmore, and Daigh office building. The morning stock quotes were just being posted, industrials from New York, stock and grain from Chicago, and mining from San Francisco. The mining stock had everyone talking.

"North Star was three dollars last Thursday. Look at it now! It's over two hundred dollars. I shoulda bought it on Thursday," one man said.

"It's not too late to buy now. Why, I reckon it'll go on up to a thousand dollars a share," another said. "I hear the vein is the richest yet."

"I bought stock in North Star when it was a hundred dollars a share. I'm goin' to sell this morning and double my money."

"You'd be a fool to sell now. I'm telling you, it's going up to a thousand dollars a share."

Susanna recognized the voice of the last speaker, and though she was just passing, she stopped and looked back. It was Jesse.

"Yes, sir," Jesse said, "I've got fifty shares and I'm holding until they reach a thousand."

"Jesse," Susanna called.

Seeing Susanna, Jesse came over to join her. "Hello, Susanna."

"Mr. and Mrs. Kirkland missed you yesterday afternoon." It wasn't a harsh condemnation, merely an observation.

"Oh, yeah, I forgot about that."

"How could you forget? Mrs. Kirkland makes cake and coffee every Sunday."

"I know. But tell me, truthfully, Susanna, do you enjoy going over there every Sunday?"

Susanna chuckled. "Not really."

"Ha! I thought so. But better you than me. Are you headed for work?"

"Yes."

"Would you like me to walk with you?"

"Yes, that would be nice."

"What do you think about North Star?" Jesse asked. "I told you to buy it a couple of weeks ago. Did you do it? I bought it at fifty and I'm a rich man."

"You'll be a rich man if you sell right now, today. But if I were you, I wouldn't hold on to your stocks any longer."

Jesse laughed out loud. "Ha! Listen to yourself. Who's

made more money in the market, me or you?" Then he paused, giving Susanna a quizzical look. "Wait a minute. Does old man Loudin know something the rest of us should know?"

"No, nothing that I am aware of."

"Then, why do you think I should sell North Star?"

"It's just a feeling I have," Susanna said.

"A feeling."

"Yes."

"You're giving me advice based on a feeling you have. Well, I've got a feeling, too, and my feeling tells me North Star's going to a thousand dollars a share. I've made a lot of money trading in the market."

"And you've lost a lot of money. You take too many risks, Jesse."

"I guess you agree with Pop, that I should stop all this and just work in his damn store."

"Why not? The store makes a good living for your parents, as well as for your sister and her husband. You know your father is worth as much money as any one of those yahoos. And he doesn't have to stand there every day in front of Barry, Patmore, and Daigh acting like a bee at a Brobdingnagian hive trying to strike it rich."

"Listen to her, trying to show off her fancy education with her big words," Jesse said. "Think how much more money Pop would be worth if he had put his money in mining stocks."

"Mr. Kirkland is smart not to invest in mine shares. So is Harold."

"And you think I should be like Harold, a little mouse that sells hats to ladies?"

"Yes."

"That'll be the day," Jesse said with a scoffing laugh.

Susanna took a deep breath. If she was going to honor Kirkland's request, this discussion had just presented the perfect opportunity. "Jesse, do you ever think about marriage?"

"What do you mean?"

"I mean having a wife and a family. Do you ever think about that?"

"Not all that much. Anyway, what does that have to do with investing in mining stock?"

"It's just that if you ever did get married, your wife wouldn't want you to be risking everything you have on mining stocks. They're like smoke in the wind, here now, gone a moment later. A woman needs security. She wants her husband to have a steady job, and she wants a roof over her head. If she has children, she wants clothes for them and she needs food for the table."

Jesse's lips twisted into a cynical smile. "Hold on, Susanna, you've got me with a wife and younguns already when my gettin' married is a long way off."

"It needn't be."

The expression on Jesse's face changed from cynicism to bemusement. "What are you tryin' to tell me, little sister? Do you know something I don't know?"

"Well, I know what women want."

"Ha! I know, too. Take your friend Annie Biggs, for

example. I don't have to marry her to get her in bed. All I need is money."

"Jesse, there's more to marriage than sex. There are children to think about, and there's the companionship of a good woman."

"If I need sex, I'll pay for it. If I need children, I'll spend more time with Betsy. If I need the companionship of a good woman, I'll spend time with you. That's what we've been doin' for most of our lives anyway, isn't it?"

"Yes, we have, haven't we?" Susanna replied with an enigmatic smile.

When Rab went into the Bonanza Saloon, it was nearly empty. One of the saloon girls was sitting back at the piano, picking out a tune, one note at a time. A Chinese man was sweeping the floor, and a man was sitting in the far corner with his chair leaning back against the wall. His arms were folded across his chest and his eyes were closed. Rab didn't know if he was sleeping, but if not, he was giving a good impression of it.

Another man was drinking a beer. For Rab, it was a little too early to be drinking, but he had come here for breakfast.

When Rab stepped up to the bar, the barkeep was polishing glasses and took one of them over to the beer barrel. "Beer?"

"Breakfast," Rab replied. "You do serve breakfast, don't you?"

"Ham, biscuits, coffee, is all."

"That's good enough." Rab found a table, which wasn't difficult to do because only two tables were occupied.

Rab was aware that the man who was sitting alone, drinking beer, had been keeping a close eye on him from the time he came into the saloon. So when he stood up and brought his drink over to Rab's table, he wasn't surprised. Rab dropped his hand down to rest his fingers on the butt of his pistol as the man approached. But the expression on the man's face did not cause alarm.

"Mind if I jawbone with you a bit?" the man asked.

Rab raised his foot and pushed a chair away from the table. "Sit."

"Thanks."

The man looked to be in his late forties, though he might have been younger. It was difficult to tell because he had obviously seen hard times; his clothes were tattered, his hair and beard unkempt, his hands gnarled.

"You're that detective fella folks is talkin' about, aren't you? Trudeau I think they said your name is?"

"I am, and it is."

"Are you wantin' to take a look inside the North Star Mine?"

Rab's eyes narrowed in interest. "What makes you think I might want to do that?"

"Well, you are here lookin' for cheatin' and wrong-doin', aren't you?"

"Yes."

"The North Star Mine is cheatin' and doin' folks wrong."

"Who are you, and how do you know this?"

"The name is Posey. Otis Posey. Me 'n' Sheehan come out here from Missouri together, started diggin' together. We had us a mine goin', was payin' off, too. Oh, not like some of the mines here that's makin' folks rich. But it was payin' enough to make it worth somethin'. Then Sheehan, he says we needed to borrow some money to expand our operation, so that's what we done. Only later I found out that the money we was borrowin' actually come from Sheehan his ownself, and when I couldn't pay it, he took over my share of the mine. And that's what he took in to North Star with him."

"Would you like another beer?" Rab said. "Or maybe you would rather have breakfast? Have you eaten?"

"Yes, sir, I ate me a bite yesterday mornin', I think it was. Or maybe the day before."

"You haven't eaten, but you spend your money on beer?"

Posey smiled. "This beer?" He held up the glass. "Hell, I didn't buy this beer, mister. Someone left it last night, and it was sittin' on the table when I come in here this mornin'."

When Rab's ham, biscuit, and coffee was brought to the table, he slid it over to Posey. "I'll have another," Rab said, and the Chinese man who had delivered it nodded, then shuffled back to the kitchen.

"You asked if I wanted to get a look inside the North Star Mine. The answer is yes, I would love to, but it's shut down and heavily guarded right now."

"That don't mean nothin'," Posey said, his words muffled because his mouth was full of biscuit and ham. "I know how you can get in."

"How's that?"

"They's a back entrance. It's the same one we used when me 'n' Sheehan was workin' together. Once you get down inside, the main drift will lead you into a crosscut, and that crosscut will take you over into the North Star Mine."

"You'll show me this entrance?"

"Yes, sir, I will."

"How much is that going to cost me?"

"I ain't askin' for no money nor charity." Posey held up his hand. "This here breakfast is charity enough, and I'm shamed to be takin' it. Soon as I get enough money together, I'm goin' back to Missouri. I got a little farm back there that I abandoned when I come out here, and I plan to go back and work it. And I aim to marry the girl I left behind, too, if she'll still have me."

"I don't consider paying for information to be charity. It's done all the time in the detective business."

"Is it? Well, would it pay enough for me to buy a railroad ticket back to Missouri?"

"What would the fare be?"

"Thirty-five dollars. I done got me fifteen dollars saved up, but it's been hard to save money 'cause I need to keep usin' what little I can earn, now and then, for food and such."

Rab pulled five twenty-dollar bills in paper money from his money clip, put them on the table, and slid them across to Posey.

"What's this for? This is a lot more than the railroad fare would be."

"You're going to have to eat on your way back home, aren't you? And you don't want your girl seeing you like this, do you? You're going to need a bath, a shave, and some new clothes."

A broad smile spread across Posey's face. "Yeah. Yeah, that's right, ain't it?"

Posey scooped up the money and dropped it in his pocket at about the same time the Chinese man returned with Rab's breakfast.

"Soon as you get your food et, I'll take you out and show you how to get into the mine." Posey giggled. "Truth is, I woulda show'd it to you for free, just to see Sheehan get his comeuppance."

When Posey looked longingly at Rab's biscuit and ham, he pushed it across to him as well. The way the man wolfed down the food, he obviously needed it a lot more than Rab did.

An hour later they were a thousand feet farther up the side of Mount Davidson. "This is it," Posey said.

Rab looked around, but saw nothing that resembled a mine entrance. "What is it?"

"Right there." Posey pointed. "Don't nobody know 'bout this entrance but me and Sheehan, and I'm pretty sure he's all but forgot about it. It was our first dig, but we abandoned it pretty quick, and we closed it back up. If Sheehan does remember it, he'll probably think it's still closed up. But when I found out Sheehan stole my share of the mine, I come back out here and opened it up again."

Rab could see how the mine entrance could go undiscovered. It was impossible to see from as close as ten feet away. The opening was just on the other side of a rock outcropping, and some low-growing sagebrush covered it.

"You don't even have to move the bush aside; all you got to do is push a couple of branches out of your way and go on down in there."

"Are you going with me?"

"No, sir, I done my part. I showed you how to get in. But I ain't goin' no farther 'n this."

"I thank you for your help."

Rab started down into the narrow shaft, lighting a candle from the box he carried. He followed the gradually descending corridor until he reached the passageway Posey had told him about. From the moment Rab reached the crosscut, he knew he was in the North Star Mine. He walked on until he saw a dim, yellow glow ahead. Extinguishing his candle, he continued forward, feeling his way carefully by measured footsteps and by keeping his hand on the wall.

As he got closer, he saw that he was approaching one of the North Star's main drifts. He knew that because unlike the bare crosscut corridor he had just come through, up ahead he saw the honeycomb support boxes that held the roofs up and the walls out.

"How long we goin' be locked up down here?" Rab heard one voice ask.

"What difference does it make as long as we're gettin' paid?"

"Yeah, not only that, we ain't even doin' no work," another man said.

Rab heard the ruffle of cards being shuffled.

"How come we're on shutdown anyway? Ain't nobody found no new vein that I heard of. And the one we're workin' ain't hardly worth comin' down here every day."

"Hey, you're gettin' four dollars a day, ain't you?"

"Yeah."

"And all we have to do for the next few days is lay around and play cards, or sleep. What are you complainin' for?"

"What happens when Van Cleve and them other two bastards open 'er up again?"

"Who knows, but I reckon they'll let us know when the time comes. Hey, are you in this game or not? King bets."

"It's goin' to get pretty ripe down here if we stay much longer."

"What's the matter, Jacob? You afraid your whore's gonna jump the fence on ya?"

The mine chamber echoed with the laughter of the scores of miners, and Rab used the sound to cover his withdrawal.

North Star Mine Reopened
No New Strike
by
B. D. Elliott

North Star Mine has been reopened after being shut down for six days. It was widely

thought that the shutdown was because a new
vein of silver had been located, but Colonel
Burdick, speaking for the mine owners, said
that no such claim had been made. He let it be
known that the shutdown was merely to give
the workers an opportunity to build some new
boxes so that the drifts could be made safer.

Because of the widespread speculation as to
a potential new silver discovery, the share value
of North Star increased to over three hundred
dollars. With the reopening of the mine, and
the realization that there was no new discovery,
the stock today was trading at six dollars per
share.

Colonel Burdick wants the general public
to know that at no time during the previous
week did he, Mr. Van Cleve, or Mr. Sheehan
make any such claim that would lead the public to believe that they had struck a bonanza.

The article that had informed hundreds of investors
that their speculation was unwise told not a few that they
had lost everything.

When Jesse read the paper, he groaned. He had bought
fifty shares of North Star at fifty dollars a share. Susanna
was right. He should have sold when the stock reached a
hundred dollars, but he had gotten greedy. He just knew
it was going to reach a thousand, and it would have if it
hadn't been for Elliott's article in the *Pioneer*. The shares
had risen to just over three hundred dollars, and now

the quote was six dollars. Overnight, Jesse's holdings had gone from over fifteen thousand dollars to just three hundred dollars.

Jesse hurried over to check the morning quotes at Barry, Patmore, and Daigh. A crowd of people were standing in front of the window, watching as the clerk, wearing a green visor and a button-up shirt with thin, vertical red and white stripes, put the latest numbers on the big board.

At first there were groans as everyone watched the share values of every mine on the Comstock go down. Consolidated Virginia—12½; Belcher—4½; Ophir—49¼; Mexican—14½; Silver Falcon—3¾; California—15¾. Then came the quote everyone was looking for—the price for North Star. Was there a prayer that the article had been wrong, that the North Star was really in a bonanza?

"No!" someone shouted in anger.

"That's impossible!" another said. "They had a big strike, the paper said so!"

"This ain't right! There's somethin' goin' on here!"

Jesse had to squeeze through several people to get close enough to read the quote for himself.

North Star—3¼.

Turning away from the window, Jesse felt the need for a drink, even though it was not yet noon. He started walking with his head down, and he ran right into an attractive young woman.

"Oh!" she said as she tripped over an uneven plank in the boardwalk.

"I'm sorry," Jesse said, grabbing her to keep her from falling. "Are you all right?"

"Yes, I think so."

Jesse smiled. "I know you. You live in the same house with Susanna, don't you?"

"Yes, I'm Mary Beth Chaney. You're Jesse Kirkland, Susanna's brother."

Jesse shook his head. "I'm Jesse Kirkland, but I'm not Susanna's brother."

"Oh, that's right, I know that. It's just that she calls you her brother. I know she is very fond of you."

Jesse laughed. "That's good to know. She may be the only one in the whole family who is."

"There seems to be quite a crowd in front of the brokers' office. Has another big strike been found?"

"I wish. It looks like everyone got taken in because of an article in Susanna's newspaper. Just about everybody standing there lost a lot of money on North Star."

"My mother wanted to buy some shares, but Susanna persuaded her not to, and thankfully she listened," Mary Beth said.

Jesse got a strange look on his face. This was the second time he had wondered whether Susanna might have known something ahead of time about this particular stock. Did the *Pioneer* have some way of getting information before anyone else did? If it did, that wasn't right.

"Yeah, Susanna seems to know best. I wish I would

have listened to her," Jesse said, nodding his head. "Maybe we'll run into each other again sometime."

Mary Beth laughed at his little joke. "Oh, thanks for catching me." She watched him walk away, wondering what he meant when he said he wished he had listened to Susanna.

❧ 11 ❧

At the Trail's End Saloon in Reno, a thin, wiry man named Asa Teague was standing at the bar. Teague's skin was so tight across his face that it looked almost as if it were stretched over a skull with no flesh beneath it. The skull-like idea was enhanced by his bald head. Only the well-shaped Vandyke beard interrupted the illusion.

A mug of beer sat on the bar before him, and he had both hands wrapped around it as he stared down at the head, which was slowly receding. At the opposite end of the bar, holding court, was Joshua Broadman, a ranch owner from the surrounding area. His ranch didn't have many acres, and he wasn't running many head of cattle, but he was doing well financially because he controlled a commodity that in this part of the country was precious: water.

Boardman's ranch sat alongside the Carson River, and he charged neighboring ranchers a healthy fee to access the water. The ranchers didn't like that, and after all reasoning with him failed, a few of the cattlemen secretly vowed to take extreme measures.

Asa Teague was the extreme measure.

"Yes, sir," Broadman was saying, "what I got is better than silver or gold. You can live without silver and you can live without gold, but you can't live without water, and I got water."

"The river don't belong to you," one of the other saloon patrons said.

"The river don't," Broadman said, "but unless you're a bird, there ain't no way you can get to the river without comin' across the Broken B Ranch. And the Broken B does belong to me."

Asa Teague turned toward him. "Mr. Broadman, I've been asked by some of your friends to convince you to listen to a reasonable offer for your property." Teague's voice was low, sibilant, and that, combined with his looks, gave one the impression of a snake.

"Really? And just what are they calling a reasonable offer?"

"Five thousand dollars."

"Five thousand?" Broadman responded incredulously. "Are you crazy? I've already been offered ten thousand, but I turned that down."

"I know. That offer was from the same people I represent."

"Just what in hell makes them think I would sell it

to them for five thousand dollars when I wouldn't take ten for it?"

"Because they've added a bonus."

"A bonus? What kind of a bonus?" Broadman asked.

"Your life."

"What? What do you mean, *my life*?"

"If you agree to sell, you will have five thousand dollars, and you will live. If you don't agree, I will kill you."

"Who—who are you?"

"The name is Teague. Asa Teague."

When Teague spoke his name, it got the attention of everyone. Asa Teague was a well-known, and much-feared, regulator, someone who hunted men for money. He specialized in those who were wanted dead or alive, and he seldom brought someone in alive.

Broadman had heard of him as well, and now he grew visibly nervous. Beads of perspiration erupted on his upper lip. "You—you can't just threaten me. I've got witnesses."

"I think I can. When I force you to draw on me, every one of your witnesses will see it my way. And they will all testify that you drew first."

Teague turned to the few men left in the saloon. "Ain't that right?"

"I ain't gonna draw on you, mister, and I don't have to sell my property. You got that?"   .

Teague drew his pistol, fired, and had it back in his holster almost before the sound of the gunshot had died away. When everyone looked toward Broadman, they saw the pain on his face, and his hand was clasped over his ear.

"You—you shot off my damned ear!" he shouted.

"No, I shot the tip of your earlobe." Teague raised his gun to take aim again.

"You can't do this; you're crazy."

"I'll take another piece of that one, then I'll start carving up the other one until you draw on me."

"I'm not gonna draw on you, mister!" Broadman pointed at Teague, the palm of his hand red with blood from his wounded ear.

Teague fired, and this time everyone in the saloon saw a little spray of red mist around Broadman's already wounded ear.

"Draw, sell, or I start on the other ear," Teague said coldly.

"No, no! I'll sell, I'll sell!" Broadman shouted, his words contorted by terror.

Teague turned back to his beer. "I thought I could talk you into listening to reason."

Broadman, now holding a blood-soaked handkerchief over his shredded ear, hurried out of the saloon. Absolutely no reaction came from anyone else in the place, out of either shared embarrassment and shame for what Broadman had been subjected to or fear of Teague. Nobody approached or said anything to the gunfighter.

Except for one person.

John Sheehan, part owner of the North Star Mine, asked, "Could I buy you a drink, Mr. Teague?"

"I've got a drink," Teague replied as he continued to stare at the top of his beer.

"I must say that I like the way you handle yourself."

"What do you want?" Teague turned toward him. "An autograph?"

"I think I'd like to hire you. That would be me and my partners."

"To do what?"

"I've got somebody that won't listen to reason, and I think you're the man to bring him around."

"I don't come cheap."

Sheehan smiled. "If you did come cheap, we wouldn't be interested in you. We only want the best, and we're willing to pay."

"Five thousand dollars."

"I'm prepared to give you twenty-five hundred now, and twenty-five hundred when the job is done."

"Where's this job?"

"In Virginia City."

Teague lifted the beer mug to his lips and began drinking. He didn't set it down until the mug was empty.

"Ahhh," he said, then wiped the foam from his lips with the back of his hand. "What do you say we go to Virginia City?"

When an iron flagpole was raised on the side of Mount Davidson, small cannons were hauled up the slope of the mountain and fired in salute of the large American flag that now flew proudly from the staff. Hundreds of people from both Virginia City and Gold Hill were there, for this had been a joint project of all the service organizations in both communities.

All three publishers from the area newspapers were there: Alf Doten from the *Gold Hill News,* Dan DeQuille from the *Territorial Enterprise,* and James Loudin from the *Pioneer.* Mr. Loudin had asked Susanna to accompany him because he knew Doten and DeQuille were both jealous of his attractive young typesetter. Alf had even at one time suggested to James that he would like to, in his words, cruise with Susanna, but James had never even broached the subject. He knew that she was as straitlaced as they come.

"Tell me, Susanna," Doten said. "Did you ever find this Rab Trudeau?"

"I found him."

"And yet, I don't think I've seen a story in the *Pioneer.*"

"It would seem that Mr. Trudeau is loath to grant an interview."

"And you let that stop you, my dear?"

"How can I write a story about him if he won't grant me an interview?"

"Oh, Susanna, my dear, innocent Susanna. Has Loudin failed to teach you how it works in this business? An enterprising newspaper reporter doesn't need to be granted anything. Don't let a little thing like that get in the way of a good story," Doten said. "I daresay you've met him, have you not? You've spoken to others who know him, have you not? Look how many stories have been written about the great bard, and yet I doubt that one reporter ever interviewed Shakespeare."

Susanna laughed. "I must confess that I never considered writing about him without interviewing him first. What if I write something that he finds offensive?"

"What if you do?" Doten replied. "I take it that you've offered him the opportunity to be interviewed?"

"Yes, more than once."

"Then, no matter what you write, he will have no reason to complain. Simply by making the offer, you have provided yourself and the newspaper with all the cover you need."

"Thank you for your advice, Mr. Doten."

"If you really wanted to thank me, you would accompany me to the theater tonight. We could watch *Lucrezia Borgia* together."

"Shame on you, Mr. Doten," Susanna teased. "You are a married man, with a family."

"True, but there is always room for another beautiful woman," he said with a chuckle.

"Hello, Alf," Jesse said, coming up to stand beside Susanna. Easily, familiarly, he put his arm around her, resting his hand on her shoulder. "You wouldn't be bothering my sister, now, would you?"

"Your sister? I was under the impression that Susanna isn't actually your sister," Doten said.

"She isn't my birth sister, but as far as I'm concerned, she's my sister. Enough so that I would not hesitate to come to her aid if I thought she needed me, such as, oh, maybe a married man making unwanted advances toward her."

"Look here, I'm doing no such thing," Doten said, sputtering his denial.

"I didn't think you would," Jesse said easily. "But in a crowd like this, you never know what might happen."

"Oh, there's Thomas Edison," Doten said, pointing out the famous inventor. "I understand he went down in the Consolidated Virginia today because he thinks he may have come up with a better way to illuminate the mines. If he has, you'll read about it in the *News*."

Susanna laughed as Doten hurried on his way. "My big brother coming to my rescue. Just as you did the day the awful Darrel tore up all the flowers I had picked."

"Awful Darrel? I guess you know he's a preacher now," Jesse said, laughing with her. "Oh, there's a couple of friends. If you need rescuing again, just let me know."

After both Doten and Jesse left, Susanna began moving through the crowd. By now the salute cannons had been fired, the band had played a few patriotic airs, and a series of speakers were taking their turns to address the crowd.

"I saw you with Jesse."

Turning toward the speaker, Susanna saw a smiling Gus Kirkland. "You are a good girl, Susanna. You always have been. You will be so good for Jesse. I'm glad you are beginning to spend some time with him."

"He considers me his sister."

"It is just a matter of misplaced affection. Of course you aren't his sister, and that is the whole point. You know, now that I think back on it, it may be that I have always had it in mind that you and Jesse would marry. That is why we have been so insistent that he not think of you as his sister."

"I see." Susanna didn't know how else to respond to that.

"Oh, I see Mr. Manning. I need to talk a little business

with him. Keep up the good work, Susanna. I want to hear the wedding bells soon."

As Susanna watched Kirkland walk away, she tried to deal with the conflicting emotions that were coursing through her. She had promised Kirkland that she was going to marry Jesse, and she would do so. But she was having a hard time accommodating herself to that.

With so many people attending the flag-raising ceremony on top of Mount Davidson, Rab took the opportunity to look through the mines again. Approaching the Nevada Syndicate Mine, he saw a huge building with several wings extending from it, one of which was the boiler house. Beside this building were immense piles of wood that fed the boilers and provided the steam needed to operate all the machinery. He knew the wood was a necessity, but Rab did not like what it did to the adjacent scenery. When one looked to the east, north, or south from Virginia City, one could not see a tree. Now, because the nearby trees were all gone, most of this timber had to be hauled by rail from high in the Sierra Nevada.

The stamping mills were in full operation, and when he went inside, he spoke to no one, but simply stayed out of the way and observed. It wasn't hard to avoid being noticed; working the stamping mills was dangerous work that required the attention of all concerned.

The noise was deafening with the steady thump, thump, thump of the huge rock crushers. Rab stayed for a few minutes watching the operation, then left and went into the carpenter shop. He thought that he could judge the productivity of the mine by the work in this shop, for if they were continuing to dig, thousands of supports would be required.

As it had been in the stamping mill, the noise was so unbearably loud that it was painful, and he wondered how anyone could work there day after day. Rab was about to leave, but since he was here, he decided to check the main building. Once inside, he was met by the column of steam that rushed up out of the mine. Even in the middle of summer, the surface air temperature was so much cooler than that of the air coming from the mine that this cloud of condensation formed above the twenty-foot-wide shaft that stretched from nine hundred to two thousand feet below the surface. One end of the shaft contained the giant pump that brought the ever-present hot groundwater out of the mine and emptied it on the mountainside.

As it was not time for a shift change, Rab saw few people. The engineer was on his platform operating the hoists that lowered the men and the ore carts into and out of the mine. The three cages running up and down were all coordinated by this one man. He never took his eyes off his dials that told him the position of the cages, and his ears were always alert for his signal bells, the only communication those in the bowels of the earth had with the outside world. Rab was watching the engineer do his work. His was truly the most important job in the whole mining operation because the safety of all below depended upon him.

Suddenly Rab felt a blow to his back that propelled him forward. Pitching over the edge of the shaft opening, he felt himself falling into the abyss, his arms and legs flailing.

When Susanna returned to the newspaper office, she had to unlock the door, as both B.D. and Loudin were still with those who were up on the mountain, gathered around the new flagpole. After she let herself into the empty office, she stood there looking around for a moment.

Susanna believed something about a newspaper office was almost sacrosanct. There was the editorial bay, where B.D. had his desk; the publisher's office, the private sanctum of James Loudin; the composing room, with its tables and drawers of type; and the pressroom, where reposed the steam-powered rotary press.

Susanna thought about what Alf Doten had said. Could she really write an article about Rab Trudeau without actually interviewing him? That wouldn't be right, would it? On the other hand, maybe if she did write such an article, it would force him to submit to an interview.

With that in mind, she went into the back with a paper and pen and started writing an article.

Our Mysterious Visitor

Our readers may have noticed a man who has been seen about Virginia City, Gold Hill, and the entire Comstock area. Indeed, those who have seen him have no doubt questioned who he is, and why he appears to observe everything with a keen and detached eye.

The Pioneer has learned his name is Mr. Trudeau, and he claims to be from San Francisco's Great Western Detective Agency. What, may you ask, needs investigating in our fair cities? It would appear that he is snooping around the Comstock Lode. Will his investigation accrue to our advantage, or to our detriment?

If one thinks that an investigation of the mines has little import in his life, for his occupation may be not connected to the mines, one would be wrong. For in truth, every business here located is connected to the mines— be it the butcher, the tailor, the green grocer, the clothing merchant, the tinker, the doctor or lawyer, the schoolteacher or preacher, even the journal in which you are now reading these words—owes its continued existence to the output of the mines. For that reason, an investigation that would insure honest operation of the business would be welcomed even by the most trusting among us. But the question remains, will the investigation being conducted provide more security by uncovering any fraud or misconduct? Or is the investigation being conducted by someone who has a personal motive for disrupting the operation of the mines?

Mr. Trudeau has refused to grant this newspaper an interview, so it is not known who has employed the detective agency. Is it a mine owner? Is the purpose sinister, meant to collapse the mines and the economy so that one with malevolent intentions could then move in and profit upon the misery and misfortune of others?

Is Rab Trudeau an honest investigator against the fraud and deceit that, unchecked, could harm us all? Or is he an agent for evil?

This we do not know, and cannot know, unless Mr. Trudeau makes his purpose known by submitting to an honest and open interview, and that he has thus far refused to do.

As Susanna read over the article she had just penned, in which she had questioned Rab's motives, she began questioning her own. Why had she written it? Was she really trying to give voice to the concern that many felt about Rab's investigation? Or did she have another reason? She had no doubt but that this article would provoke Rab.

Is that what she wanted? Did she write this article to irreversibly create a rift between them? Then there could be no more thoughts of what-if when she considered the commitment to marry Jesse that she had made to Gus Kirkland.

Susanna knew that sometimes one took steps in life that could not be called back. Was this such a step? Susanna considered showing the article to Loudin, but decided against it. To publish this article or not would have to be her choice.

She set the article, then put in B. D. Elliott's byline. She stared at the byline for a moment, then removed it. This was her article, and she would succeed or fail with it.

When he was pushed, Rab was fortunately standing near the shaft that housed the water conduit. The twelve-inch pipe that brought the mine water to the surface had large counterweighted balance bobs that prevented the pipe from collapsing from its own weight. These were cut into the rock adjacent to the shaft wall as needed.

The first of these projecting levers was about twenty feet below the opening, and making a desperate reach for it, Rab managed to grab hold. The balance bob broke his fall, but now he was hanging from it, with his feet dangling over open space, knowing that if he lost his grip, he would fall two thousand feet to his sure death. Gradually, he improved his hold, then was able to move from the balance bob to the timber braces that kept the walls of the shaft from caving in. Looking down, he could see nothing but darkness. Looking up, he could see light from the opening of the shaft.

Slowly, laboriously, he began climbing. Climbing tall objects wasn't foreign to him; he had climbed to the top of the tallest mast on board ships that were lurching about in storm-tossed seas, but masts were made to be climbed, and there his footholds and handgrips were evenly spaced and clear before him. The timber supports in a mine shaft, however, were not built for this, and in the dim light, diffused by the twenty-foot projection down into the shaft, finding footholds and handgrips was difficult.

Suddenly, down in the mine, a heavy charge of "giant powder" was detonated, and the sound and shock wave rushing up through the open shaft nearly dislodged him. Finally he reached the top, pulled himself over the opening, then lay on the ground for a moment taking heaving breaths.

"What the hell?" the hoist engineer said, barking the words out in surprise. "Where did you come from?"

"I was—pushed, fell—fell into the shaft," Rab said, gasping for air. "Did you—did you see it?"

"Mister, I didn't see anything."

"You must have seen! You're sitting right here!" Rab said, regaining control of his breathing.

"I didn't even see you. I was sending a cage down and I was watching my gauge."

"Are you sure you didn't see someone do this?"

The engineer pointed to a placard on the platform where he was sitting:

IT IS UNLAWFUL TO CLIMB ONTO THE ENGINEER'S
PLATFORM OR TO SPEAK TO THE ENGINEER.

"Sorry," the engineer said. At just that moment an ore cart arrived and a carman pulled it off the cage onto the track, sending the ore to the stamping mill.

Rab shrugged his shoulders in frustration. Who was behind this? No one survived a fall down a mine shaft. Someone wanted him dead.

*   *   *

"We'll pay you the rest of the money when we know the job is done," Van Cleve said.

"The son of a bitch is dead, all right," Teague said. "The Nevada Syndicate shaft is two thousand feet deep."

"And you are sure he fell into it?" Burdick asked.

"He didn't fall, I pushed him."

"What about the hoist engineer? Did he see anything?" Sheehan asked.

"Nobody saw anything. I followed him in, pushed him down the shaft, and left. It was that simple. I want the rest of my money."

"Look," Van Cleve said. "You've got half of it. Why don't you just hang around town for a while, go to one of the shows, enjoy the saloons, visit the whores? As soon as we know for sure that Trudeau is dead, we'll give you the rest of your money."

"All right." Teague smiled. "I like the part about visiting the whores."

❋ 12 ❋

Rab slept fitfully that night. Every footfall in the hall-way, every creak of the floor, every closing of a door, awakened him. He tried to go over in his mind every contact he had made since coming to Virginia City. Who or what was he getting close to discovering? Whom had he crossed? Maybe he should send David DeLoitte a telegram, inquiring if something was going on in San Francisco that had nothing to do with Virginia City. He had to check every possible reason why someone wanted to kill him.

He needed to spend some time at the Silver Falcon. Benton McQueen could help him find out some infor-mation. His superintendent was the only one at the mine who knew Rab's purpose for being here, and McQueen had played his part well, not letting on to anyone who he was. But that might have to change. Rab was not going to lose his life over a mine. He had enough money to keep him comfortable for the rest of his time on earth, and he didn't need this.

But then he thought about Susanna Ward or Susanna Kirkland or whatever she called herself. He smiled when he thought about her unbridled spontaneity and laughed out loud when he remembered her comment about eating like pigs at a trough. She had turned down his invitation to go to the Independence Day dance with him, but he would ask her again. He would turn on the old charm and win her over. Today, he would ride Rebel out to the mine, and when he returned he would go to the Chaney House and be waiting for her when she came home from work. Quickly he dressed and left his hotel, going to the livery stable to get his horse.

Rab rode to the best hotel in town, the International. He had money—he was proud of what he had accomplished—and he wasn't going to deny himself the small pleasures anymore. He would have the best breakfast the hotel had to offer.

"Good morning, sir, would you like one of our fine papers to read while you have your morning coffee? The *Enterprise* and the *News* are hot off the press."

"I'm a *Pioneer* man," Rab said.

"Oh, well, that's an afternoon paper."

"Do you have a copy from yesterday?"

"I'll see what I can find."

Rab ordered a porterhouse steak and eggs, and when his order came, the waiter handed him the paper. Rab cut into his steak, took the first bite of the succulent meat, cooked rare to perfection. He took a sip of his coffee and picked up the paper and began to read.

"What the hell?" he sputtered, hot coffee spewing from his mouth, when he read the first few lines of Susanna's article. He pushed back from the table and rose from the chair, tipping it backward as he did. He heard the clatter as he stormed out of the dining room. Rebel was tied to the rail waiting for him. He vaulted into the saddle and raced down C Street, causing men, women, children, dogs, cats, and even the burros that sometimes roamed the busy street to get out of his way.

He reined in Rebel and threw the reins over the banister outside the *Pioneer* office without even securing his horse. Pushing open the door, he stepped up to B. D. Elliott's desk and slammed the paper down in front of him.

"What in the hell is this?" Rab demanded.

"It's nothing but a quaint," B.D. said. "They are written with tongue in cheek, meant to be entertaining. Good Lord, man, you aren't supposed to believe them."

"You think pillorying me like this is entertaining?"

"Pillorying you? Maybe you had better tell me what you are talking about? I don't even know you," B.D. said. "Who are you, anyway?"

"You haven't met him, but you have heard of him," Susanna said. She had come to the front office from the press and composing room and was now standing nearby with her arms folded across her chest. "This is Rab Trudeau, the detective everyone is talking about."

"Mr. Trudeau, apparently you are upset, but I must tell you, I have no idea why," B.D. said.

"You're damn right I'm upset." Rab tapped his finger on the article in question and held the paper out toward B.D. "Wouldn't you be if someone wrote this about you?"

B.D. read the article, then looked up and shook his head. "Mr. Trudeau, I did not write that article."

"Then, who did? Loudin?"

"Ha," B.D. said. "Loudin couldn't write come to Jesus if the Blessed Mother was dictating the story."

"I wrote it," Susanna said.

Both B.D. and Rab looked toward Susanna. By the expression on their faces it was difficult to tell which of the two was more surprised.

"You?" B.D. said. "Susanna, are you saying you wrote this article?"

"Yes."

"Did Loudin tell you to write this—this piece of . . . ?" Rab stopped in midsentence, checking his language.

"He doesn't know I wrote it."

"Oh, my," B.D. said. "I don't think it would be wise for you to be around here when he finds out. If you want, I'll tell him that I wrote the article."

"No, I'll take the credit, or the blame," Susanna said.

Rab gripped the paper in his right hand and held it out toward her. "How could you do this to me, Susanna? How could you betray me like this?"

"Betray you? Mr. Trudeau, one cannot betray another unless there is some sort of relationship. No such relationship exists between us, except that of journalist and news subject."

"But this isn't even good journalism," Rab said. "You have implied by your article that I am in cahoots with some son of a . . . some nefarious mine owner who has as his purpose the destruction of the mines. How could you write such tripe? You know that isn't true."

"No, I don't know that," Susanna said. "As I clearly stated in the article, you have, thus far, refused to grant me an interview."

Rab's face reflected his rage: his mouth was drawn tight, and a throbbing was visible in his temple.

"All right," he finally said, the words cold and clipped. "Let's just see how much of a journalist you are."

"What do you mean?"

"Do you want the truth? Or do you want to continue to publish fiction?"

"I want the truth," Susanna said. "Does that mean you are ready to grant me an interview now?"

"An interview won't do it. With an interview you will have only my word for it. I'll give you a firsthand look at what I'm doing."

"What exactly is a firsthand look?"

"I'll take you down into the mine with me. That is, if you have the guts to go."

"Impossible. They rarely let outsiders into the mines, and I've never heard of a woman going into one of them," Susanna said.

"I can get you in."

"How are you going to accomplish that?"

"You let me worry about that. All that matters is that I can, and I will do it."

Susanna was quiet for a moment. "I couldn't go anyway. I have to get today's paper set."

Rab stared at her for a long moment before he responded, the expression in his voice halfway between condescension and regret. "I must say, Susanna, that I am a little disappointed. I thought you had more gumption than that."

"I want to go," she replied quickly. "And I would go in a heartbeat if I didn't have work to do."

"Susanna, if you really want to go, I'll set up the paper," B.D. said.

"I couldn't ask you to do that."

"Don't worry about me. I was setting type before you were born."

"It's up to you, Susanna," Rab said. "The decision is yours now. Do you really want the truth, or are you afraid of it? The truth is easy enough to find if you have the will to go down into the mine with me."

Susanna nodded. "All right, I'll go."

Rab turned and strode out of the newspaper office, not waiting for Susanna.

She followed him.

By the time Susanna got outside, Rab was already sitting astride a big, beautiful Arabian bay. This was the same horse she had seen him with the first time she had ever encountered him—the day he had rescued her from the runaway wagon.

"Am I supposed to trot along behind like some Indian squaw? Or do you have a horse for me?"

"You'll ride with me."

"How is that going to work?"

"Give me your hand and I'll show you."

Susanna offered her hand tentatively. Rab grabbed it and began to pull.

"Wait, what are you doing?"

"Work with me or against me, Susanna, but I'm hauling you up onto this horse." Rab held out the stirrup and Susanna put her foot into it. She had no idea where she was supposed to sit. She knew that with her skirt she wouldn't be able to sit behind him, and she couldn't very well straddle the horse in front of him.

Rab picked her up as easily as he had the day he had rescued her in the street. He sat her sidesaddle in front of him, her bottom resting on his muscular thighs, her legs hanging to the side of the horse.

"Put your arm around my neck," Rab said.

"I will not!"

"Your neck or mine."

"I beg your pardon?"

"If you don't want to fall and break *your* neck, you'll put your arm around *my* neck and hold on."

Susanna did as he directed.

Rab slapped his legs against Rebel's side and the horse broke into a brisk trot. Surprised, and a little frightened, Susanna had no choice but to hang on with both arms.

When Rab had learned that Susanna had written the article, he was angry with her. He knew that it would not be comfortable for her down in the mine; it wasn't comfortable for anyone. He was taking her down there not just to give her a close look, as he had said, but also to punish her for her betrayal. And part of that punishment began now, as they rode up to the mine.

Except, it wasn't working out quite the way he had expected. She was leaning into him, with her arms around his neck—and he was very aware of the way she was sitting, with her body pushed against him, from his chest to his stomach to his groin.

He felt himself reacting to her.

He had to get her down off this horse, or all his plans would go awry. He wasn't punishing her, he was punishing himself. Damn, there was no way he could hide this!

Susanna's initial anger and fright gradually gave way. She could feel the strength of his arm around her, the musculature of his chest, and his powerful legs. And something else as well. She was inexperienced, yes, but not totally ignorant. Annie had told her what happens when a man gets aroused. And from the hard pressure that was digging into her thigh, she knew that Rab was aroused. Susanna couldn't help but feel a sense of satisfaction—more than that, a sense of triumph.

But that sense of triumph and satisfaction began to slip away from her, and she started feeling something new. The horse's gait made her breasts move against Rab's chest through his clothes and hers, and she felt her nipples harden. Even though she knew she shouldn't do it, she leaned into him, allowing the friction to build. Her breasts began to throb with pleasure. She repositioned herself, pressing her body even more tightly against his. The satisfaction, even the delectation, was there. But the sense of triumph was gone.

Rab slowed Rebel to a walk, and Susanna felt a loss when the movement stopped. She lowered one arm from around Rab's neck and tried to adjust her position, but Rab caught her waist and held her tightly against him.

He dropped his head and inhaled the aroma of the perfumed soap she had used, as well as the scent of lemon that came from her luxuriant sable hair, now fluffed by the wind. When he looked at the soft color of her parted lips, he knew he would kiss her. More than anything, he wanted to give her a deep, demanding kiss, but now wasn't the time or place. Instead he kissed her full on the lips, a tender whisper of a kiss that Susanna returned.

"Rab," she said, mouthing the name even as their lips were together. Susanna knew that the anger he had felt toward her was gone.

"Oh, Susanna, what are we going to do about this?"

Susanna had no answer. Her dark eyes invited Rab to do more, though she was unable to articulate or even conceive what more would be. All she knew was that she didn't want it to stop. What had just happened was wonderful, and she felt a sense of unrestrained recklessness. She put her hand down on the bulge that still protruded from Rab's pants.

"Put your arms around my neck," Rab said. Unlike earlier, this was not a demand, but a plea, and the words could not have been more caressing if they had been mouthed by a poet.

Unbidden, a picture of Sophia and Byron Ward came into her mind. Was this feeling what love was all about? She wished she knew.

As they approached the scattered buildings of the mine—the hoisting works, the stamping mill, the boiler house, and the other components—Susanna twisted around to see which mine they would be visiting. At least six high smokestacks extended from the center of the main building, pouring forth smoke and steam. She could hear the sound of the rock being crushed in the stamping mill. She was familiar with the sound, for the grinding of the ore, the buzz of the saws, and the discharge of the air compressors competed for audible dominance all over town. But now she was actually on the Comstock, and the sounds multiplied by more than a dozen different mining operations were deafening.

Above the main building, Susanna saw a big signboard: SILVER FALCON MINE—SUNSET ENTERPRISES.

"We're going to the Silver Falcon?"

"Is there some reason we shouldn't?" Rab questioned.

"I thought we would go to a richer mine, like the Consolidated or the California. I didn't think we'd come to a mine that's about to play out."

"What makes you think it's playing out?"

"All the reports have said so, and of course the value of the stock is so low now. Mr. Loudin made B.D. write an article about it, but I must say, B.D. was hopping mad when he had to do it."

"What made him so mad?"

"He said he didn't think we should write a story like that unless we had absolute confirmation from the owner of the Silver Falcon."

"Well good for B.D.," Rab said.

"But of course, Mr. Loudin said that the owner would naturally deny that his mine was failing, so it would be better to get it from some other source."

"Who do you think was right?"

"I don't know. I can certainly see B.D.'s point of view. We probably should have gotten the mine owner's input."

"Why didn't you?"

"From what we've been able to determine, the Silver Falcon is owned by a San Francisco consortium called Sunset Enterprises. For all we know, there is no such thing as a mine owner, per se. So if you look at it that way, then Mr. Loudin has a point."

"Why don't we just see for ourselves who was right?" Rab suggested.

Riding up to the hitching rail in front of the mine, Rab helped Susanna slide down from the horse, then he dismounted as well. With a motion of his arm, he indicated that she should go to the door that led into the mine office. She hesitated for a moment.

"What's wrong?"

"I still don't feel right about this," Susanna said. "I told you, they don't like strangers out here."

"Don't worry about it."

At the moment he was standing with Rebel between them. He made himself busy by adjusting saddle cinches, testing the harness, and rubbing Rebel down until the pressure in the front of his pants subsided. He had no intention of going farther until he could display himself without embarrassment.

"Are you coming? Or must I go in alone?" Susanna asked.

Believing himself to be in control now, Rab tied Rebel off, then joined her. "Go on in. I'm right behind you."

Rab reached out to open the door, then stood to one side to allow Susanna to enter.

The mine superintendent, Benton McQueen, stood up and, seeing Rab, smiled broadly. "Mr. Trudeau. Good to see you."

"Hello, Benton."

"Really, good to see you from what I hear. You're the talk of the lode, you know. Not many have done what you did yesterday and lived to tell about it."

"What happened yesterday?" Susanna asked.

McQueen started to say something, but Rab cut him off with a look. "Nothing to tell. . . . This is Miss Kirk— that is, Miss Susanna Ward. She wants to go down in the mine with me."

McQueen shook his head. "I don't know—that doesn't sound like all that good of an idea to me."

"There's no reason why she can't, is there?"

"No, sir, I was just thinking of Miss Ward, that's all. Does she have any idea what it's like down there?"

"You've never been in a mine, have you?" Rab asked.

"No, but I'm ready," Susanna said as she smiled timidly.

"Mr. McQueen, she is a *journalist*." Rab came down

hard on the word *journalist* as if mocking her and her profession. "She is a *Pioneer* journalist."

"Aha, so that's what this is all about," McQueen said with a chuckle.

"What do you mean, 'that's what this is about'?" Susanna asked, but both men ignored her question.

"Come on," Rab invited. "We've got to get dressed."

"Get dressed?"

"You don't think you can wear a dress down there, do you?"

"I don't know. I guess not. I guess I just hadn't thought about it."

Rab directed Susanna into the dressing room, a commodious and open room located in the main building. She saw what seemed like hundreds of identical blue flannel pantaloons and gray woolen shirts hanging from hooks on the walls. Shelves contained several kinds of hats, and dozens of pairs of shoes, all neatly paired and marked with sizes.

"Pick out your Sunday best," Rab said, motioning toward the clothing. He grabbed the first shirt and the first pair of pantaloons and tossed them to Susanna.

She looked over the oversize clothing. "Is there any size besides giant?"

"That's it. One size fits all." Rab took the next set of clothing for himself and began unbuttoning his shirt.

"Wait a minute. Where do we change clothes?"

Rab had a mischievous grin on his face. "Why, right here, Miss Ward. I don't have anything you haven't already seen, do I?"

Susanna's eyebrows shot up in surprise, causing her brown eyes to appear even larger than they were. She turned and started to run for the door.

"No, no, no," Rab said, catching her hand in his. "I'm only teasing. We do change right here, though." Rab enjoyed the feel of her soft hand in his, and he was reluctant to let it go.

"Here? In front of everyone?"

"What do you mean *everyone*? Do you see anyone here?"

"No, not at the moment."

"Then, don't worry about it. I'll keep a lookout for you," Rab offered.

"Really? And who will keep a lookout for you?"

He flashed a devilish grin, then brought her hand to his lips and kissed it before he let go.

"You first," Rab said, turning his back to her. "And one more thing—when I say change clothes, I mean take off everything."

"You don't mean my . . ."

"Yes, I do. Believe me, you'll be much more comfortable."

Susanna took off her dress and rolled it into a neat little package because she couldn't see hanging it on a hook. That, she thought, would call attention to the foreignness of a woman in a world that so obviously was the domain of men. She hesitated over removing her camisole and drawers and decided to leave them on. She placed one foot in the voluminous pant leg.

"You'll be sorry," Rab said.

Susanna jumped. How did he know what she was doing? He had not turned around once, he could not have seen her, but she obeyed, removing her foot from the pantaloons. Taking a deep breath, she removed her underwear. The air seemed to sensitize her naked skin, and the feeling surprised her. Why had she never felt like this before when she was naked?

A smile tipped the corner of her mouth as she answered her own question. She had never been naked in the same room with a man. She looked over at Rab, who was, ever the gentlemen, standing with his back to her.

What if he turned around, right now?

She stood there for longer than she should have, trying to decide if what she was feeling was concern that he might turn, or a wish that he would turn.

Finally, with a sigh, she pulled on the flannel pantaloons, then put on the woolen shirt.

"I'm ready," she said.

Rab turned, took one look at her, and laughed uproariously.

"What is it? What's wrong?"

"You look so fetching. As big as those clothes are, I could almost get in there with you."

"Don't you dare!" she replied, trying to sound indignant, though she did find the thought rather titillating.

"You can't wear those shoes either." He pointed to the shelves of brogans. "Those are in different sizes. Find something as close to your size as you can."

Susanna found a pair of work boots that were close enough to her size, and she put them on.

"Stand over here while you're on guard for me," Rab directed. Susanna turned her back to him to afford him the same courtesy he had shown her, wondering why he had moved her position.

Rab dressed quickly, pulling on the same uniform, and in his own way he looked every bit as outrageous as Susanna did.

"Grab a hat, and tuck as much of your hair under it as you can," Rab said. "When we get in the drifts, there will be sand and gravel falling all the time. There's a mirror over there if you need it."

Susanna found a skullcap similar to that worn by a Chinese cook. As she was looking in the mirror stuffing her hair into the cap, she saw Rab in the background watching her.

"You didn't," she screamed, realization hitting her. "You stood right there, the whole time, didn't you?"

He looked at her with amusement flickering in his eyes. "Turnabout is fair play. Now we're even."

✻ 13 ✻

Once they changed clothes, they were ready to proceed to the hoist room. There, Susanna saw three huge pulleys positioned over the shaft opening. One of the pulleys was turning, drawing up a cage that was suspended beneath it. When it arrived on the surface, Rab turned to Susanna.

"Our carriage has arrived, madam." He stepped into the cage and executed a sweeping bow.

Susanna appreciated all the silliness because it definitely took her mind off what she was about to do. She looked around to see if anyone was going to accompany them on their tour. Thinking it strange that she saw no one else, she stepped into the heavy iron cage wondering how a detective from San Francisco knew so much about the workings of a silver mine. Being more than a little nervous, she instinctively knew she should hang on to something, so she grabbed the side rail.

"No, don't do that," Rab said gently. "If you hold it there, you might get your hand torn off by some unseen rock outcropping as we go down. Put it here." Taking her hand in his, he moved it to the front rail. He stepped behind her, then gave two jerks on the bell rope.

The engineer, who was standing up above them on a platform, responded to the ringing bell by pulling a lever on the engine, putting the machine in motion.

When they first began to drop, Susanna felt a fluttering in her stomach that caused her to feel weightless, as if she were about to come up off the floor. The smallness of the cage and the darkness in the shaft, lit only by a small, swaying lantern suspended from the crossbar at the top of the cage, caused her a moment of panic. Rab sensed that she was uncomfortable, and soon she felt his light touch on the small of her back. Instantly she was calmed, and she wasn't afraid anymore.

She didn't know how fast they were descending, but she did know that they were moving quickly. The timbers on the sides of the shaft appeared to be darting rapidly upward, much as trees and telegraph poles seemed to be running backward when one rode on a fast-moving train.

As they hurtled down through the shaft, they passed the first of the upper-level tunnels, a lantern-lit room where Susanna saw men standing around. She could hear the sound of their voices and the clank of machinery, but the room and the sounds were there but for a fleeting moment; then they were gone, the sound rising, then receding. Several seconds later there was another flash of light, more men, more sounds, then as quickly as the first station it, too, zoomed up as they continued down.

Susanna felt a bobbing action in the cage, not unlike that of a ball tied to an India-rubber string, and involuntarily she reached out to grab Rab.

"Nothing to be worried about," he said soothingly. "That's just the natural spring in the cable."

Finally the velocity of the cage's descent began to decrease, slower still, until the timberwork on the sides of the shaft was barely creeping by. Then the cage settled to a complete stop.

"Are you all right?" Rab asked, still holding her close.

"I think so. But how do these men do this every day?"

"You just got here, you've not seen anything yet." Rab ushered her out of the cage.

Immediately Susanna's senses were assaulted with the extreme heat. It was like being in the steams at Steamboat Springs, but there was no steam, and she gasped for air.

"Do you need some water?" Rab asked.

"Yes, I would like that."

Rab led the way through the station room toward a large cask containing ice water. Susanna was impressed by the general orderliness and cleanliness of the area, but most of all she was struck by the extreme quiet. The only noise she heard was the sound of their footsteps on the wooden floor, as fine as might be found in most homes.

And then she saw it. Susanna screamed as a rat darted across the floor, disappearing behind a box of candles.

"Don't be alarmed," Rab said. "There are always rats in mines, and they serve a very useful purpose because they're scavengers for any crumb of food that may be dropped. There can't be any foreign smell because you have to be ever vigilant for the smell of smoke."

"Bloody 'ell, wot was that?" a miner asked, coming into the room quickly from the crosscut that led off the chamber.

Susanna was a little surprised to see that the miner was shirtless.

"Nothing, the lady saw a rat, is all," Rab said.

"A rot, is it? Blimey, miss, did you think you would be seein' a bloody robin two thousand feet below the queen's own?"

Rab laughed. "The queen owns nothing here, you bloody Cornishman. Back into the mine with you, now."

"Aye." The Cornishman touched his eyebrow in a sort of salute. "Aforeego, miss, ye'd best be watchin' your toes that the rots don't decide to take a nibble." He laughed at his own joke as he hurried back out into the drift from which he had come.

Rab removed a dipper from a hook on the wall, scooped up some of the cold water, and offered it to Susanna.

"That is so good," she said as she wiped the perspiration off her brow.

"Drink plenty. You'll need it."

"Hey! What the devil is going on? Who said you could be down here? This is my level," a gruff-voiced man said as he entered the station.

"Hello, Gabe," Rab said as he turned to address the man while extending his hand.

"Mr. Trudeau," the miner replied, shaking hands vigorously. "I'm sorry, sir, I didn't recognize you."

"That's all right. This is Miss Ward. Miss Ward, this is Gabe Singleton. He is the foreman of this level."

"It's good to meet you, ma'am," Gabe said.

"I thought I might show Miss Ward around the mine, if you don't mind?"

"Ha!" Gabe said. "If *I* don't mind."

"We will try to stay out of your way."

"You'll not be a bother."

Unlike the first miner she had met, Gabe was wearing a shirt.

Rab led Susanna down a long corridor. This was Susanna's first trip into a mine, and she had always imagined them to be dark, dreary places. To her surprise the corridor was as well lit as Piper's Opera House.

"Rab, how is it that everyone here seems to know you?"

"This isn't my first time down here," Rab answered easily.

"It's more than that. They not only know you, they seem to respect you."

"You're imagining things. Come on this way."

Rab led her down the tunnel or "drift." A set of rail tracks ran along the center of the drift, and here she saw the square support boxes, or cribs, invented by Philip Deidesheimer, a local engineer. It was such a simple idea, yet it worked so well. All the boxes were interconnected, and they could be built up to any height, thus supporting the roofs, preventing cave-ins. Susanna thought they looked like honeycombs.

As they passed through the drifts, she was again struck by the eerie sense of quiet, until ahead they could hear the clanking sound of pickaxes at work. Then they came upon the men, and Susanna gasped at the sight. All of them were naked to the waist, many from the middle of the thighs to their feet, and no small number of them were wearing nothing but breechclouts. They were all gleaming in a patina of sweat, which reflected the light of the many candles. With broad shoulders, muscular arms, large chests, and flat stomachs laced with muscle, they looked to Susanna like exquisite statues come to life.

"Excuse me," Rab said to one of the miners. "Why don't you rest for a few minutes? I want to take a core sample."

"Want my gab?" the Cornishman asked, offering his pick to Rab.

Rab took the pickax, then began swinging it hard against the side wall, dislodging large chunks of rock with each swing. After a few minutes he stopped and leaned his pickax against the wall. Susanna thought that he was about to quit, but was surprised to see him strip out of his shirt. Like the others, his skin glowed with a light covering of sweat, which emphasized his muscled arms, strong shoulders, and flat, ribbed abdomen.

"Catch," he said as he tossed his shirt to Susanna.

When Susanna caught the shirt, she felt a little charge of electricity such as that felt between two people when they touch after walking across a wool carpet. She wasn't prepared for the reaction she was experiencing. She had

seen him naked, yes, but that had been a quick, accidental, and somewhat embarrassing encounter.

This was something entirely different. She was very
aware of his masculinity, and of the scar like a purple flash
of lightning. Seeing him like this, and surrounded as she
was with an entourage of beautifully sculpted, half-naked
men, she found the entire thing incredibly erotic.

As Susanna watched Rab swing the pickax, she felt
her own body perspiring, and beads of sweat were rolling
down between her breasts and down her stomach. She
could feel the rough texture of the cloth of her shirt, now
wet with moisture, rubbing against her nipples, which
were taut, extremely sensitive buds.

And that wasn't the only place where the texture of
the cloth was eliciting pleasurable sensations, for she was
feeling a tingling in that most private part, free from
any clothing except the voluminous folds of the oversize
pantaloons. The feeling was so intense that her knees felt
weak, and for a moment she wasn't sure she wouldn't
buckle.

After a few more swings of the pickax, Rab leaned
over and began looking through the chunks of rock. He
picked up several, looked at them, then tossed them into
the ore car.

He kept one of the rocks and showed it to Susanna.
"Look. This rock is rich with quartz deposits. Quartz is
the host for silver. Do you see this crystalline with the
white or almost clear color? When you find bright white
quartz with streaks of gray, that means it is rich with silver." He handed the rock to Susanna.

She looked at the rock. For all that she knew that Virginia City, in fact the entire Washoe Valley, was dependent upon the silver produced here, this was the first time she had ever seen the ore in its native state, exactly as it had been for millions of years.

"Now you tell me how your paper could have printed a story that the Silver Falcon's vein had played out." Rab picked up several other chunks of ore that looked exactly like the one he had handed to Susanna and tossed them into the hopper of the ore car.

"I—it was what we were told," Susanna answered.

The expression on Rab's face had been one of challenge, but as he looked at Susanna's face, gleaming with perspiration while the tendrils of her hair escaped from the tight-fitting skullcap, he became concerned for her.

"We need to get you back up top," he said as he took in the drenched clothing that was now clinging to her body, emphasizing all her feminine curves.

Rab walked her back to the hoist cage, holding her arm to steady her. When they reached the cage, he helped her in, stepped in behind her, and yanked on the bell cord, sending the signal to the engineer that the cage was ready to ascend. Almost immediately the cage started, going up even faster than it had come down. It went up so fast it generated a breeze, so that by the time they reached the top, Susanna shivered.

"You're not cold, are you?" Rab asked, drawing Susanna to him.

"No," she said, as she stepped out of the cage, wanting to put some distance between the bare-chested Rab and herself. "Those poor men. How can they work down there, day in and day out?"

"They work because they are men of honor, integrity, and dedication."

"And incredible strength."

"Picking rock twelve hours a day can make a person strong," Rab said. "Come, let's get you cleaned up." He removed her hat and let her hair fall loose to her shoulders. Then he directed her toward a small area partitioned off by a hanging canvas.

"Where are we going?"

"To the bathing room. It's not very fancy, but the water is great."

"Oh, I couldn't take a bath here," she said.

"Sure you can. You may as well, because I'm going to take one. And if you don't, you'll just have to stand there in your wet clothes and be miserable."

Rab led Susanna into a bathing room where stood several copper bathtubs.

Susanna had a puzzled expression on her face. "Do we take a bath here—together?"

Rab began to laugh. "Yes, we do, but I'll pull this canvas between us so that you have a sense of privacy."

"A sense of privacy? I want real privacy if I'm going to do this," Susanna said emphatically.

"And you shall have it. I'll be on guard."

"And I am supposed to believe that? Are there any mirrors in strategic places?" Susanna looked around teasingly.

"Get in there, before I really do come in with you," Rab said as he gently pushed her forward. True to his word, he pulled the curtain, making a cozy area for Susanna's bath.

"Oh, it has running water," Susanna said, surprised.

"It does. Both hot and cold water. The hot water comes up from the bottom of the mine."

"I don't suppose there's any soap?" Susanna asked hopefully.

"We don't have the perfumed bar you may be used to, but we do have some honest castile." He pulled back the curtain and handed her the bar of soap. "You still have your clothes on," Rab said, feigning disappointment.

"Mr. Trudeau"—Susanna shook her head—"I do want some privacy."

"And you shall have it." He pulled the curtain closed and immediately began drawing water in the tub adjacent to the one Susanna was to occupy. Susanna heard the drop of one boot and then the other. Then she heard a light splash as Rab entered the water. He began to hum a song that Susanna didn't recognize.

She turned on the two petcocks and water started streaming into the tub, steam billowing up as it did so. She removed the rough wool shirt and pantaloons and stepped into the tub. The warmth of the water was luxurious as she settled back into the tub, allowing her hair to spill around her. The hot water was lapping at her breasts as she shifted slightly, allowing more of her body to be submerged. She lay there without moving, listening to the soft humming. It was as if Rab was doing that to let her know that he was still there, protecting her in case someone should approach.

Rab was just on the other side of the curtain, as naked as he had been that day when she walked into his hotel room, as naked as she was right now—and they were separated by less than six feet.

That thought made her body tingle from the top of her head to the tips of her toes.

What was she doing? She couldn't lie here in this tub fantasizing about a naked man who was practically within arm's reach of her own naked body. She had to get those thoughts out of her mind.

Why was she naked anyway? Oh, yes, she was taking a bath. Tilting her head back, she reached for the soap. Something about the soap brought back a potent memory—the smell of olive oil, a smell that she associated with her mother.

She began to lather—first her arms, then her legs, lifting them one at a time from the warm bath. Her hair floated on the water, covering her breasts, and as she pushed aside the tresses, she watched, fascinated, as her nipples hardened when they were exposed to the air. She started to lather her chest and then, letting the soap drop from her hand, found herself, almost involuntarily, fondling her breasts, first one and then the other. Closing her eyes tightly, she rubbed the nipples, tentatively at first, then bolder and harder, surprised at the intense reaction this simple action caused. Almost as if self-animated, her hand drifted to that part of her body where she had never dared place it before. At first she touched it gingerly, then she began to stroke herself, each stroke bringing on spasms of pleasure.

She had never done this before, though there had been times, disquieting moments, when curiosity or newly stirring sensations, which she now realized had been caused entirely by Rab Trudeau, had made her want to explore. With her eyes closed, and her bottom lip sucked in between her teeth, Susanna continued to stroke herself, floating—no—soaring with the ecstasy of it all.

Dressed now, Rab stared at the curtain, knowing that Susanna was on the other side. Dare he look? That might not be the proper, gentlemanly thing to do, but he was feeling much more like a man now than a drawing-room dandy.

Stepping up to the curtain, he pulled it quietly, and barely, to one side, then looked in. His gasp was so loud that he wondered how she didn't hear it, because what he saw filled him with such sexual excitement that he felt as if he might explode.

Susanna was in the tub, her head back, her eyes closed in an expression that was more arousing than anything else he had ever seen in his life. He saw her breasts, twin white mounds protruding from the water, the nipples sticking up like tightly drawn rosebuds. Her legs were spread so that her knees were on either side of the tub, and her hands, both of them, were at the junction of her legs. He saw the finger of one of her hands moving in a jerking fashion, and he knew exactly what she was doing.

Sliding the curtain open a little farther so he could

enter, he stepped up to her tub, walking as quietly as he could. Then, kneeling beside the tub, he reached down to put his hand on hers.

At first, Susanna didn't know if she was actually feeling another hand on hers, or if the hand was merely a part of her fantasy, given form and texture by the strength of her imagination. Then, suddenly, she realized that it was real, and her eyes jerked open in surprise! She saw Rab, kneeling on the floor beside the tub. He was fully clothed, and he was holding a towel in one hand. His other hand was in the water, on top of her hand.

"Rab!" she gasped.

"Let me help you," Rab said huskily.

"Leave. You must leave!"

"There is no need for you to feel afraid." Putting the towel down, and lifting his other hand from hers, Rab scooped some water up in his cupped hands and allowed it to drizzle on her already sensitive skin—first her breasts, where his fingers flicked away the last vestige of soap, and then the water trailed down her stomach toward the mound of dark hair. He pulled the chain that allowed the water to drain.

"You—you have to leave," she said again, this time the words little more than a plaintive whisper.

"Do you really want me to leave, Susanna?" Rab's dark eyes burned into her own.

"No. God help me, no."

A smile crept to his lips. He picked up the towel and

made a pillow for her head as she laid it against the tub. Slowly, his hand found her breast again. He began to caress it and knead it, bringing the nipple to a taut tip, then he lowered his lips and took it into his mouth, his tongue twirling madly around it. He repeated the action on the other breast, never stopping the rhythmic motion.

The sensations that were pulsating between Susanna's legs were maddening. She instinctively knew that only Rab could relieve this ache, so she removed his hand from her breast and placed it on her mound of dark hair. He did not disappoint her. Slowly and deliberately, he began to stroke her back and forth, bringing forth a fountain from her innermost parts. He wet his finger in the moistness and drew it over a small bud that seemed to strain under his touch. Her whole body was aflame and she began to quiver with excitement, drawing her legs closer together.

"Let it happen, my love, let it happen," Rab said as he opened her legs to continue his caressing. Now he moved his fingers faster and faster, and all at once a tremor seemed to ignite and radiate out from her core as she became more and more breathless. She grabbed for Rab, as eddies of pleasure washed over her whole body, while small sounds of enjoyment escaped from her lips. Then it stopped and she fell against Rab, not knowing what had happened to her, yet wanting more. He held her tightly, rubbing his hand along her back and cupping her bottom, brushing her hair back away from her face, and then he kissed her—a deep kiss that was almost more than Susanna could bear.

"We've got to get you dressed," he said. "It's almost time for a shift change and this place will be crawling with Cornishmen."

"I don't want this to end. Ever."

"It doesn't have to end." Then Rab smiled at her. "But this part of it does have to end."

Rab kissed her again.

"Where are my clothes?" Susanna asked, looking around.

"What clothes?" Rab asked, again kissing her.

"My clothes. You said the miners would be here soon," Susanna said, mumbling the words even as she continued to kiss him.

"Yes, they'll catch us if we don't hurry," Rab said without hurry.

She kissed him again, torn between wanting to dress quickly enough to avoid any embarrassment, yet held, by not only the pleasure of the moment, but the titillating thrill of being caught in such a compromising position.

Finally, Rab found the strength to separate them. Standing up, he helped her out of the tub, then gave her the towel to dry off as he went for her clothes.

Susanna would never, in her wildest dreams, have expected to have had an afternoon like the one she just experienced. It was the first time she had ever realized such intense pleasure. She did not think it would be the last.

* 14 *

"He can't possibly still be alive," Asa Teague replied when he was challenged by Van Cleve, Burdick, and Sheehan. "I tell you, I pushed the son of a bitch down a two-thousand-foot mine shaft! I saw him fall!"

"Maybe he sprouted wings," Sheehan suggested sarcastically.

"Not unless they were angel wings," Teague said.

"I don't care whether he is angel, ghost, or devil," Van Cleve said. "He was over at the Silver Falcon mine today. He went down into the mine, and he took the newspaperwoman with him. This I know for a fact."

"I'm going to have to see him with my own eyes before I can believe that," Teague said.

"Good. You see him with your own eyes. Then you take care of him," Van Cleve said. "I'm not used to paying for something and not getting my money's worth. And so far, Mr. Teague, you haven't performed."

"You'll get your money's worth, Mr. Van Cleve," Teague said. "I guarantee you that."

Van Cleve smiled. "That's what I like. A man who stands behind his work."

When Susanna returned from her visit to the mine, she went not to the newspaper office, but directly to the Chaney House. Mary Beth was not in the parlor, and Susanna was glad, because who she really wanted to talk to was Annie. And she wanted to talk to her in private. She hurried up to Annie's room, then tapped lightly on the door, hoping that Annie was not away.

"Yes?" Annie's muffled voice called from within.

"Annie, it's Susanna. I need to talk to you."

Annie didn't answer, but a moment later her door opened. "Come in. Come in."

"Thank you," Susanna stepped into the room.

Although she had known Annie for quite a while now, this was the first time she had ever been inside her friend's room. As she looked around, she was a little surprised by the decor.

The room was much more modest than Susanna would have thought, especially given Annie's flamboyant public persona. A sampler was on the wall, bearing the embroidered words GOD BLESS THIS HOME. Next to it was a framed teacher's certificate issued by Kansas State Agricultural College. On the chest of drawers stood a framed photograph of Annie, much more sedately dressed than Susanna had ever seen her, standing alongside a rather serious-looking, well-dressed man. Susanna knew Annie's history and realized that here, in this room, Annie was holding on to a part of her life that was special to her, a haven from the world in which she now existed.

"Have a seat," Annie said, motioning toward a chair upholstered in blue-and-yellow chintz fabric.

Susanna sat in the chair while Annie settled on the bed.

"Now," Annie said, "to what do I owe the pleasure of your company?"

"Annie, how can you tell when you are in love?"

"Oh my. Have you met someone?"

"Yes. No. I mean, I don't know."

Annie laughed. "That's a good sign."

"What is a good sign?"

"It's a good sign when you don't know whether you're in love or not. The very fact that you are asking questions means that you probably are."

"Oh. No, that's terrible."

"What's terrible?"

"I can't be in love with anyone. Not now. Not after the promise I made to Mr. Kirkland."

The smile left Annie's face. "What promise? Honey, what are you talking about?"

"I promised Mr. Kirkland that I would marry Jesse."

Annie gasped. "You did what? Susanna, what on earth would cause you to make such a promise?"

"Mr. Kirkland is concerned about Jesse. He thinks that

if Jesse would get married, maybe he would settle down. He asked me to marry Jesse, and I said I would, because I owe the Kirklands my life."

"No, honey, you owe them a debt of gratitude for taking you in. But you do not owe them your life. Your life is yours to live as you see fit. And you certainly don't have to marry Jesse."

"I'm afraid I do. I have already given Mr. Kirkland my word."

"When you asked how can you know if you're in love, you weren't talking about Jesse, were you?"

"No."

"Who is it? Is it Rab Trudeau?"

Susanna looked toward the floor without answering.

"It is, isn't it?"

"Yes." Susanna spoke so quietly that Annie could barely hear her.

"Have you had—don't get angry and don't get upset with me for asking this question—but have you had any . . ."

"No." Susanna thought about what had just happened at the Silver Falcon bathhouse. "That is, not exactly."

"What you mean is, you have not slept with him."

"No, I have not."

"But you have come close?"

"Oh, yes." Susanna's tone expressed the pleasure she had experienced. "Oh, Annie, I never knew it could be like that. Is it like that with you? I mean . . ." Susanna paused in midsentence, realizing that she was coming close to prying too much into Annie's affairs.

"It is always like that when you are with the right man.

With my Keith, it was like that because I loved him and he loved me. But with the men who buy my time?" Annie paused for a moment, then looked at the floor, almost as if in apology. "It is not like that with them. I've never experienced anything with anyone like what I felt with Keith."

"It was . . ." Susanna stopped, unable to come up with the word she was looking for.

"You don't need to explain it to me, honey, I know. Let me ask you this. Have you ever kissed Jesse?"

"Of course, we grew up together."

"That's not what I mean, and you know it. I know he isn't your brother, but what I mean is, have you ever kissed him in any way other than a sisterly kiss?"

"No."

"Susanna, when you came in here, you asked me how you could tell if you are in love. I think the only way you are going to be able to tell is if there is any way Jesse could make you feel the way Mr. Trudeau made you feel. If he can, fine. If he can't, and you marry him just to please Mr. Kirkland, you will be miserable for the rest of your life. And so will Jesse."

"How am I going to find that out? I'm certainly not going to . . ." Again Susanna paused in midsentence. What she was going to say was that she had no intention of letting Jesse take such liberties with her body, certainly not just to check how he made her feel.

Annie chuckled. "You don't have to do that."

"You don't even know what 'that' is, do you?" Susanna challenged.

"Not exactly, but I have a pretty good idea. Look, Susanna, you're a big girl. I'm going to leave that up to you."

By the time Susanna returned to the newspaper office, the paper had already been run off, and Mickey was just picking it up for the afternoon delivery.

"How was the trip to the mine?" B.D. asked.

"Fascinating." Susanna looked around. "Has Mr. Loudin been in today?"

"He came in a couple of hours ago, going on about your article," B.D. said.

"Oh," Susanna said in a frightened voice.

B.D. laughed. "You can put your mind to rest, girl. He thought the article was so good that it was all I could do to keep from taking credit for it myself."

Susanna smiled.

"Now, tell me about your trip to the mine."

"We went way down inside it," Susanna said. "B.D., do you have any idea how hot it is down there?"

"I've never experienced it myself, but I've heard the lads speak of it. Six feet from hell, they say it is."

"An apt description I would say."

"Will you be writing about it?" B.D. asked.

"Yes, I suppose so. Mr. Loudin did want me to get an interview with Rab—uh—Trudeau, and write it under your byline, so that's what I'll do."

B.D. shook his head. "Oh, no. When you write it, you'll write it under your own byline."

"I've already asked. Mr. Loudin said no."

"Susanna, you've earned the right. Write it, set it, and print it, just as you did the last article. If you say nothing to him until it comes out, it'll be too late for him to stop it."

"He may not like the tone of this one."

"Will you be writing the truth?"

"Yes, of course I will."

"With apologies to Shakespeare and King Henry for perverting the quote, 'We few, we happy few, we band of brothers, for he today who speaks the truth with me shall forever be my brother.' Or, in your case, it would be 'forever be my sister.' And it is to a greater authority than the mere owner of a newspaper that you and I owe our allegiance, Susanna. We owe our allegiance to the truth, and to the public we serve."

Susanna laughed. "You do wax eloquent, B.D. But the bottom line is, if I write something Loudin totally disagrees with, I'll lose my job."

"The *Pioneer* is not the only fish in the sea, nor is it the only newspaper on the Comstock Lode. Don't forget the *Enterprise* and the *Gold Hill News*. I would be willing to bet that either one of them would hire you."

"Ha. Mr. DeQuille would use me no differently than Mr. Loudin, and Mr. Doten would hire me not in spite of the fact that I am a woman, but precisely because I am a woman, and you know what I mean."

B.D. laughed. "I fear you may be right about that. Mr. Doten does perceive himself as a bit of a lothario."

"But there is something to what you say. Perhaps I will write the article anyway."

B.D. held up his finger. "I have an idea. The day after tomorrow is Independence Day. I think you should write an article about the celebration. It will start tomorrow night—but you can wait and write the article on the morning of the Fourth. There will be so many people in town on that day, we will double the number of issues we print. It will be a noncontroversial article that will win you a following, and James will have no choice, then, but to acknowledge you."

"Maybe you are right."

"Susanna, one thing that does come with age is that when I am right, I have the confident and certain determination that I am right."

Susanna laughed and shook her head. "I'm sure, B.D., that there is a grain of wisdom in that rather convoluted remark, so I am going to let it stand. I'll see you tomorrow."

Leaving the newspaper office, Susanna planned to go to Kirkland Emporium to see if Jesse was there, but it wasn't necessary. As she passed the Boar's Head Saloon, she saw Jesse coming out.

"Jesse," she called out to him.

Smiling, Jesse crossed the street to her. "Hello, Susanna."

"I was about to have my dinner. I wonder if you would join me?"

Jesse looked surprised. "What? You are asking me?" He smiled. "Aren't you afraid I might push your plate off in your lap?" He was referring to an incident that had occurred during a Thanksgiving dinner when they were both much younger.

"That wasn't funny," Susanna said, but she eased her censure with a smile. "Anyway, you were twelve years old then. I would hope that you are a little more mature now."

The smile left Jesse's face. "I am. Although my father doesn't think so. Pop thinks I'm still a boy."

"Maybe if you made a concerted effort to show him otherwise, he wouldn't think so."

"You mean like not getting arrested for throwing a chair through a window, or knocking someone in the head?"

Susanna started to agree with Jesse, then thought better of it. How was she going to "win him over" if she found fault with him? "Jesse, I'm not here to chastise you. All I asked was if you would like to have dinner with me tonight."

Jesse reached out and took her hand in his. "Thanks, Susanna. I have always been able to count on you to be on my side. I guess I haven't told you how much that has meant to me over the years."

"You have always been special, Jesse." In this tender moment, Susanna felt affection for him. She put her arms around him and pulled him to her in a hug.

There was nothing there—certainly nothing like the feeling she had experienced with Rab earlier today. Could she actually go through with this? She thought of what Annie had told her, how a marriage like this would be bad for her, and for Jesse.

But even as she was thinking of all the reasons why it couldn't be, she was unable to free herself of the promise she had made to Mr. Kirkland.

"You know what, Susanna?" Jesse said as they separated from the quick hug. "I'll even buy the dinner tonight. It can't hurt my reputation to be seen with the prettiest girl in town, even if she is almost my sister."

"Almost isn't exactly the same thing as actually being your sister."

For a moment, Jesse got a confused look on his face, as if he was wondering exactly what she meant by that. But almost as quickly as the thought formed in his mind, it slipped away.

Jesse took Susanna to the Rustic Rock, one of Virginia City's best restaurants, its name derived from its construction. The façade was made of rock from the tailings of the mines and was described, in the words of a newspaper advertisement, as "perfectly fit together to present a most pleasing appearance."

A waiter arrived at their table.

"I'll order, since I know what you like," Jesse said, "unless your tastes have all changed since you left home?"

"I still like the same thing."

"We'll have grilled Tahoe trout, with tartar sauce," Jesse said. "Fried potatoes, English peas, and for dessert, bread pudding." Jesse put the menu down, then looked across the table at Susanna. "Did I miss anything?"

"No," she said. "You ordered the perfect dinner."

Jesse seemed to be making a concerted effort not only to be on his best behavior, but also to please her. Perhaps there was something to be said for a relationship that was based upon a lifetime of shared experiences and intimate knowledge of each other's likes, dislikes, and habits.

The meal was delivered, and Susanna genuinely enjoyed the food, and the conversation, most of which was memories of their growing up together. Some of it brought laughter.

"It wasn't always just what I did to you and Alice, you know," Jesse said. "You weren't always Little Miss Good Girl. I remember one time when you hid in the bushes and watched my friends and me swimming naked in the pond, don't you?"

Susanna gasped and put her hand to her mouth. "How did you know that? You didn't see me," she said, mortification in her voice.

"We all saw you, Susanna. How else would I have known you were there?"

"Oh, I'm so embarrassed. Why did you never say anything?"

"I don't know. Maybe because I knew it would really make you uncomfortable and, somewhere down inside of me, deep, deep down inside, there breathes a sensitive soul."

"I thank you for that."

"I still remember the day Pop brought you back to our wagon," Jesse said. "I thought it was great, having someone besides Alice around. I'll be honest with you, Susanna, I didn't even think about the fact that you had just lost your entire family. I was that selfish, and I apologize for that."

"There is no need for an apology." Almost involuntarily, Susanna reached across the table and put her hand on his. She felt a warmth—not the heat she felt when she came into contact with Rab, but a genuine warmth of affection, such as she would have for a brother. Was that enough?

"Jesse, that sensitive soul you mentioned? It isn't that deep down inside."

"Maybe I don't lack the sensitive soul as much as I lack plain old common sense. If I had some, maybe I wouldn't always be just on the edge of trouble," Jesse said self-deprecatingly.

"I think you've got enough common sense. Perhaps what you have is an overabundance of free spirit."

Jesse laughed again. "'An overabundance of free spirit.' Leave it to a writer to put it so well."

Susanna took a breath and held it for a moment before speaking. "Jesse, there is to be a dance on the night of the Fourth."

"Yeah, at the Miners' Union Hall. I'm going."

"With someone?"

"Nah. Well, just with a couple of friends is all," Jesse said.

"I wonder if you might call for me at about seven and escort me to the dance?"

"What? You want me to take you to the dance?" Jesse asked, surprised by her request.

"Yes. That is, if you wouldn't mind."

A broad smile spread across Jesse's face. "Now, why should I mind taking the prettiest girl in town to the dance? I'll be there at seven."

*   *   *

When Susanna returned to her room, she opened the bottom drawer of her chest and pulled out the little gutta-percha bag that she had saved from the burning wagon the day her family had died. In addition to her mother's diary and a crucifix, there was a packet of letters. The letters were bound by a small ribbon that might have been purple at one time, but had now faded to near gray.

Susanna's mother was an Italian immigrant, and her maiden name had been Romani. As a child, Susanna used to make up stories about her real family. Her parents would take her to Italy to see her maternal grandmother, the woman for whom she was named. In her childish imagination, she was certain that they lived on a huge estate and grew grapes for wine. Susanna particularly liked it when a real opera came to Piper's Opera House, because she believed that to be a part of her heritage. That, and the letters her father had written to her mother.

Dear Miss Romani:

With the trust that you will forgive my presumption, I take pen in hand to be so bold as to write to you. I do not know if you remember me, and indeed there would be no reason for such hope to spring to my breast. You may recall that as you departed the boat in St. Charles, Missouri, there was a man standing nearby who gazed upon your beauty with no sense of decency or proper comportment.

I am that man, and by this missive and apology, I cannot help but hold the most earnest aspiration that I can erase any bad feelings you may have for one who was so lacking of manners.

*I hope this letter, written in total sincerity and humil-
ity, will elicit pity and a favorable consideration of this
most lowly scribe. I remain,*

                                        Your Most Obedient Servant,
                                        Byron Ward, Esq.

Susanna smiled at the stiff formality of her father's first
letter. Her mother had saved all of the letters Susanna's
father had ever written, from this tentative epistle to the
letter in which he had proposed to her. Over the years
Susanna had read the letters many times, but now this
chronicle of the love affair between her mother and father
seemed more poignant than ever before.

Could she fall in love with Jesse? She already loved
him, but she wasn't "in love" with him. And what, exactly,
did that mean, anyway?

She knew that she did not feel about Jesse the way she
did about Rab. When she was with Rab, even when she
just thought about him, she felt a tingling all over, hot
and cold and shaky all at the same time. She never felt
that way about Jesse.

As Susanna removed her clothes to go to bed, she
was totally naked for a moment before she put on her
nightgown. Even though she did this every night, she
was much more aware of her nudity this night than she
was normally. Her skin seemed sensitized by the very air,
and as she thought of being naked earlier today, she felt a
shiver pass through her.

Was she in love with Rab? She thought of a line in
her father's letter where he had said he had no sense of

decency. Was what she had done today an example of someone who had no sense of decency? She knew that if her mother were still alive, she would not have been able to discuss this with her. She couldn't even discuss it with Annie. It was much too personal. She did know, though, that she felt no sense of shame. How could something that felt so right possibly be wrong?

As Susanna lay in bed, she tried to force Rab out of her mind by thinking of Jesse. But no matter how hard she tried, images of Rab kept crowding out any notion of Jesse. Finally, a fitful sleep ended the unsettling thoughts.

It might have comforted Susanna to know that Rab was having his own problems going to sleep that night. He had sensed from their very first meeting that Susanna was a woman of spirit and spontaneity, and he had believed she could also be a woman of passion. That suspicion was proven correct by her reaction to him in the bath.

How different Susanna was from Margaret. Susanna was effervescent, exciting, generous, and vulnerable. Margaret was arrogant, self-centered, dull, and parsimonious.

Rab was especially aware of Susanna's vulnerability, and he would have to take care to do nothing that would hurt her. He had been so angry when he found out that Susanna had written that article. But during the day that anger had vanished, to be replaced by a yearning that had developed into unbridled desire. It had culminated with the bath, where he helped her explore her sensuality in a way that enflamed his own, testing the limits of his self-control.

He had never once touched Margaret in this way. Nor had he ever wanted to.

But what was he going to do about Margaret?

Rab needed more time to answer that question.

At two thirty in the morning, Asa Teague stepped into the lobby of the McAuliffe House. The lobby was dimly lit by two gas lamps. It was even darker behind the desk where the night clerk was unabashedly sleeping in a chair that was tilted back against the wall.

Walking quietly, Teague stepped over to the desk, examined the registry, and found the entry he was looking for.

Mr. Rab Trudeau—San Francisco—204

Leaning over the desk, Teague removed a key from a hook that was marked 204. Smiling, he clutched the key in his left hand and started up the stairs. When he reached the top of the stairs, he pulled his knife, then looked down the hall.

The single wall-mounted gas lantern hissed as it cast a dim, greenish glow. The hall was even more poorly lit than had been the lobby. Holding the knife out in front of him, he started down the hall.

At that moment, in room 202, Nathan Parker was just closing his grip and his sample bag. A traveling drummer, his next stop would be Reno, and it was time for him to walk over to the railroad depot to catch the 3:00 a.m. train. As soon as he stepped out into the hall, he saw a man moving stealthily and determinedly up the hallway.

His first reaction was to the man's face. It was so narrow and angular and had such a lack of flesh that it looked almost like a green, glowing skull. His second reaction was to the knife the man was carrying.

Parker reacted quickly.

"Help! Man with a knife! Help!" Parker shouted at the top of his voice.

Teague was as startled by the sudden and totally unexpected appearance of Parker as Parker was upon seeing an armed man in the hall.

"You bastard!" Teague shouted, and he slashed out at Parker, cutting Parker's arm.

The commotion in the hallway awakened Rab, and, grabbing his pistol, he moved quickly to the door, then opened it to look down the hall. He raised his pistol, but by now several other doors had opened as well, and the hall was too crowded for him to shoot. The man with the knife turned and ran down the stairs.

"This man is bleeding badly!" someone said.

"I'm a doctor," a second man said.

The doctor hurried to Parker's side, then knelt on the floor beside him. By now Rab had pulled on his trousers, and he joined some of the other hotel guests who were gathered around, watching the doctor tend to Parker.

"We must stop the bleeding!" the doctor said.

The door was still open to Parker's room, and Rab stepped into it and pulled the sheet from the bed.

The doctor applied some bandages, then put his hand on Parker's shoulder. "I'm sure it is painful, but the cut isn't deep, and no arteries were severed. You'll be all right."

Rab saw a key lying on the floor and picked it up. A round, wooden disk attached to the key read ROOM 204.

Damn, he thought. *That son of a bitch was after me.*

❊ 15 ❊

Although it was only the third of July, Independence Day celebrations were already starting, and the streets of Virginia City were crowded. Storefronts, saloons, and business offices were festooned with red, white, and blue bunting.

Rab wandered around town, hoping to get a glimpse of the assailant he'd seen last night, though the corridor of the hotel had been dimly lit and he wasn't sure he would recognize him if he saw him. After the confrontation with the drummer, the would-be assassin had run. Parker, the man who was attacked, had seen him, though, and Rab listened to the description the wounded man gave to the policeman who came in response to the attack, hoping that would be all he would need to identify him.

Rab decided not tell the policeman about the key he'd found lying on the floor after the attack—the key to his room. He thought for the time being it was best to keep that information to himself. As a result, people assumed that Parker had just happened onto a burglar, and the burglar, in frustration and desperation, had slashed out at him.

As Rab wandered around town, he realized that he was looking not only for the assailant from the night before, but also for Susanna. He could go to the newspaper office, but he didn't want to do that. He wanted to see her, but he didn't want his attentions to be unwelcome.

Rab took his lunch in the Silver Dollar Restaurant not only because he liked the food, but also because he had seen Susanna there once and he thought—hoped—that he might see her again.

She wasn't there.

When Rab came out of the restaurant, he saw four men stretching a banner across C Street: HAPPY BIRTHDAY AMERICA.

A fifth man was standing out in the middle of the street, waving his arms and shouting directions.

"Danny, lift your side higher," the "supervisor" shouted.

"How's this?" the man called back.

"Higher."

"Here?"

"Higher."

"Damn, George, why don't I just get a balloon and pin my side up on the moon or something?"

Rab chuckled as he continued his fruitless search.

That night nearly the entire town turned out in front of the Post Office, where a band had set up on the steps and was playing patriotic music. Here, Rab did see Susanna, but she was with B. D. Elliott and he thought it best not to disturb her.

What was he doing looking for Susanna anyway? Was he not already engaged to a woman who was both beautiful and determined? A woman who knew her way around San Francisco society? A woman who, he was told, would be good for his business? True, she had never excited him the way Susanna did, but he tried to convince himself that there was surely more to marriage than sexual excitation. But there was also more to a marriage than societal obligation.

What it all came down to now was honor.

For the entire day Susanna had been unable to get Rab out of her mind. The most innocuous thing would remind her of him—even the spot where he had stood when he came in to challenge the article she had written. At one point during the day she set an advertisement for the International Hotel, and when it said that their restaurant featured lamb, she recalled the lamb she and Rab had shared at the Washoe Club.

Her memories were not all that benign, either. As she moved through the office going about her work, she would feel residual quivers of pleasure. The sensation was more than lingering ghost sensations; it was quite real, for the normal pressure of her dress, now against her breast, now against her thigh, which would ordinarily go unnoticed, sent shivers of arousal through her. At times she even had to hold on to the composing table just to stay on her feet.

Susanna did not see Rab for the entire day, and that surprised her because she had thought that he might come by the newspaper office. She did see him that night when she and B.D. had gone to the band concert. It was only a fleeting glimpse; Rab was standing on the other side of the crowd. She didn't know if he saw her or not, and for a moment she considered going to him. Then she thought better of it. Given what had happened between them, she wasn't sure how she would react to him. And she could not forget that she was committed to going to the dance with Jesse.

Susanna had asked Jesse to take her to the dance, and now she knew if she saw Rab, she would subconsciously be comparing the two men. That would not be fair to Jesse because he would lose. Even now it was not going to be easy to keep her commitment to Mr. Kirkland. If she had too much more exposure to Rab Trudeau, it would be next to impossible, but Susanna felt that she owed Mr. Kirkland, and Jesse, too, a fair consideration. In her heart, she knew that all Rab would have to do to take her away from here would be to ask her.

He had but to say a word, crook a finger, or even lift an eyebrow toward her, and she would run away with him to San Francisco, to Denver, to Paris, to Timbuktu. But, no, she would not, she must not think about that.

*   *   *

The next morning was Independence Day, and Susanna was able to put Rab out of her mind because, fortunately, she had an article to write. B.D. had approached James Loudin suggesting not only that Susanna write the article about Independence Day, but also that it be written under her byline. Loudin agreed.

Susanna felt a slight thrill and was almost giddy as she wrote, then composed the story. At first she set the byline as Susanna Kirkland; then she hesitated, looking at the type she had just placed. She was not a Kirkland; she was a Ward. In acknowledgment of her true heritage, she removed the type for *Kirkland* and reset the name to read *Ward*.

Our Nation's Birthday
by Susanna Ward

At an early hour on the 3d of July, businessmen began, one day early, making preparations to celebrate the birthday of our nation. Businesses and private houses were clothed with flags, and the town presented a brilliant appearance. At 7:00 p.m. last night, the brass band took position upon the porch in front of the Post Office and performed National airs, while the Stars and Stripes were run up on every housetop, and a cannon salute told everyone that festivities had begun.

The remainder of the day, and into last

night, was given to cheers, shouts, and a general good time. About 12:00 midnight the fires for the barbecue were lit and the cooking of the goats began.

When the sun rose this morning, its golden rays fell upon the American flag that waved with glorious majesty from the top of Mount Davidson, encompassing the entire city with its spirit of freedom and bravery. The flag was saluted with 102 guns, one for each year of our nation's existence, as well as church bells and mine whistles, all of which vied with each other in welcoming this day of all days. As these words are being written, the new day has barely begun, yet already the town is thronged with people. C Street is almost impassible because of the surging crowd. This morning the firemen marched in procession, followed by the children of the schools. There is a constant rattle and explosion of booms. Chariots, pulled by six horses, are, as often as paying passengers can be arranged, racing around the town, while at Piper's Opera House, Tony Pastor is providing entertainment. Tonight the glare of torches, bonfires, and Roman candles will light the whole heavens with a ruddy glow, while, at the Miners' Union Hall, there will be a dance.

This is a time of great joy and celebration, and all Americans and Nevadans should pause to honor the struggle of those brave men who over a century ago left their bloody footprints in the snow to secure for us the blessings of freedom.

Forever float that Standard sheet
Where breathes the foe that falls before us
With Freedom's sword at our feet
And Freedom's banner streaming o'er us

The streets of Virginia City were redolent with the aroma of cooked meat, primarily goat, because that creature was in almost endless supply. Goats wandered freely on the mountainside and through the town, providing milk and cheese to those who would take the time to milk them. The cooking had been done by a combined effort of the Knights of Pythias and the Red Men Club, as well as by the Miners' Union Hall, and it was served in a townwide picnic. The goat was augmented by potato salad, coleslaw, baked bread, pies, and cakes, all offered by citizens of the town. Lemonade and tea were also furnished, but beer and hard liquor had to be bought at one of the many saloons, which did a brisk business throughout the day as the celebration continued.

Firecrackers frequently exploded, often near the skirt of some unsuspecting female. For the most part the firecrackers were set by young boys who would run away giggling as the fuses sputtered.

Senator Jones made a speech in front of the Post Office, where, the night before, and again earlier this morning, the city band had played. Jones spoke of patriotism, heroism, and the impact the silver from Virginia City had on the economy of the rest of the country.

Tony Pastor was a nationally known show-business personality who, during the summer months, left the New York theater to tour the country. He presented shows that were popular with both male and female audiences. On this Independence Day he was in Virginia City with his show and delighted the audience with his comic singing of "The Upper and Lower Ten Thousand."

> *If an Upper-Ten fellow a swindler should be*
> *And with thousands of dollars of others make free*
> *Should he get into court, why, without any doubt,*
> *The matter's hushed up and they'll let him step out.*
> *If a Lower-Ten Thousand chap happens to steal*
> *For to keep him from starving, the price of a meal,*
> *Why the law will declare it's a different thing—*
> *For they call him a thief, and he's sent to Sing-Sing!*

Rab watched the matinee performance, then went back out onto C Street, which, if anything, was even more crowded than earlier. The firecrackers were still exploding, young women were still squealing in fright and fun, and young boys were still laughing.

Asa Teague had seen Rab Trudeau going into the theater, so he climbed up onto the roof of the Silver Queen Saloon to wait for him to come out. The Silver Queen was perfect for two reasons: it was directly across the street from Piper's Opera House, and it had a false front that provided concealment for him.

Asa waited in the sun for nearly two hours. Then, hearing the laughter and conversation of the departing matinee theatergoers, he got into position and waited until he spotted Trudeau.

If Rab Trudeau had not been in the war, and if he had not heard the sound a bullet makes when it passes by so close—oh so close—he would not have known that a shot had been fired at him. The report of the gun that fired the missile was lost in the pops, booms, and blasts of all the pyrotechnics being used in the city.

But the telltale angry buzz of the bullet passing but a few inches from Rab's head recalled old fights on distant battlefields. The bullet plunked into the wooden wall of the building behind him. Because of the angle of the bullet's path, Rab had an idea where to look, and glancing across the street, he thought he saw a puff of smoke drifting above the false front of the Silver Queen. Was the shooter there? Or was that just part of the huge cloud of gun smoke that filled the street from all of the fireworks?

Rab didn't want to draw his pistol in front of everybody, so he darted across the street toward the Silver Queen.

Teague was about to take another shot but saw that Trudeau was coming across the street. Teague ran to the back of the building, dropped down into the alley, then slipped in quickly through the back door of the saloon. He stepped up to the bar, pushing his way through the crowd.

"Hold on there, mister," one of the patrons said. "Who do you think you are, crowdin' in here like this?"

Teague stared at the complainer, his dark eyes set deep in the sockets of his skull-like head. It unnerved the customer, who, without another word, turned quickly and moved to the other end of the bar.

Teague ordered a beer and stood there, holding the mug with both hands. From this position he could see the entire saloon in the mirror. He watched as Rab Trudeau came into the bar, paused for a moment to peruse the customers, then left.

That bastard has nine lives, Teague thought.

"Oh, what a wonderful piece in the paper!" Mary Beth said, setting her glass of lemonade on the table. "And with your name, too! It's about time the editor let you sign your own work."

"Thank you," Susanna said. "Several other people have commented on it as well. And even B.D. said he thought it was a fine article."

"Did you know Annie is going to the dance tonight?" Mary Beth asked.

"No, I didn't know. Good for her," Susanna said.

"I thought perhaps we could all three go together," Mary Beth suggested.

"Oh, honey, I can't. Jesse will be coming by for me."

"Jesse is coming? Jesse, and not Mr. Trudeau?"

"Yes," Susanna replied without further elaboration.

"You are going to the dance with your brother?"

"He is not my brother."

"Well, no matter." Then Mary Beth smiled. "We will all be there together. It's going to be so much fun."

Annie came into the room. "Did you hear? I'm going to the dance tonight."

"Yes, and I'm glad," Susanna said. "Would you like some lemonade?"

"There'll probably be a lot of old fogies who won't be too happy to see me there," Annie said as she took the glass. She smiled. "But I doubt there will be too much stink raised, since a lot of them have—uh. . . . I'll be interested in seeing the expressions on their faces when I come in."

Susanna laughed. "That will be something to see."

The three talked about the dance as they finished their drinks, while outside they could hear the continual bang of firecrackers and the whistling of rockets. Then they left to get dressed.

As Susanna sat in the tub feeling the warm water caressing her skin, she couldn't help but recall her bath at the Silver Falcon. For this evening to work she could not think about Rab and how he had made her feel. Not even a little bit. She had to concentrate on Jesse. She took the washcloth and scrubbed her skin with such vigor that it actually hurt, but it succeeded in putting the bath out of her mind.

Wrapped in her dressing robe, Susanna considered the three dresses she had laid out on her bed. The first one had a blue-and-white-chintz-patterned overskirt with a looped-up cambric skirt beneath it. The high neck and long sleeves made the dress quite modest, but she put it aside, thinking it would be too warm for a midsummer's dance. The second dress, with two ruches and a fringe, was made of salmon silk, but to be effective, the dress needed fullness in the back. Susanna hated the constraint that a bustle imposed, so she passed on the salmon dress as well. She looked at her third choice the longest, wondering if the time had come for her to wear the crimson dress, the dress she had contemplated wearing to the Washoe Club. With its short, capped sleeves, low neckline, and formfitting torso, she knew to wear it would be almost indecent.

"You have to wear the crimson dress," Mary Beth had told her before the three of them had left to get dressed. "For if not now, when would you ever wear it?"

Susanna put the dress on, then examined herself in the mirror, turning first one way, then the other.

"Oh, my," she said quietly. "It does cling to the form."

The dress did something else as well, and when looking directly into the mirror, she saw it. So low cut was the dress that she could see not only the tops of her breasts, but her cleavage as well. She heard a light knock.

"It's me," Mary Beth said.

"Come in, it's not locked."

"Oh," Mary Beth said, clearly enthralled by the image Susanna presented. "I've never seen you look so beautiful."

"But I can't wear it." Susanna began removing the dress.

"Why?"

"Look at this."

"Look at what?"

"This." Susanna motioned with her hand to take in her décolletage. "I can't be seen in public like this. I'm half-naked."

"Nonsense, that is the style. I saw a dress at Manning and Duck's almost exactly like this one, and if I had the money, I would be wearing it tonight. Instead I am wearing a dress that my mother could wear."

"That is a beautiful dress and you look perfectly exquisite," Susanna said, noting the soft lines of the rose-colored dress. "Your mother's pearls are just the right accessory."

"Next to you, I look like a little gray mouse," Mary Beth complained. "Let's arrange your hair."

"Arrange my hair?"

"Yes, you have such a lovely neck. And you must let it show. Especially with this dress."

Mary Beth swept Susanna's hair up into a topknot, leaving ringlets around her neck and her ears. Tendrils of curls cascaded onto her forehead.

"What do you think?" Mary Beth asked, handing Susanna a mirror.

"Oh, dear."

"You don't like it?" Mary Beth asked, sounding disappointed.

"Oh, you did a wonderful job." Susanna reached up to

touch her hair. "It's just that somehow this seems to make my—nakedness—all the more apparent."

"Nonsense, Susanna. You're a beautiful woman. One of the most beautiful in this town. What would be the harm in showing it off a bit?"

"Well, I can't— Wait. I know how to wear it." She went to her clothespress, then pulled out a lace chemisette.

"Oh, no, that'll ruin it."

"It's the only way I'm going to wear this dress," Susanna insisted, carefully arranging the lace to cover her exposed breasts.

"That's not right, but if you want to look like an old lady, then, that's fine with me. After all, you are two years older than I am."

The two women were laughing as they walked down the stairs to where Annie was waiting for them. Both Susanna and Mary Beth were surprised by Annie's gown. Though they were accustomed to seeing her in provocative attire, tonight she was wearing a modest dress that accented her red hair and green eyes while playing down her curvaceous body.

Annie laughed at the expression of surprise on their faces. "I'm being brazen enough just by going to the dance. I'm not about to wear something that will give everybody an opportunity to gape at me any more than they will already."

She looked at Susanna and Mary Beth. "Though I could probably go naked tonight and no one would notice, as pretty as you two look."

"Do you see that she is finally wearing *the* dress?" Mary Beth asked.

"That's not it, is it? I thought the crimson dress was—oh, you spoiled it! What are you doing with a tucker?"

"There's no sense in arguing with her," Mary Beth said. "I've tried."

At that moment there was a knock on the door.

"That must be Jesse," Susanna said.

"Jesse?" Annie asked.

"Yes. Jesse is taking her to the dance," Mary Beth said.

Annie smiled. "Jesse doesn't know it, but he's taking all of us to the dance." She was walking to the door as she was speaking.

"Good evening, Annie," Jesse said. "Is Susanna ready to go?"

"We're all ready," Annie said.

"All?"

"Yes, all." Annie looked back into the house. "Come, ladies. Our escort is here."

❋ 16 ❋

It had been two days since Rab had last seen Susanna, and he was now beginning to worry that she was having second thoughts about what had happened at the mine. Was she purposely staying away from him? If so, would that matter to him? Yes, he knew that it would matter. She had been on his mind constantly, and he knew that he had to see her again.

The dance! He had asked her if he could escort her and she had turned him down, but he would be willing to bet that she would be there. And he was going to be there, too.

Before he left San Francisco, Margaret, insisting that men had no idea of how or what to pack, had helped him. Against his protest, she had packed some formal wear, the same thing he had worn at Judge Conrad's party.

"Now if you have occasion to wear this, you will think

of me and remember the night we announced our engagement," she said.

Rab took the apparel out and looked at it.

Should he wear this tonight? The only reason he was going to this dance at all was to see another woman. If he wore this, would he be betraying Margaret, or would he be betraying himself? Right now he knew that Margaret and love had nothing to do with it. He put the formal wear back and reached for the same thing he had worn when he and Susanna had gone to the Washoe Club.

When he left the hotel, the Fourth of July celebrations were still going strong. Looking up toward Mount Davidson, he saw the giant flag, flapping in the breeze, while rockets were shooting into the air, then bursting high over the city. Firecrackers were going off in the town itself, and some were firing their guns into the air.

It was a short walk from the hotel to the Miners' Union Hall, where the dance was being held. Although the dance had not yet started, several people were there. Van Cleve, Burdick, and Sheehan were already present when Rab arrived. Van Cleve and Sheehan were both in tuxedos; Burdick was wearing the blue dress uniform of an army lieutenant colonel.

"That's him," Sheehan said, nodding toward Rab.

"Why is the son of a bitch still walking around?" Burdick asked, looking at Sheehan. "Weren't you supposed to take care of that?"

"Don't worry," Sheehan said. "I have confidence that Teague will get the job done."

"And if he doesn't?" Van Cleve asked.

Sheehan lifted his drink, took a swallow, then wiped his mouth with the back of his hand.

"If he doesn't, I will."

At that moment Susanna, Jesse, Mary Beth, and Annie arrived at the Union Hall.

"Wait a minute," Annie said. "I'm beginning to have second thoughts about this."

"What do you mean?" Susanna asked.

"Maybe I should let the rest of you go in first, while I wait out here for a moment or two."

"Why?" Mary Beth asked.

"It might be better for you if you aren't seen arriving with me. I shouldn't have come. I don't know what I was thinking."

"Don't be silly," Susanna said. "You are our friend."

Susanna took Annie's arm and was surprised to feel that she was trembling. Susanna didn't think Annie was afraid of anything, but here, standing in front of the Miners' Union Hall, Annie was clearly terrified.

"We're going in together," Susanna said.

Suddenly, Mary Beth reached over and pulled the chemisette out of the top of Susanna's dress and stuffed it down her own bodice, making it impossible for Susanna to recover.

"Don't worry, Annie," Mary Beth said. "Now nobody

will notice you or me. They won't be able to take their eyes off Susanna."

Jesse smiled broadly. "You got that right."

Annie laughed. "That very well may be."

Although Susanna was shocked when Mary Beth first jerked the tucker out, she laughed with the others. She gripped Annie's arm. "Now we'll have to support each other."

When they stepped into the Miners' Union Hall, Susanna made a quick perusal of the guests. James Loudin was there. So, too, were Dan DeQuille, Alf Doten, and Billy Virden, Doten's partner at the *Gold Hill News*. The banker John Welch and his wife; Jack O'Brien, the superintendent of the Ophir Mine, along with his wife; and Rufus Kellogg, who owned the Consolidated Virginia Mine—all were there. It appeared as if everybody who was anybody in the Comstock was present, for this dance was a benefit for the widows and orphans of miners who had been killed in accidents.

And, Susanna thought, everyone in the hall was looking directly at them. Were they looking at Annie? Or were they looking at her? She noticed that no other woman was wearing a gown that was nearly as revealing, and that made her even more self-conscious.

Rab was standing by the wall near Benton McQueen when he saw Susanna enter. He had a quick intake of breath. Had she come in totally naked, he did not think she could have presented a more provocative appearance.

The low-cut dress, clinging to her figure as it did, took him back to the scene at the bath, and he knew that he would have to get his mind off that or risk embarrassment by displaying his reaction to her.

She was with a man and two women, and at first he didn't recognize any of them. Then he realized that the woman in white was Annie Biggs. He was somewhat surprised to see her at the dance and even more astonished to see her with Susanna. The way Susanna was holding her arm, Rab surmised the two were friends.

"Do you remember Susanna Ward?" he asked McQueen.

"She's the woman who works for the *Pioneer*. The one you brought to the mine. Isn't that her coming in now?" Benton asked. "My God, I didn't know she was such a handsome woman! Who's that she's—oh my goodness!"

"I know, I recognize the woman in white," Rab said. "And I recognize Miss Ward. But who are the other two?"

"The young woman is Mary Beth Chaney. I knew her father. He was killed when a tunnel collapsed in the Justice Mine a few years ago, and the young man is Jesse Kirkland. He's a real hooligan."

"What is that whore doing here?" someone close by asked. Looking toward the speaker, Rab recognized the banker John Welch.

"She's got some nerve," the Ophir superintendent replied.

"Someone should tell her to leave. This is no place for her kind," Welch suggested.

"Do you want to do it?" O'Brien asked.

"Me? Uh, no, that's not a good idea," Welch said, looking toward his wife who was conversing with Mrs. O'Brien.

"I know what you're saying. I won't do it either."

"Well, someone should. It's just not Christian for her to be here."

Rab continued to watch Susanna, Annie, and the others. As they came deeper into the hall, the guests parted like the sea before Moses, and Rab could see the expression of mortification on Annie's face. He felt sorry for her and proud of Susanna for standing by her side.

Dan DeQuille walked to the platform and signaled for the bandleader to play a trumpet fanfare that got everyone's attention.

DeQuille held up his arms. "Ladies and gentlemen, may I have your attention please? First of all, thank you all for coming. As you know, this dance is to be a benefit for the widows and orphans of the miners who have lost their lives in the mines over the last year. And to raise money we are having a silent auction with dozens of donated items to bid on, so please stop by the table where Mrs. Kellogg and Mrs. Clayton are sitting. Make generous bids on whatever catches your fancy. Mr. Loudin, Mr. Doten, and I are offering the very best items—one year's subscription to our newspapers, though why you would want to read any other than the *Enterprise* is beyond me."

His comment elicited a smattering of polite laughter.

"We have a fine suit of men's clothing from Kirkland Emporium, and Mr. Manning has donated a woman's dress. Sikes Hardware gave a wood-burning stove—why, we have lots and lots of stuff. Even the beautiful candelabras you see are a generous donation from the Yellow Jacket, and the grand prize is the beautiful punch bowl being used tonight. Its silver was taken from the Silver Falcon Mine."

At the conclusion of the announcement, there was generous applause.

"Now if you would, choose your partners for the grand march."

As the music began playing and everyone chose their partner, Rab watched as Annie, with a forlorn expression, started to drift over to one side of the hall to be out of the way of the dancers. Rab moved quickly to her.

"Miss Biggs," he said with a slight bow. "Would you be my partner?"

Annie looked surprised. "Mr. Trudeau, you do remember encountering me at the hotel, don't you?"

"Yes. You waved at me."

"I did indeed wave at you. Just before I went into a man's room," she added pointedly.

"As I recall, he was rather short and he had a bald head."

"Then, you do remember. Which means you must also know what I am."

"I know that you and Susanna came in here arm in arm. And if you are her friend, you are my friend as well."

"Oh, my. It sounds like you both have it bad."

"Have what bad?"

"Infatuation? Maybe more. It's not for me to say."

Rab wanted to ask Annie for an explanation, but the grand march was forming quickly, so he offered her his arm.

"You are sure you want to do this?"

"Absolutely sure," Rab said, leading her out onto the floor, where they got into line behind Susanna and Jesse.

The music started and the procession began as they marched, two by two and arm in arm, to the far end of the floor. Curving around, they came back to where they had started. Then, as the music continued, the marchers weaved back and forth until their numbers increased to four. This time, Rab was between Susanna and Annie.

"Hello, Susanna," Rab said. He felt her stiffen slightly, but he didn't know why.

On the next pass, the numbers in the file increased again, and Annie found herself marching side by side with John Welch.

"Good evening, Mr. Welch," Annie said quietly.

"How did she know you?" Mrs. Welch asked, angered by Annie's innocent comment.

"I'm a banker, dear. Everyone knows me."

"Hrmmph," Mrs. Welch said.

In his peripheral vision, Rab saw Annie grinning broadly.

Several quadrilles followed, and Rab, dancing first with Annie, then Mary Beth, got himself in Susanna's set every time. Because the intricacies of the dance required the exchange of partners within the square, Rab was able to dance with Susanna almost as often as he danced with his own partner.

Susanna found it a most unusual evening. She was enjoying the company, the music, and the sequence of steps that made up the dances. But there could not have been a more pronounced difference between the way she felt when she was dancing with Jesse and when she was dancing with Rab.

When she was with Jesse, he was but a player who functioned as no more than a placeholder when the leader called for such moves as the chassé, the grand chain, or the promenade—no more important than any other man or woman in the quadrille. But when she danced with Rab, she could feel a transfer of heat and energy that penetrated to her soul from the touch of his hand, even from his look. Every sensory point in her body was awakened.

Between the sets of the spirited quadrilles, the band played some waltzes. This gave the more sedate attendees a chance to participate, and the more active dancers a chance to catch their breath. For a few of those waltzes, Jesse danced with Mary Beth, his sister, Alice, and even Annie.

When Susanna saw Rab approaching her, she quickly turned to Alice's husband, Harold, and asked him to be her partner. She then danced with several other older gentlemen, aware that each of them was ogling her breasts, and rather than being embarrassed, she was enjoying the attention. As she was twirled around the dance floor, she was ever cognizant of where Rab Trudeau was, but she managed to avoid him.

Then, a short time later, Rab moved ahead of Harold to claim her for the next dance. She could not refuse him without making a scene.

"Why have you been avoiding me?" Rab asked.

"I'm not aware that I was." Susanna stepped back and did a pirouette; then, after she held her hand out toward his, he drew her back to him.

"Really?" he asked as he pulled her tightly against him for just a moment. They glided around the room in time with the music.

"Mr. Trudeau . . ."

"*Mr.* Trudeau? Now you're hurting my feelings."

"Rab, please, you don't understand."

"No, I don't understand. You can't tell me that you don't feel something between us."

"What is happening between us can never be. It just— can't."

After the next pirouette, Rab pulled her close to him and held her, not allowing her to separate as the dance required.

"Susanna, I can feel you trembling. Do you think I don't know what you are feeling? I'm not going to deny it. I feel the same way."

Susanna didn't answer verbally, but her eyes betrayed her.

"Rab, oh, Rab," she said as the music stopped. She went no further because she didn't know if it was a request for him to leave her alone or a plea for him to take her away.

After that dance, Susanna did not want to dance with anyone. She headed for the refreshment table, in shadows now because many of the candles in the candelabras had sputtered out. She thought about leaving, but she knew with the holiday revelers, it would not be safe to be on the streets unaccompanied, especially not the way she was dressed tonight. Getting a cup of punch from the large, silver punch bowl, she sat on a bench that had been pushed up against the wall and hoped that she was hidden from view. She could not risk another dance with Rab, knowing the way he made her feel.

Susanna saw James Loudin nearby, conversing with Van Cleve, Burdick, and Sheehan. Susanna knew that the three men were owners of the North Star Mine. She did not know them intimately, but she had heard enough about them to know that some of the other mine owners didn't think too highly of them. The trick that they had pulled with the shutdown of the mine—and Susanna was now certain that it was just a trick—tended to validate what Susanna had heard about them. Their conversation with Loudin was so intense that none of them even noticed Susanna back in the shadows. She was close enough to hear every word that was being spoken.

"We need another article," Van Cleve was saying.

"I shouldn't have run the one about you shutting down North Star," Loudin said. "It caused a lot of people to lose a lot of money."

"Except you," Burdick said. "You were paid well."

"Yes, I will admit that, but I don't think people will believe it if we run that again."

"That's not what we want this time," Van Cleve said. "What we need is an article that says the Silver Falcon has run out of silver and they're closing down for good."

"Oh, I don't know. Before I print something like that, I'd have to hear it directly from the owners of the Silver Falcon."

"You've heard it from us," Burdick said. "That's all you need."

"No, I'm sorry, that's not all I need," Loudin said. "If I printed a story like that, why, you couldn't give Silver Falcon stock away. You've caused the price to drop to practically nothing as it is, just because of the stories I've already run for you."

"And for which, I might remind you," Van Cleve said, "you were amply compensated."

"I know, and I'm not overly proud of myself for that. I don't feel good about this. I don't feel good about it at all."

"Mr. Loudin," Van Cleve said, "are you aware of the principle of the carrot and the stick?"

"Yes, of course I am."

"Let's apply that principle here," Van Cleve said. "I'll start with the carrot. If you print the story we are asking you to print, we'll give you five hundred shares of the Silver Falcon Mine."

"If I print this story, five hundred shares of Silver Falcon stock will be practically worthless. So what would be my incentive?"

"It won't be worthless after we take over the Silver Falcon," Sheehan said.

"Why would you want to take it over if—wait a minute. I think I see what's happening here. Your mine is right next to the Silver Falcon. My God, you've discovered a new vein, haven't you? But it runs into the Silver Falcon."

"You're a smart man, Loudin," Sheehan said.

"Maybe a little too smart," Burdick added.

"Now you see the value of the incentive we are offering," Van Cleve said.

"I don't know," Loudin replied. "I've gone along with you boys before because it's been nothing but a little stock manipulation, and everyone does that."

"And you were paid for it," Van Cleve said.

"Yes, I was paid for it. But what you're asking me to do now is help you steal a silver mine. I think that's further than I want to go."

"We've told you the carrot part," Van Cleve said. "Perhaps I should have Mr. Sheehan tell you the stick part."

"I don't care what the stick part is, I'm not going to help you steal a silver mine."

"Oh, yeah, well, what you may not know is that during the war Mr. Sheehan here rode with Quantrill's guerrillas for a while—that is until Quantrill kicked him out, and do you know why he did that? It wasn't because he was a Sunday-school teacher, you can bet on that," Van Cleve said. "Sheehan taught even those bad boys a thing or two. Now, Mr. Loudin, shall I have Mr. Sheehan teach you a little about the stick part of our offer?"

"I think I get the picture," Loudin said.

"That's good, that's very good, because I don't like to get my hands dirty these days. You see, I'm respectable now," Sheehan said, "and I like it."

"If you take over the Silver Falcon and prove out that

new vein, how much do you think this stock will be worth?" Loudin asked.

"By this time next year, it should be worth at least a thousand dollars a share."

"Half a million dollars," Loudin said.

"I don't think we'll be needin' the stick, now will we, Mr. Loudin?" Van Cleve asked.

"No. You will have your article."

Susanna knew she should leave before any of the four men saw her, but she was determined to stay long enough to hear everything. Then, stunned, she slipped away from the punch table. She knew now what Rab was investigating. Should she tell him? Would he believe her? Would having the information that she now had put him in danger?

Susanna had one more opportunity to dance with Rab before the evening ended, and she sought him out.

"Make sure you read tomorrow's paper," she said as they were dancing.

"I read it every day. But today, I was especially pleased with your article about the celebration. It was well written, but do you know the part I liked best? The byline."

"Read it tomorrow. I think you will find it particularly interesting."

Not until Rab realized that Susanna had not reacted to his compliment did he notice the serious expression on her face. "What is it? What are you trying to tell me?"

"I'll just say that it has to do with your investigation."

Before Rab could reply, the music ended, and Susanna turned quickly to walk away before he could ask any more questions.

"Ladies and gentlemen!" the bandleader called, shouting through a megaphone. "Choose your partners for the last dance!"

During his dances with Annie and Mary Beth, Rab had learned that the two women lived with Susanna at the Chaney House. When the last dance ended, Rab offered to walk them all home.

"That won't be necessary," Susanna said as she and Jesse joined the others. "Jesse will walk us home."

"Well, uh, Susanna, if this fella is going to walk with you, then, there's really no need for me to come along, too," Jesse said. "Michael O'Malley wanted me to stop by after the dance. We're goin' to set off some fireworks."

"Jesse, I think—"

"That would be quite all right," Rab said, interrupting Susanna's reply. "I'll be happy to see the ladies home safely."

"Great." Jesse started to leave, then stopped and turned toward Susanna. "I'll see you this Sunday for the chocolate cake."

"Good." Susanna wanted to say more, to tell him how rude it was of him not to walk her home—yet a part of her was glad that he wasn't.

"We'll walk a little ahead of you," Annie offered. "That way you two can talk all you want, and we won't be in the way. And, Mr. Trudeau, I thank you for being such a gentleman tonight."

"Oh, it's no problem. I'm happy to walk you home."

"That's not what I meant," Annie said. "I'm talking about dancing with me and making me feel welcome."

Rab smiled. "It was my pleasure, ma'am."

They walked down Union on the way home. With no business establishments on the street, and few houses, for long stretches it was completely isolated. It was also very dark and would not have been the way the women would have returned if they had been by themselves.

But it was the quickest way home, and because Rab was with them, none of them was frightened.

"Tell me about this article that's going to be in the paper tomorrow," Rab said.

"I'd rather not," Susanna said. "I have to think very carefully about what I'm going to say."

"But you said it had something to do with my investigation."

"Yes, it does. I know you've been down in the Silver Falcon more times than when we, uh—" She stopped because, even as she mentioned the Silver Falcon, ribbons of heat flashed through her body. "Many times," she amended. "Do you think the silver has played out in that mine?"

"No. Don't you remember the ore samples I showed you?"

"Yes. But that was from just one section. I'm talking about the entire mine. Do you think there's any chance it's playing out?"

"Does this have anything to do with what's going to appear in the paper tomorrow?" Rab's voice had an angry edge. "Is the paper going to publish another lie about the Silver Falcon? It's already caused the stock to drop down to less than five dollars a share. Isn't that enough?"

"Trust me, Rab. The story tomorrow will set that straight."

"I—I do so want to trust you. But I don't know how the paper is going to be able to undo the damage that has already been done."

Stopping, Susanna turned to Rab, taking his hand in hers. "This time, you will see."

When they reached the house, Annie and Mary Beth turned to tell Rab good-night, and to thank him for walking them home.

"Wait," Susanna called. "I'm coming in with you."

He looked at her, and even in the subdued light of the half-moon, she could see a longing in the gleaming depths of his eyes.

"Will you stay outside a minute?"

"I can't." She bit down on her bottom lip. More than anything else in the world, she wanted to be held by this man—to be kissed over and over, and then to do more. Even now as she said the words, her body was betraying her. She knew she could not trust herself to be alone with him even for a moment.

"Good night," she said in a bare whisper

Rab's lips curled into an easy and knowing smile that told Susanna he had read her eyes as clearly as if she had spoken to him.

"Good night," he said as he dropped her hand and turned to leave.

Asa Teague had seen Trudeau leave the Union Hall with the three women, and he followed, staying well behind them, hidden by the darkness. He waited until he saw Trudeau coming back; then he hid behind the berm where the railroad crossed the street. At first he thought that he would just shoot him as he came across the tracks, but Teague had second thoughts about it. After all, he had tried three times before to kill this man and had failed every time. This time he was going to be damned sure. He would be standing no more than six feet from him. He knew Trudeau was not wearing his pistol, so this should be an easy way to collect his money.

Rab had seen a shadow within the shadows just on the other side of the railroad track. It had not been light enough for him to be certain, but he had a strong feeling that it was someone who didn't want to be seen. Because Rab now knew that someone was trying to kill him, he decided that he should be cautious when he started across the track. For that reason, he wasn't particularly startled when a man suddenly stepped up from behind the berm, right in front of him.

"That's far enough, Trudeau."

It was too dark to make out the man's features, but Rab could see that he had about the same general physique as the knife-wielding intruder who had come into the hotel the night the drummer was slashed. Rab could also see, quite clearly, the pistol in the man's hand.

"You're a hard man to kill."

"I try to be," Rab replied.

The man laughed, a low, guttural laugh.

"Who are you?" Rab asked.

"The name is Teague. Asa Teague. I reckon you've heard of me," he added with a hint of pride.

"I can't say that I have. Tell me, Teague, why are you trying to kill me?"

"I ain't tryin'. This time I aim to do it."

"Why?"

"Because you're a five-thousand-dollar payday, that's why."

"Only five thousand? Damn, I would have thought I was worth a lot more than that."

"I'm through jawin' with you." Teague raised his pistol and thrust it toward Rab.

Seeing that it wasn't cocked, Rab quickly reached down and wrapped his hand around the cylinder of the pistol. If the cylinder couldn't turn, the pistol couldn't be cocked. And if the pistol couldn't be cocked, it couldn't be fired.

"What the hell?" Teague said as he tried unsuccessfully to pull the hammer back.

Rab smiled at Teague, his smile mocking and dangerous. "You seem to have a bit of a problem."

"Let go! Let go, you bastard!" Teague shouted.

Rab brought his right knee up, hard, into Teague's groin. With a gasp, Teague went down, releasing his grip on the pistol. He lay on the ground doubled up in pain. Holding the pistol, Rab stood looking down at him.

"I take it this has a bullet in it?" Rab cocked the pistol, the sear engaging the cylinder with a deadly click in the night. He aimed at Teague's head.

"Don't shoot, please don't shoot," Teague said, still writhing in agony.

"Then, get on your damn feet. We're going to take a little walk."

"Take a walk? Take a walk where?" Teague replied, his voice still strained with pain.

"To the police station."

❋ 17 ❋

"Susanna, here's a story from the *New York Tribune*," Loudin said. "Please set it for our paper."

"All right," Susanna replied.

The story was about Nevada's own Senator Jones being complimented by former president U. S. Grant. "Senator Jones is a man of much force of character, and daily growing as a statesman," Grant said.

As Susanna worked in the composing room, setting the type, she couldn't help but overhear a heated discussion between B.D. and Loudin.

"Would you tell me what this is all about, James?" B.D. asked. "You know damn well this is a lie. Is it a newspaper we are running? Or would it be an organ for printing lies to promote the schemes of such despicable scoundrels as the devil's own Van Cleve, Burdick, and Sheehan?"

"Mr. Van Cleve, Colonel Burdick, and Mr. Sheehan are fine, upstanding businessmen," Loudin said. "They are the kind of men who have built Virginia City. And I would further remind you, Mr. Elliott, that *we* aren't running a newspaper. I am. And you will write exactly what I tell you to write."

"I'll be damned if I'll write such prevarications and try to pass it off as news!" B.D. said angrily.

"You'll be fired if you don't."

"Fire me. I'll go to the *Enterprise.*"

"Do you really think DeQuille will hire you? At least here, when you are so drunk that you can barely walk, you have Susanna to write your articles for you. Who will write for you over at the *Enterprise*?"

"I'll work as a printer's devil for Mr. DeQuille if I have to. At least I know I'll be working for an honest newspaper instead of the purveying, lying broadsheet you are publishing. I weep for God's own noble trees that have been sacrificed to print this disgusting broadside you would call a newspaper."

"That's it, Mr. Elliott! You are fired!"

"You can't fire me, because I quit!" B.D. stormed out of Loudin's office, walked over to the hat rack, grabbed his hat, and stuffed it down onto his head. Then he pulled open a drawer on his desk and took out a full bottle of whiskey. He uncorked the bottle, started to raise it to his lips, then stopped halfway. Holding the bottle out, he looked at it for a moment, then put it back down, untouched.

"You'd better take your whiskey with you."

"You know, Loudin, I have a feeling I'll have no more use for the creature. I think I've found the courage I've been looking for."

B.D. looked back into the composing room where Susanna, stunned by the unfolding events, stood transfixed by the drama she was witnessing.

"Susanna, I bid you a fond adieu and beg that you watch yourself around this heathen that he does not corrupt your sweet innocence with his perfidious iniquities. Remember, *se méfier de ses mauvaises intentions*."

"And good riddance to you, you self-righteous bastard!" Loudin shouted. He stood there looking at the door for a moment, then he stepped back into his office, and Susanna returned to setting the story they would be running from the *New York Tribune*.

A few minutes later Loudin came back into the composing room, carrying a piece of paper.

"Susanna, you are now my reporter." He thrust the paper toward her. "Write this story, and see to it that the paper gets out. I probably won't be back today. Fill the paper with articles and bits from anywhere you can find them."

Susanna took the paper from him and began reading it as Loudin left.

> This newspaper now has it on unimpeach-
> able authority that the Silver Falcon Mine
> will be shutting down all operations within
> the week. It has been reported that the drift

of silver that passes through the Silver Falcon
has been completely worked out, and there is
nothing left.

Susanna finished composing the story about Senator
Jones, then started working on the Silver Falcon story,
composing it even as she was writing it.

When Rab went downstairs that morning, he was surprised to see David DeLoitte in the lobby. "David, what
are you doing here?"

"I arrived on the five o'clock train. Too early to wake
you so I decided to just sit here and wait."

"Well, I'm glad to see you, of course, but why are you
here? Is anything wrong back home?"

"I haven't eaten yet," David said. "Suppose we talk over
breakfast?"

"All right. I've been having my breakfast at the Silver
Dollar. It's just down the street."

"How about the International Hotel?"

Rab chuckled. "I remember the time when you were
my first officer on the old *Falcon,* and we were in Calais.
All of our money was tied up in cargo with practically
nothing left for food. What did we have for breakfast that
morning?"

"As I recall, we had a fish and onion brioche."

"And now the Silver Dollar isn't good enough for you?
You want to have breakfast in the best restaurant in town."

"I do."

"All right, that's fine by me. How are Lila and the girls?"

"Lila and the girls are doing fine." David paused for a moment, then with a big smile added, "And so is little Davey."

"What? When was the baby born?"

"On July first. He came a little earlier than the doctor thought, but he's my son so, by God, he set his own schedule."

Rab grabbed David's hand and shook it. "Well, congratulations! I can't tell you how happy I am for you!"

"I'm pretty pleased myself. In fact, the reason I want to have breakfast at the International Hotel is because I want to treat you to a champagne breakfast."

"A champagne breakfast, is it? Well now, that's even better than a cigar."

A few minutes later, after they ordered their breakfast and a bottle of champagne, David pulled an envelope from his pocket. "I have two letters for you. This one from Margaret, and this one from your sister. I would have forwarded Emmaline's to you, but it just came day before yesterday, so I decided to bring it myself."

"Thanks." Rab opened Margaret's letter first.

My dearest Rab,

How I wish I could accompany David to Virginia City to see you, but with so much to do in preparation for our wedding, I simply cannot take the time. This letter will have to be a poor substitute.

Yesterday I visited Lila and held the new baby. Little

David is just precious. I can hardly wait until we start our own family, though I would hope that it not be too soon. Before I am forced into the role of motherhood and dutiful wife, I want some time to enjoy life.

Darling, I can hardly keep my imagination in check. I see us obtaining a private box at the theater with a brass plaque marked "Mr. and Mrs. Rab Trudeau," I see us being introduced at societal balls, and especially, I see us hosting parties so lavish that the Chronicle will be hard-pressed to do justice to the event.

I do hope your work there ends soon so you can return to me in time to be fully rested before the final round of activities begin prior to our wedding.

Sincerely,
Your Margaret

Rab folded the letter and returned it to the envelope. He tapped it on the table contemplatively for a moment before he picked up Emmaline's letter.

My dearest brother Rab,

Yours in hand, I undertake to answer the questions posed. I have delayed my response because I was not sure whether you wanted my validation of a decision you have already made, or whether you wanted an honest answer from me.

I have decided that you seek the latter, so I will answer you honestly, and as a sister who loves you dearly. I am sure that the young lady of whom you wrote is of the finest character and would make a wonderful wife.

Rab folded the letter over and tapped his fingers on it for a moment as he looked around the room.

"Bad news?" David asked, concerned by the expression he saw on Rab's face. "Your father?"

"What? Oh, no, nothing like that."

David chuckled. "I'm sure Emmaline intended for you to read the whole thing."

Rab turned his attention back to the letter.

> *But I do not think she would be such a wonderful wife for you. By your own admission, your regards for her are more an obligation of honor than an expression of love. You have your own interpretation of honor, Rab, an interpretation that has led you down paths you would rather not have taken. You fought a duel against a kinsman that you did not want to fight, and I know that because of that, until this very day, you feel pain in your heart.*
>
> *Do not marry this woman out of a sense of honor or obligation. Marry her only if you love her. If you cannot say that you love her with all your heart and all your soul, then marrying her would condemn both of you to a lifetime of misery and regret, and that, my dear brother, would be dishonorable.*
>
> *It was the Trudeau perception of honor, you will recall, that has caused the great rift between you and our father. And you suffer yet because of that as well. Father grows more frail with each passing day. Did you know that he now speaks of you with affection? The harsh tones of his past remonstrations are no more. In fact, he subscribes,*

by mail, to the San Francisco Chronicle, so that he may follow the affairs of Sunset Enterprises, and thereby keep an account of you. You may want to consider a return to New Orleans before it is too late for you and Father to make your final peace.

I do not know if this be the response you wished to receive, but I feel it my responsibility to speak only the truth to you. This, my dear brother, from a sister who adores you.

I remain affectionately.

　　　　　　　　　　　　　　　　　　Your Sister,
　　　　　　　　　　　　　　　　　　Emmaline

Rab folded the letter, returned it to the envelope, then put it in his pocket just as breakfast was delivered.

"To your son," Rab said, holding his goblet up.

They drank the toast, then began their breakfast of steak and eggs.

"I'll bet you're wondering why I'm in Virginia City," David said.

"I am."

"I received a disturbing letter from Benton McQueen. He said that there had been an attempt on your life and that someone had actually pushed you down a mine shaft. How did you survive that, by the way?"

Rab chuckled. "I just started grabbing and managed to find something to hang on to."

"It's not funny. If this lunatic tried once, he'll try again."

"He did try again, three more times."

"What?"

"Don't worry about it. He's in jail now." Rab told David about his adventure the night before.

Now David chuckled. "If he had checked with me, I could have told him you weren't someone to mess with."

"I appreciate your concern though."

"Rab, you have no idea how big your wedding is going to be. Mayor Bryant is going to be there of course. Governor Irwin is also coming, and so are both senators and Adolph Sutro. Margaret is determined to make it the biggest social event that has ever hit San Francisco."

Rab stared into his glass, but didn't answer. He was trapped. Regardless of what he felt about Susanna, regardless of the advice given him by Emmaline, there was no way out of this marriage. Margaret was as unstoppable as an avalanche, expanding the parameters until it was no longer a marriage between two people, but an event so large that it could rival the nominating convention of a major political party.

Regardless of how he felt, the conclusion to this drama was ordained. He would marry Margaret.

"Are you all right?" David asked.

"Yeah. Let's get out of here. What do you say we go visit Benton out at the mine?"

Back at the office of the *Pioneer,* the newspaper had been put to bed and the papers were now in two stacks, one for Mickey to deliver and another for him to take to the Post Office to go out by mail. Susanna had one of the papers in her hand, and she was sitting at B.D.'s desk reading today's issue.

Technically she supposed that this was her desk now, though she knew it wouldn't be for long. She had no doubt that after today's issue, she would no longer have a job either.

B. D. Elliott Resigns from the Pioneer

by

Susanna Ward

Mr. B. D. Elliott is no longer a Reporter for this newspaper, a difference of editorial philosophy having developed between Mr. Elliott and James Loudin, the publisher of the Pioneer. Mr. Elliott was ordered to print a story about the Silver Falcon Mine that had no basis in fact and he refused to do so.

Had the story been printed, it would have been but one of many false stories the Pioneer has printed, the purpose of which has been to manipulate the cost of mining shares.

Mr. Elliott, a man of great talent and strong moral character, made his disapproval of such nefarious activity known by submitting his resignation. This scribe has learned much from Mr. Elliott and believes the newspaper and the community of Virginia City will be the poorer for his absence.

Susanna figured that story alone would be enough to bring about her dismissal, but the next one would give Loudin apoplexy.

Dishonest Dealings in the Mines

by

Susanna Ward

Virginia City, all of Washoe Valley, indeed the entire state of Nevada, are dependent upon the workings of the silver mines extant on the Comstock Lode. Honest men, who toil at jobs not related to the mining, milling, and processing of silver, owe the very existence of those professions to the mines.

It is imperative, then, that if this prosperous intercourse is to continue, it must be, like Caesar's wife, above all suspicion. Unfortunately, that is not the case, for four of Virginia City's most prominent businessmen are engaged in a scheme of fraud, dishonesty, and corruption that would put to shame the betrayal of our Lord by Judas Iscariot.

These businessmen by name are Sam Van Cleve, William Burdick, and John Sheehan, owners of the North Star Mine, and James Loudin, owner and publisher of the very journal in which you are now reading these words. The mine owners have engaged Mr. Loudin in perpetrating their deceit, by way of compensating him for publishing spurious information that accrues to their benefit by undervaluing the true worth and production of other mines.

The most recent example of their iniquity is in making the false claim that the Silver Falcon

Mine is on the verge of collapse, when in fact silver production remains at its peak. Why, the reader may ask, would the owners of the North Star Mine do this? The answer, dear readers, is that Mr. Van Cleve, Mr. (though he calls himself Colonel) Burdick, and Mr. Sheehan have discovered a new and very rich drift that departs their mine and goes into the Silver Falcon.

This vein will, no doubt, greatly increase the value of the Silver Falcon. But if the scheme these nefarious men would perpetrate would succeed, Van Cleve, Burdick, Sheehan, and the publisher of this journal would realize great profits by buying the Silver Falcon for pennies, then capitalizing on its rich resources.

This will be the last article that I write for the Pioneer, for I will no doubt be terminated as soon as the publisher of this newspaper discovers the article herein printed. But with my last public pronouncement, I call upon the law to bring to justice these four men whose illicit and scandalous activities equal the outrage of the most infamous of all bank robbers, train holdup artists, and road agents.

Not until early evening did Rab and David return from their visit to the mine. They took their dinner at the Silver Dollar, and while there, Rab bought a copy of the *Pioneer*, which remained unopened as the two men were discussing business.

"We're going to need some more timber out at the mine," Rab said. "Those new winzes need to be shored up so we can access that lower level. Gabe tells me you won't believe what the assays look like down there."

"If we hit something big again, that should bring the stock back with a roar, no matter what lies somebody tries to tell. If you'd like, I can go see Bliss before I start back to San Francisco," David offered.

"No, I'll take care of it. You need to get back to Lila, and besides, I could use a little relaxation about now, just to get out of Virginia City. Glenbrook is the perfect place for that, you know."

"You need to get back to San Francisco. I'm sure Margaret would love to see you."

"I'll get there soon enough," Rab said with a resigned sigh. He opened the paper and began to read.

"I figure we will need about half a million board—"

"What the hell? How did she know all this?" Rab blurted.

"How does who know what?" David asked, clearly confused by Rab's outburst.

"Hold on to your stock, David," Rab said with a huge smile spreading across his face. "By this time a week from now, our stock will be trading at a thousand dollars a share."

"You've got to be kidding."

"Read this article." Rab passed the newspaper across to his friend and stood up. "Can you stay a few more days?"

"Sure."

"Good. Get with Benton while I'm gone and find that new drift."

"What new drift?"

"Read," Rab said, then he started toward the front door.

"Where are you going?" David called after him.

"I have to see a man about a goat," Rab replied with a twinkle in his eye.

Leaving the restaurant, Rab walked quickly to the Chaney House. When he knocked on the door, it was answered by a plump, gray-haired woman in her early sixties.

"Oh, I'm sorry," she said. "This lodging house is for women only."

"Yes, ma'am," Rab said. "But you have a lady guest I would like to speak with. That is, if she is home."

The expression on the woman's face hardened somewhat. "Miss Biggs does not conduct business in this house."

"It's all right, Mama," Mary Beth said, coming into the lobby. "I know this gentleman. He isn't here to see Annie. Mr. Trudeau, if you'll wait in the parlor, I'll get Susanna."

"Thank you," Rab said as he stepped into the house.

Realizing her mistake, Harriet became more hospitable. "Would you like a cup of coffee?"

"Yes, thank you, that would be very nice."

Harriet brought the coffee to Rab just as Susanna came into the parlor. He rose to greet her.

"Rab. What a surprise to see you here."

Rab smiled. "Now, how much of a surprise can it be when you consider that article you wrote?"

"You read it?"

"I read it. It was beautifully written. And I might add,

it was a courageous thing for you to do. This was what you were talking about at the dance last night, wasn't it?"

"Yes," Susanna said. "I overheard Mr. Loudin talking with Van Cleve and the others. I—you were right, Rab. The *Pioneer* has been a part of this deception from the beginning. I didn't know it, and I didn't begin to suspect anything until we ran the story about the shutdown of the North Star Mine. But even then, I had no idea that it was as bad as it is. And I had no idea how deeply involved Mr. Loudin was."

"How did you manage to get that story by him?"

Susanna smiled. "He wasn't there. After B.D. resigned, Mr. Loudin left me in charge. For one day I was a full-fledged reporter, editor, and publisher. And I gave it all up."

"To write the most important article written in the history of the Comstock. I'm so proud of you, Susanna."

"Thanks," Susanna said, feeling an unexpected pleasure from the comment.

"So, what are you going to do now?"

"I don't know for sure. After that article, I don't think Mr. DeQuille or even Mr. Doten would hire me. I suppose I'll be working at Kirkland Emporium."

"You don't have to do it tomorrow, do you?"

"Tomorrow? No, I don't suppose so. Why? What's so important about tomorrow?"

"It might not be a bad idea for you to be out of town for a day. Tomorrow I'm going to Glenbrook to take care of a lumber contract. I'm going up on the first train in the morning, and I'll come back on the last train tomorrow afternoon. I'd like for you to go with me. We can spend some time at Lake Tahoe."

Susanna couldn't believe the invitation. She couldn't accept it, could she? Wouldn't that be considered scandalous? What would Mr. Kirkland think if he found out about it? No, she couldn't possibly accept it. What kind of woman did he think she was?

"I'd love to go," she said.

❊ 18 ❊

The *Genoa*, a 4-4-0 engine, was sitting in front of the Virginia and Truckee depot, its steam up, waiting for the morning run. The brass fittings of the green-and-red engine shone brightly in the morning sun, which was just now full-disk up on the eastern horizon. To the west, purple shadows still lay in the draws and crags of Mount Davidson.

Susanna shivered slightly as she stood alongside Rab on the brick platform, and she pulled her shawl more tightly around her.

"Are you cold?"

"A little," Susanna said. It was cool in the still morning air at this altitude, but it wasn't really cold enough to make her shiver. That, she knew, came from anticipation—not only of this day, but of her future.

She had enjoyed her work at the newspaper, finding

it exciting to be in the center of everything. Then, when she'd finally reached her goal, she threw it away by writing that article. She didn't regret it, though. She didn't think she could live with herself if she became a part of the fraud.

Susanna had not told the Kirklands of her unemployment yet, and she wanted to put it off for as long as possible. For the first time, she began to understand why Jesse did not want to work at the store, as spending her days there had to be the most boring job she could imagine.

Susanna had tried to convince herself that her only reason for accepting Rab's invitation to accompany him to Lake Tahoe was to revisit the beautiful countryside. But if she was truthful with herself, she knew that wasn't her reason for going. She wanted to be with Rab one more time before it was too late.

No, this was all wrong. What was she doing? She had no business going with this man. She had given her word to Mr. Kirkland that she would marry Jesse, and she would honor that commitment. But here she was standing on the depot platform, about to leave town with another man. And not just any other man—but the only man who had ever caressed her naked body, evoking the most intimate and intense pleasure she had ever known.

It was ironic, she thought. She had just exposed Loudin as a fraud, but wasn't she just as big a fraud in going off with Rab, wanting Rab, when she was to marry Jesse? She should turn and run away from him right now, because if she did not do it now, she might never be able to do so.

The conductor stepped down from the train and took

his watch from his vest pocket and stretched out the gold chain, which glistened in the morning sun.

"Board!" he called.

In addition to Susanna and Rab, the eleven other passengers started toward the train. The conductor stood by the boarding steps as they got on, occasionally reaching out to help a passenger board. Rab put his hand on Susanna's arm to help her up. When she put her foot on the first step, she hesitated, knowing that this was her moment of truth. Her mind and sense of propriety told her this was wrong, but her heart and her body told her that if she turned back now, she would regret it for the rest of her life.

"Are you all right?" Rab asked.

Susanna took a deep breath, then stepped on into the car. "Yes. I'm fine."

The route from Virginia City to Carson City covered thirteen miles, but had scarcely one mile of straight track. That winding railroad did not seem to concern the engineer as he took the train down the incline at what Susanna thought was breakneck speed. The engine darted through tunnels, which were lined with zinc to prevent belched sparks from igniting the wooden support trusses.

As the train hurtled around the curves and the car rocked back and forth on the uneven tracks, Susanna began to feel a little woozy. Then, on a particularly sharp curve that almost completed a circle, Susanna was pushed by centrifugal force into Rab.

"I didn't know you wanted to sit so close to me," Rab joked as he slid his arm around Susanna and squeezed her closer.

"I'm not sure you want to do that," she said, not chastising him as much as alerting him that she was getting nauseated.

Rab realized what she was saying. "I think the engineer is trying to get us off this mountain as fast as he can," he said reassuringly. "It will only be a few more minutes. Here, I'll keep you from lurching about as much as I can." He left his arm around her shoulders.

Then, mercifully, the train slowed, until finally it came to a full stop at Carson City, where they were to change trains. She was glad that Rab held her arm as they walked through the aisle.

As they stepped down from the train, wisps of steam from the drive cylinder floated by, dissipating quickly. She could hear the snaps and pops of overheated bearings and journals as they cooled.

"Are you feeling better?"

"A little," she said.

"Come with me, I have just the thing to settle your stomach."

Rab led her into the depot and over to the lunchroom.

"Sir, the lady could use some sarsaparilla, if you have it," Rab said.

The man behind the lunch counter chuckled. "Come down from Virginia City, did you?" He drew the drink from a keg and handed it to Susanna. "Yes, sir, we get a lot of queasy stomachs here after that ride."

Susanna took a slow drink of the sweetened root beverage.

From the lunchroom they walked over to the ticket counter.

"How long before you expect the Lake Tahoe train?" Rab asked.

"Shouldn't be more than an hour, I'd say." The man took his watch out of his pocket. "But it could be sooner, you know."

"Thanks," Rab said. "We'd better hurry."

Carson City was like an oasis, not only because of the groves of cottonwood and willow trees in the lush Eagle Valley that spread beside the Carson River, but because of the silence. There were no stamping mills, no sawmills, no ore wagons, no whistles blowing, no mules braying, no ruckus from miners—the only sound was the hissing steam from the V&T locomotive as it pulled out, headed toward Reno.

Rab hurried Susanna to the small building that served as the depot for the recently completed Lake Tahoe Railroad. He was right to hurry her on, because the train was already boarding.

Settling into the car, Susanna realized that she was hungry. She hadn't taken the time to eat before leaving Virginia City, and she was glad that she hadn't. She was certain she would not have been able to take the twisting and turning of the trip down from the mountain on a full stomach.

Beside her, Rab withdrew a red-checked napkin from his pocket. "Hungry?"

"Yes, I'm starving! You have food?"

"Sort of. I have pilot bread." He handed her one of the hard crackers.

"You think of everything," Susanna said. "I don't suppose you have a piece of cheese?"

"You won't need it; you'll find this filling enough. Pilot bread was a staple on board ship, and many are the times that I've gone for days with nothing but this. I do have dessert, though."

"Dessert?"

"Yes, one that, given your delicate stomach now, will be quite good for you." He produced a peppermint.

A man and a woman were sitting opposite Rab and Susanna, and as the train slowly climbed the grade of the mountain, the woman leaned across the aisle. "I've been watching, my dear. Do you know how lucky you are to have such a thoughtful husband?"

Susanna started, "Oh, he's no—"

"—saint, I admit," Rab interrupted her as he clasped her hand in his, "but I keep trying to tell her what a fine man I am. She just won't listen." Rab lifted her hand to his lips and kissed it.

"Are you from these parts?" Susanna asked, trying to change the subject.

"Oh, no, we are the Wisemans from Philadelphia. I am Lily, and this is my husband, Jacob."

"We came here to see what made us rich," Jacob said, "and we weren't disappointed. I thought we were out of the silver-mining business, but now I'm not so sure."

"Did you own a mine?" Rab asked.

"No, just stock. Every time we doubled our money, we sold, no matter how high the stock climbed after that. The Comstock has been good to us," Jacob said, "and now I'm ready to get back into the market."

"I don't suppose we should tell you this," Lily said,

"but we met some men at the Washoe Club back in Virginia City. As soon as we get to San Francisco, we're going to buy a lot of one particular stock. This mine has been on—what do they call it, Jacob?"

"Shutdown?" Susanna asked.

"Yes, that's it!" Lily said enthusiastically. "Then, you know about the North Star Mine, too."

"Yes, I do," Susanna said, but she did not elaborate further. It had been her experience that it was hard to influence people once they had made up their minds about something. Anyway, she didn't have to warn these people about the folly of North Star stock because she knew there would be no further trading in it.

"Excuse me, sir," another gentleman on the train said, "aren't you Rab Trudeau, from San Francisco?"

"Yes, I am. Do I know you?"

"Lucky Baldwin's the name." The man extended his hand to Rab. "I've seen you around town. Last time was at Judge Conrad's the night of your big announcement." The man gave an exaggerated wink to Rab.

"What you see is not what you think," Rab said.

"Tick a lock on my lips," Lucky said, making a motion as if he were locking his mouth.

Susanna wondered about the strange conversation, but because she knew that Rab was a detective, she thought perhaps it had to do with some investigation he had conducted.

The scenery was changing as the train was climbing, and Susanna was feasting on the beauty that surrounded her.

She remembered coming through here on the trip to Virginia City ten years ago, when the Kirkland family had left San Francisco. Mr. Kirkland brought enough supplies to open his store, and the big prairie schooners required as many as sixteen mules to get over the steep grades of the Sierra Nevada. It had been a long, exhausting trip.

As she thought back to that move, she recalled that Jesse, then a man of just twenty, had worked hard during the journey, loading and unloading the wagons as needed when they were too heavy for the teams. He had managed the mules and maintained the wagons. When they reached Virginia City, Jesse had worked beside his father building the new store, assuming it would be established as Kirkland and Son.

It was not. Gus Kirkland expected Jesse to work for him as a salaried employee. That was when Jesse decided he would make his mark at some venture other than Kirkland Emporium.

Susanna could not help but think how different things would be had Gus Kirkland not disappointed his son then. Jesse would no doubt have settled down and been married long before now. Susanna would not be bound by some coerced promise to marry him, and she would be free to love Rab, without reservation, and to win his love in return.

She did love Rab, whether she was free to do so or not. Marrying Jesse would not change that. Susanna reached over to take Rab's hand, and he squeezed hers reassuringly as Mrs. Wiseman looked on, beaming. Susanna blinked several times to hold back the tears as she thought of what could have been.

*   *   *

Once they crested Spooner Summit, Susanna caught her first glimpse of the shimmering blue surface of Lake Tahoe as it peeked out from between the tall pines.

"Thank you, Rab, I'm really glad I came," Susanna said softly. "I think sometimes I can almost forget how beautiful the world really is, when all I see is rocks and barren dirt."

"I'm glad you came, too."

When the train stopped on Spooner Summit, Rab and Susanna were the only ones to get off.

"My business won't take long," Rab said, "then we can go on down to the lake and explore. But I expect you had better stay with me because there are men everywhere, and in case you haven't noticed, every one of them is looking at you."

Rab walked over to the Carson and Tahoe Lumber and Fluming Company office, where he entered without knocking.

A tall, thin, gray-haired man looked up from his desk, then smiled broadly. Getting up, he came across the room with his hand extended.

"Rab Trudeau, you old son of a gun! What are you doing way up here in God's country? It's been a while."

"What do you mean *old*? I'm not the one with gray hair."

The man ran his hand through his hair. "It's not gray, it's brindled."

"Duane, I'd like you to meet a special young woman. Susanna Ward, this is Duane Bliss."

"How do you do, Mr. Bliss?" Susanna said, recognizing the name of one of the main financiers of the lumber operation and the V&T Railroad. She did not know what else to say.

"Very well, thank you, ma'am. And what may I do for you, Rab?"

"I need to sign some more contracts, and then we'll get out of your way. I could have sent David, but you know how it is with him and Lila. They just had a new baby and he needs to get back to San Francisco as soon as possible."

"Boy or girl?"

"Boy."

"Ha! I'll bet David is happy about that, after that house full of girls. Will you be here for long? You've seen the new Glenbrook House I've built, haven't you? People are calling it the Saratoga of the West."

"We will more than likely have our lunch there, but we're taking the last train back to Carson City this afternoon," Rab said.

"That's a shame. I'm sure Miss Ward—it is *Miss,* is it not?—would appreciate the evening. But I'll get the paperwork ready for your signature and have someone meet the last train."

The telegraph keys began to rattle, and he turned toward the operator. "Market report?"

"Yes, sir," the telegrapher replied.

Bliss turned his attention back to Rab. "How large is the contract?"

"Half a million board feet of lumber and twenty thousand cords of wood should do it for now," Rab said as he ushered Susanna out the door.

Susanna was furious when she left the office of the CTLFC, as the fluming company was known.

"There is something you have not told me about who you are. The superintendent at the Silver Falcon, the men down in the mine, the man on the train—they all know who you are, and yet you say you are a detective. And you just committed to a half million board feet of timber. Mr. Trudeau, I may not be a detective, but until recently I was a newspaper reporter. Mr. Duane Bliss is a very important man, and he doesn't know every jackass that comes along."

Susanna hurried across the marshaling yard, dodging men and mules.

"Wait, where are you going, Susanna?" Rab called.

"I'm going to be on the next train that comes over that hill on my way back to Carson City."

"Please, don't go," Rab said, overtaking Susanna. He turned her toward Lake Tahoe. "Look down onto this beautiful site. You said yourself how glad you were to be here. Let's enjoy it together, and I will try to answer any question you may have about anything."

Susanna saw the image of the snowcapped mountains reflected in the most brilliant blue and green water of the lake. Then she looked at Rab, his eyes seeming to plead with her. For the first time since she had known him, she sensed an uncertainty, a vulnerability, about him. It touched her. The anger she had toward him seemed to melt away.

"Now you'll give me an interview? It's too late. I was fired, you know," Susanna said, her face softening into a grin.

"This isn't about work. I want to spend the day with a woman I find to be spirited and refreshing and beautiful. Will you spend the day with me?"

Susanna didn't answer.

"Even if I am a jackass?"

Susanna flushed with color. "I can't believe I said that, but . . ."

"On the other hand," Rab said, with a flash of humor in his eyes, "if you really want to go back to Carson City, you could ride a log down the flume and be there in about fifteen minutes. But as for me, I'm ready to catch a ride with the next whistle punk we see going down the hill."

"Whistle punk?"

"You'll see," Rab said without further explanation.

"I could write a great story about all this," Susanna said as she looked around at all the activity.

"You loved your job, didn't you?"

"Yes. While I had it," she added with a sense of regret.

"Susanna, the article you wrote about Loudin and the North Star owners had to be written, and it had to be written by someone who had not only the talent but the courage and great strength of character. Someone like you. Do you have any idea how proud I am of you? How proud the entire Comstock is going to be of you when the story gets around?"

"I don't know; I didn't think about that."

"No, you didn't think about that. But you certainly

knew you would lose your job when the paper came out, didn't you?"

"Yes, I knew that."

"But you did it anyway. That's what I mean about showing courage. But that brings up a question. What are you going to do now?"

Susanna looked away, not daring to look at him, for fear he might be able to read what she would really like—to be taken away by a prince, a prince who in her imagination looked exactly like Rab Trudeau.

"Mr. Kirkland has always wanted me to work at the store. I suppose I will do that."

"But you don't want to, do you?"

"No."

"Have you ever thought about leaving Virginia City? You could go anywhere you wanted to."

"That's easier said than done. Look at Annie. She is one of the most intelligent, caring women I have ever known, and look what she has to do. Some people are in a trap of their own making."

Susanna thought of her own trap, then she consciously put it out of her mind. For this one day she was going to be free of any sense of guilt, any self-recriminations. For this one day she was going to build memories that would last a lifetime.

They heard an engine starting.

"You wanted to know about a whistle punk?" Rab asked. "There it is, but we'd better hurry."

Both Rab and Susanna moved quickly between the logs, reaching the train before it reached the incline and picked up speed. Rab hoisted Susanna unceremoniously, exposing her legs as she landed on the flatcar. Then he bounded up beside her. "Madam, I believe you are exposed," he said as he pulled down her skirt, restoring her modesty.

If Rab only knew how exposed she really was.

When the little train reached the bottom of the hill, Rab and Susanna hopped down, then started walking through the towering pines. The air was perfumed with the smell of pine bark and pine needles. Susanna was pleased to see that great as the demand for lumber was, so far little impact seemed to have been made on the woods that skirted the lake.

"Listen," Susanna said. "Isn't that the most beautiful sound you have ever heard?"

Rab cocked his head, trying to hear what Susanna was referencing. "What? I don't hear anything."

Susanna smiled. "I know, and that's just it. It's like we are in a cocoon."

At that moment, a stellar jay with its deep blue feathers and crested head began to squawk a greeting.

Susanna chuckled. "All right, we are in a cocoon with a blue jay. My, do you have any idea how long it has been since I have heard a bird that isn't a vulture? It makes you wonder why anyone would stay in Virginia City, no matter how much money can be made there."

"I said it before, and I will say it again. You don't have to stay in Virginia City. You've lost your job, and you don't want to work at Kirkland Emporium. Why don't you come with me to San Francisco?"

Almost as soon as he spoke the words, Rab wished that he could call them back. It was what he wanted; he realized that, now more than anything. He wanted this woman, and not just for the moment, but for the rest of his life. But his life in California was so complicated. He could not subject Susanna to all that—not until he was able to extricate himself from his predicament, and that he intended to do.

Emmaline's answer to his questions about love had given him all the confirmation he needed to break off his engagement. He now believed that there was more honor in telling Margaret he did not love her than in committing her to a lifetime of unhappiness.

"Do you truly mean that?" Susanna asked, her eyes glimmering as tears of happiness began to gather. So moved was she by the request that she had not even noticed Rab's introspection.

Rab said nothing. He took her in his arms, his eyes penetrating into her soul. Then his lips found hers. His kiss was as gentle as a summer breeze, and then it deepened, causing shivers of delight to race through her.

She returned the kiss with a hunger she was not aware she had. In her entire life she had never felt such happiness, such a sense of satisfaction. She knew, too, that this was not an act on Rab's part. This was genuine, and this was exactly where she was supposed to be.

When at last they separated, Rab began to lead her out of the trees. "How about lunch?"

"Lunch? You kiss me like that, then you ask if I want lunch?"

"Kissing makes me hungry," Rab said.

Susanna laughed. "All right, we'll have lunch. Do you have another piece of pilot bread in your pocket?"

"No, this time we will have a proper lunch at the Glenbrook House."

The Glenbrook House was made of logs, but it was the largest log structure Susanna had ever seen. Inside the lobby there were etched-glass panels, a large stone fireplace, timber columns, and handcrafted furniture. Buffalo rugs were strewn about, and the walls were festooned with antlers and stuffed trophy heads.

A maître d' met them at the entrance to the dining room, and they were escorted to a table.

"I know that there are many places in Virginia City that pride themselves on having no Chinese working for them, but Duane has an outstanding Chinese chef."

"Duane? You are on a first-name basis with Duane Bliss?"

"Well, we've known each other for a while," Rab said dismissively. "Have you ever eaten Chinese food?"

"No, but I'm sure you have."

"Sure. Remember, San Francisco has a big Chinese district. But you might be surprised to know that I've also eaten Chinese food in Shanghai and Hong Kong."

"Rab Trudeau, I'm not sure there is anything about you that could surprise me now," Susanna said, the words not testy, but deferential.

"Shall I order?"

"Don't tell me you can speak Chinese?"

"I can get along in restaurants."

When the waiter arrived, Rab ordered. "We'll have wonton soup, ma yi shang shu, and chow fun."

After the waiter left, Susanna laughed. "The only word I understood was 'soup'."

"I ordered wonton soup—which is soup with stuffed dumplings—ants climbing trees, and rice noodles."

"What? 'Ants climbing trees'? You can't be serious!"

Rab laughed. "That's just what it's called. Actually it's spiced pork, and it's very good."

During their meal, Lily and Jacob Wiseman stopped by their table.

"We're taking the excursion boat across the lake into California, and then on to Yosemite," Jacob said. "We were wondering if you would like to join us."

"Thank you for the invitation," Rab said. "But I have some business I must attend to in Glenbrook."

"Do have a pleasant trip, though," Susanna added.

❊ 19 ❊

After the meal, they walked down to the edge of the lake.

"Beautiful, isn't it?" Rab asked.

"That word is almost inadequate," Susanna replied. "If God made any place more beautiful than this, He kept it for Himself."

"How would you like to take a boat trip? I'd like you to meet someone. Be prepared, he is an old curmudgeon, but he is a friend of mine. Yank Clements."

"All right."

Several rowboats were pulled up onto the pier, and Rab made arrangements for one; then he and Susanna got into the boat and Rab rowed them about a hundred yards out into the lake. The shore of the lake wasn't straight, but had several bays and coves, along which were narrow strips of sandy beaches. The lake was surrounded by mountains that rose blue and purple from a wooded area, thick with tall pines, and crowned with snow, even in midsummer.

Susanna looked down into the water, amazed at how clear it was. She could see pebbles that were at least twenty feet down as clearly as if they were on the other side of a glass. She could also see speckled trout, which because of the transparency of the water had the appearance of hanging in midair.

They had gone about a mile when Susanna saw on the shore a field of bursting color from its many wildflowers.

"Oh, Rab," she said, pointing. "Please put in over there. Aren't the flowers beautiful? I'd like to gather a bouquet."

"Your wish is my command, madam." Rab turned the boat, then rowed it ashore.

"Better let me get out first so I can pull it out of the water," Rab said when the bow of the boat touched the sand. Picking up the rope, Rab stepped easily over the prow and onto the ground.

Watching the grace and ease with which he did this, Susanna laughed.

"Why are you laughing?"

"As you were stepping from the boat, I suddenly got the image of a pirate landing on a deserted island to bury his treasure."

"Really? Would you like to go to a deserted island? Well, maybe not deserted, but a place like Pago Pago?"

"Where is Pago Pago?"

"It's in the South Pacific. Coconut trees, sandy beaches, balmy breezes—it is an island paradise."

"Oh, how wonderful that sounds! Yes, I would love to go there with you."

As Rab tugged on the rope, pulling the boat completely out of the water to make it easier for Susanna to step out, he couldn't help but compare her response with the different response Margaret had made to the same question.

About a quarter of a mile away, a dozen cows were grazing in the meadow.

"Oh, look at them," Susanna said.

"Look at the cows?"

"No, the flowers," Susanna said with a chuckle. She went immediately into the field of daisies, arrowleaf, paintbrush, larkspur, and violets. Within moments she had assembled a bouquet, artfully arranging the colors.

"What do you think?" she asked, returning with the bouquet.

"I think you would make a Japanese master of ikebana envious," Rab said.

Susanna sat down. "Let's stay for a while. I can't imagine a more lovely place on earth than this."

Rab sat with her. In the distance they could hear the tinkle of a single cowbell. Closer in was the soft whisper of nearby pines, and closer still, bees hummed as they darted from flower to flower, gathering nectar. Yellow, purple, and blue butterflies competed with the flowers in their vivid display of color.

Susanna turned and spread her shawl on the ground behind her, then lay down and looked up at the sky. "Have you ever made pictures from clouds?"

"Sure I have." He looked up, then pointed. "Look, there is a knight, riding a white charger, rushing to save his lady fair."

"Is he clutching her from the street, out of the way of a runaway wagon?"

"I'm not a knight, Susanna."

Susanna sat up. "Sure you are. The only difference is, you ride a bay."

A daisy was hanging from Susanna's hair, and Rab reached up to pull it away. As he did so, her hair began to tumble loose, and she started to put it back in her chignon.

"No," Rab said quietly. "Let your hair down. You should wear it down."

"I don't wear it down because it could get caught in the printing press."

Rab looked around the meadow. "Do you see any printing presses here?"

Susanna laughed. "No, I don't." She began taking out the pins, allowing her hair to tumble freely.

Rab put his fingers to her cheek, and Susanna was shocked by the impact of that simple touch. It was as if his fingers were magic wands sending tingles through her entire body. She reached up to put her hand on his, not to push it away, but to hold it. It was strong, hard, masculine, yes, but she knew from experience it was capable of the most divine gentleness and the most delightful caresses.

Rab looked at her, a long, slow, appraising study that caused her breathing to become more shallow. He leaned toward her and kissed her, a light kiss that disappointed her because she wanted more. Then he kissed her again, as lightly as the first time. When he kissed her a third time, she opened her lips to his and felt his tongue as he probed the cage of her mouth.

Hungrily, Susanna responded to him, running her hand through his coarse black hair, drawing him closer to her. Then, separating from him, she lay down and looked up at him, at those dark, expressive eyes—eyes that could melt her at a glance. He lay down beside her and, putting his arm out, pulled her head onto his shoulder. Not at any time since her parents died had Susanna felt more secure, or more cared for, than she did at this moment.

"Ask me," he said.

"Ask you what?"

"Ask me anything you want."

"You'll laugh if I tell you what I really want to know."

"Try me."

"What were you like as a little boy?"

Rab chuckled.

"See, I told you you would laugh."

"I'm sorry."

"Tell me. What were you like?"

"All right. I was a happy little boy, raised in the South, in Louisiana where my grandfather owned a sugar refinery. My father owned Rivière de Joie. He also had cargo ships to take sugar all over the world. Life was good. I had a loving family, an older brother that I looked up to and a younger sister that I adored. As children our lives were all planned out. My older brother, Charles, would run the sugar plantation, I would manage the shipping company, my cousin Pierre would operate the sugar refinery, and my sister, Emmaline, would marry some nice boy from one of the other plantations in the parish and have babies.

"You would love her." Rab smiled. "She married, all right, but it was to a Yankee from Ohio, and you can bet Father didn't much like that. But now I don't know what he would do without Randolph and their two boys. Little Rab and Beau run and hide in the canebrakes just like Charles and Pierre and I used to."

"Where are Charles and Pierre now? Are they still in Louisiana?"

Rab was quiet for a long moment and, sensing his melancholy, Susanna wished she had not asked the question.

"They are both dead. Charles was killed in the war." Subconsciously, Rab reached for his scar. "And Pierre was killed in a foolish and senseless duel. Honor," he said, though he practically spat the word.

"I'm sorry, Rab. I'm sorry I brought it up."

"Nonsense. You wanted to know about my history; you had every right to ask."

"Let's not talk anymore," Susanna said.

"You don't want to talk?"

"No."

Susanna lifted her head up from his shoulder and looked down at him, her long hair falling forward. She dipped down to kiss him, and when their lips touched, he responded, but took no action to push it further. She pulled away from him just far enough to be able to see him, to try to gauge his thoughts right now.

He lifted his hand and put a finger on her lips. She drew the tip of the finger into her mouth for just a moment, then bent down to kiss him yet again, taking the lead. She opened her mouth on his, he responded, and the kiss deepened as she probed his mouth with her tongue as he had hers a few moments earlier.

With a groan deep in his throat, Rab reversed their positions, putting Susanna on the ground and moving over her. He looked down at her, trembling in excitement, feeling himself growing, pushing against the restriction of his trousers, afraid that by her kisses and touch alone he might not be able to contain himself, that he might lose control like some virgin adolescent who was doing this for the first time.

Rab was not without experience, from the beautiful quadroons of the houses of pleasure in New Orleans, to the exotic flowers of the Orient, to the sophisticated ladies of France, to the bawdy beauties of San Francisco. Yet, no woman anywhere in the world had ever enflamed Rab's passions to this level.

He wanted her more than he had ever wanted any other woman in his life. He wanted her to share the heat of his passion—more than that, he wanted her to share his soul. There was only one way to do that, and that was to possess her completely.

His kisses left her lips, then trailed down her throat. When he got to the top of her blouse, he unfastened the first button and kissed her skin there.

Rab continued downward, laying open the waist, then kissing the skin beneath. When her shirt was out

of the way, he started on the ribbons that held her camisole closed. Nipping at them with his teeth, feeling the
sensation of her soft breasts against his face, he released
the camisole as well, so that Susanna was naked from her
throat to the waistband of her skirt. Her fine, firm breasts
were displayed before his eyes.

Susanna felt a wetness between her thighs; had it
not been for her experience in the bathtub at the mine,
she would not have known what it was. She knew now,
though, and was aware not only of her own excitation,
but of the pulsing sexuality that seemed to pass, like
electricity, between his body and hers. The cool and
flower-scented air on her naked breasts, as well as Rab's
ministrations, caused her nipples to harden, and when
Rab cupped one breast in his hand and began rubbing the
nipple with his thumb, she felt wave after wave of sensual
delight pass over her. Then, when he put his mouth on
her other breast, using his tongue to make circular mo-
tions around her nipple, sometimes sucking it, sometimes
biting it gently, ever so gently, she knew they were one—
she was feeling what he was feeling, and he was feeling
what she was.

Never in her life, not even in the bathtub at the mine,
had Susanna experienced an arousal this intense, a burning need that was crying out for completion.

Rab's hand moved down until it touched her navel,
and though she thought he was going to go farther, she
wanted him to go farther, as he began to explore it with
his finger, she was surprised at the sensations that evoked.
Then, loosening her skirt, he stuck his hand under the

waistband, and Susanna, lost in the eroticism of the moment, lifted her bottom from the ground to invite him to lower her clothing.

Susanna was nearly naked, outside, lying on her shawl.

Rab looked down at her. No nude painted by Peter Paul Rubens could match her beauty, her sensuality, her eroticism. Rab's hands returned to her body, one back to her breast, the other down to the little silken mound of hair at the junction of her legs. He felt the wetness as he pushed his fingers in through the fold of flesh.

When she felt his fingers slip into that part of her that was now burning with desire, aching with the need for fulfillment, she wanted to cry out in the ecstasy of it. He pushed them in through the moistness and began to massage that little nub that was the center of all her craving, and she started writhing beneath his fingers, lifting herself against them, drawing them into her, knowing that it was but a presage of what was to come.

"Rab!" she said, the word a cross between a moan and a sigh.

Then Rab's mouth left her breast, and he began working his way down her body, into the hollow of her stomach, where his tongue repeated the action his fingers had taken earlier, only this time eliciting much more sensation than had his fingers.

From her navel he moved slowly back up to her throat, his tongue leaving a trail of exquisite torture on her burning skin; then came another deep kiss while his fingers continued to elicit the most delightful sensations at her very core.

"Oh, Rab. Please, please."

Please what? She was hanging on the edge knowing there was more, wanting more, and asking for it with words that were a moaning plea.

Rab rose up then and, smiling down at her, removed his shirt and began to unbutton his trousers.

"My God, you are beautiful," he said, the words a roll of timpani that resonated in her soul.

Her eyes were drawn to the bulge in his pants, and she was mesmerized as he continued to open the buttons. She had seen him naked before, yes, but never like this, and the anticipation was almost more than she could bear. Susanna waited, ready with every fiber and nerve ending of her body for what was to come next.

He opened his trousers and she saw him then, a huge thing of fear and beauty, forcing itself free of restraint, ready for . . . she closed her eyes.

"Oh, oh," Rab said, and the quiet words broke the spell.

Susanna opened her eyes and saw Rab rebuttoning his trousers and looking away.

"Rab, what is it?"

"Get dressed. We'd better get back in the boat."

"Rab, no, not now, not now."

Rab kissed her, a gentle, calming kiss, and he held her tenderly. "I'm sorry, my love, there will be another time. But we have company."

"What?" she gasped, sitting up and drawing her shirt closed across her bare bosom.

Rab pointed. "The cows are here. And the folks that tend them are just across the field, and coming this way."

"Oh! Oh, my!" Susanna quickly sat up and reached for her skirt.

Rab laughed quietly.

"It isn't funny," Susanna complained.

She had never experienced anything quite like this. She had been taken to the edge of a great mystery, she had glimpsed a pleasure that was promised but denied. She was dangling over the edge of a precipice, her body still tingling with sensations, but aching with an unfulfilled desire for more.

As Susanna was dressing, Rab started over toward the cows. "Shoo! Get away!"

Moo.

"Get away, I said!" Rab waved his arms, but the cow that had mooed walked right up to him.

Behind him, Rab heard Susanna laughing. "I guess you aren't very frightening to them."

"Dumb cows," Rab mumbled as he came back. "You ready?"

"Yes."

"Not quite ready."

"What do you mean?"

Rab bent over to pick up the bouquet. "You forgot this."

Smiling, Susanna took the bouquet; then hand in hand they ran, like a couple of schoolchildren, to the boat.

Rab helped her get in, pushed the boat back out into the water, then leaped athletically from the shore even as the gap was widening.

A breeze had come up, and not only was the wind

against them, it caused waves to form on the surface of the lake, but it did not seem to bother Rab as he rowed effortlessly through the choppy water.

"I guess we're going to have to visit Yank some other time," he said. "If we want to catch the train to Virginia City, we'd better get back."

As Susanna watched him, almost unbidden she recalled a passage from one of her father's last letters before he and her mother were married. She had read it so many times it was now committed to memory.

> *My darling. When I think of my love for you, it is as if I have been plucked from the deepest woods on the darkest night, and thrust, suddenly, into the sunlight. Has anyone ever loved another more than I love you? I think that is not possible, for when you breathe, my lungs fill with air, when you drink, my thirst is slaked.*

For the first time, Susanna fully understood the true meaning of her father's words. She felt that Rab had plucked her from her deepest darkness, and now she was basking in his sunlight. More than anything else in the world, she wanted to be with this man, she wanted to complete what they had started.

And she knew this was love.

When they returned to the pier, Duane Bliss was waiting for them.

"Rab, I'm afraid I have some bad news for you."

"Bad news? Did something happen at the mine?"

"Oh, no, nothing like that. It's just that the engine's pony-truck axle broke, so the train won't be here until tomorrow morning."

Rab looked toward Susanna. "I'm sorry. I know I promised to get you back to Virginia City tonight."

"Don't be sorry; it's not your fault." Susanna smiled. "And it isn't as if I have to be at work tomorrow."

"Then, let's get us a couple of rooms in the hotel," Rab said. "It might be nice to spend the night out here anyway."

"Oh, I wish you could," Duane said. "But a lot of folks who hadn't planned on it have to stay now because of the train problem. I'm afraid there aren't any rooms left at the Glenbrook House. But"—he held a finger up—"I sent word to Yank. He's holding a cabin for you."

A cabin? Rab thought. *One cabin?* Again, he looked at Susanna.

"Thank you, Mr. Bliss. That was good of you to think of us," Susanna said.

"There's a man from San Francisco who is doing some business with Yank, and he'll be going down in the carryall in a minute. I'll tell him he has two passengers," Duane said. "Oh, I forgot your contracts, but I'll have them in the morning."

"Thanks," Rab said.

Just then the surrey pulled up and stopped. Lucky Baldwin, the man they had met on the train, was the driver.

"I guess we're all sorry for this little unforeseen delay," Baldwin said, a sardonic grin crossing his face.

The inference was not lost on Rab, and he looked pointedly at Baldwin as he and Susanna climbed into the backseat of the surrey. Baldwin snapped the reins and the horse started out at a brisk trot.

"How are things at Sunset Enterprises?" Baldwin called over his shoulder. "Has the spur line connecting the C.P. with the Northern Pacific come through yet? I heard you were in negotiation."

"Not yet," Rab said, feeling Susanna's quick reaction to the question.

"Well, there's no doubt in my mind that you'll pull it off. With a shipping line, a stagecoach line, and your freighting operation, you may as well get into the railroad business." Baldwin chuckled. "I swear, if they figured out how to carry freight on a balloon, why, I'm sure you'd get in on that, too."

The surrey stopped in a little clearing beside the lake. A log building served as a supply store, with three or four small cabins nestled among the trees. Rab and Susanna entered the building and were greeted by a big, barrel-chested man with a long, white beard.

"There you are," the man said. "I heard you were here. It's good to see you and to meet your young lady. She's sure a pretty little thing."

"Yank, this is Susanna Ward, and I agree with everything you just said. I hear you're saving a cabin for us."

"Yes, sir. I'm putting you in what some call the honeymoon cabin. It's set a little apart from all the rest, so nobody will bother you."

Rab shook his head as he began to laugh. "You're getting a little ahead of yourself, my friend. Give me a couple of your thickest blankets and we'll be just fine."

"Well, all right, if that's the way it is," Yank said as he handed the blankets to Rab. "It was good to meet you, madam."

"It's good to meet you, too," Susanna said.

"We'd better get a bite to eat before we go to the cabin," Rab said. "Yank only makes one pot of stew, and when it's gone, that's it."

The stew was in a large, black iron kettle that hung over an open fire. On a table beside the pot were several tin plates and spoons, and a large basket of sourdough bread, butter, and honey.

"This smells delicious," Susanna said. "I didn't realize how hungry I was."

"It's the fresh mountain air—and the activity—that always makes you hungry," Rab said.

He filled one dish and handed it to Susanna, then filled another one for himself. He carved off a couple pieces of the bread, then spread butter and honey on each piece.

"Enjoy the butter," he said. "We probably met the cow that produced it. As well as the bees that made the honey."

Susanna smiled as she placed the bouquet on the table beside her plate. She recalled the afternoon, and as she did so, she felt a small rush of pleasure. Her cheeks began to flush.

"Go ahead," he said. "Ask it. I know you're dying to. And as I told you, I will answer, truthfully, anything you ask."

"Sunset Enterprises owns the Silver Falcon Mine."

"Yes."

"So, tell me, Rab, what do you have to do with Sunset Enterprises?"

"You should try the stew with some crushed red peppers."

Susanna had made no move toward her food. Instead, she was looking at Rab, waiting for the answer. Only, she was fairly certain she already knew the answer. "May I answer for you?"

"All right." Rab made liberal use of the crushed red peppers on his own plate.

"You have stock in Sunset Enterprises."

"Sort of."

"What do you mean, 'sort of'?"

"Except for the Silver Falcon, which of course does issue stock, the rest of Sunset Enterprises is privately held."

"Who owns it?"

"David DeLoitte owns thirty percent." Rab took a bite of his stew. "Uhmm, this is good."

"And?"

"I own seventy percent. Do try your stew. It is awfully good."

Susanna's mouth dropped open. She had already determined that Rab was not who he had said he was—a detective—but she'd never dreamed he was as wealthy as any of the barons on the Comstock. Immediately, she felt intimidated. Who was she, really? An orphan who had to have someone paid to take her. She felt a sinking feeling in her stomach as the realization that she loved this man with all her heart dawned on her, and now she could never have him.

Susanna looked hard at Rab. He was sitting across the table from her, eating out of a tin pie pan. He was the same man she had known this morning, and the day before that, and the week before that. She knew he cared for her—even if he was a rich man. She made up her mind right then that she would not walk away from the joy that he had brought to her. She would make him fall in love with her, just as her father had loved her mother.

She picked up her spoon and ate her stew in silence.

❋ 20 ❋

When they entered the cabin, Susanna was struck by just how small it was. It had a bed with a headboard made of peeled tree limbs, a fireplace, and a dry sink with a bowl and pitcher of water. A straight-back chair sat in the corner, and that was it.

"I'll start a fire for you before I go," Rab said as he struck a match to the kindling. "It will probably get pretty chilly tonight."

"Where are you going?"

"I've got my blankets. I'll just go down on the sand and bed down."

"No."

"You'll be all right," Rab said as he came back to her. "I'll be just outside. If you need me, I'll hear you."

"Don't go, Rab," Susanna said in a bare whisper.

"But there isn't any room in here."

Susanna looked toward the bed, then back to Rab, her eyes conveying what words could not say.

"Oh, Susanna," Rab pulled her to him. "I want you more than you know, but this will have to be your choice."

"I've made my choice. I want you."

Susanna extinguished the lamp, but the room didn't grow dark. Instead, it was lit by the flickering glow of the flames that danced in the fireplace. A little bubble of gas, trapped in one of the logs, ignited and burst with a pop that sent up a small shower of sparks.

Susanna started to remove her blouse, for the second time that day, but as she reached for the first button, she stopped, then smiled at Rab, who, standing there, had made no motion toward removing his own clothes.

"Huh, uh," she said. "Not this time."

"Not this time what?"

"I am not the only one who is going to undress."

Rab returned the smile, then began taking off his own clothes, matching Susanna's movements, button by button. When he removed his shirt, he stood there for a moment, and now, with no pretense of accidental observation, and without embarrassment, she studied him at her leisure. His shoulders were broad, his chest powerful, his bare arms corded with muscle. His skin gleamed by the light dancing from the fireplace.

She saw the intensity with which he was watching her as she removed her camisole. His eyes shone, not only because they had captured the fire's glow, but from some inner light that reflected his desire for her. She knew that her body pleased him, as much as his pleased her.

Loosening her skirt, she waited until he pulled off his boots and unbuttoned his trousers. Then she slid her skirt and drawers down, as he slid down his trousers.

She started to lift one foot to remove her shoes, but he stopped her.

"Let me," he said, leading her gently to the edge of the bed. Reaching for her, he raised one of her feet, took off her shoe, then removed her garter and rolled down her stocking. He lifted her foot to his cheek.

Susanna had never even considered that she could experience sexual pleasure from something like this, but the feel of her foot against the rough texture of his cheek stubble sent tingles of excitement coursing through her. He did the same thing with the other foot, but then he went a step further. He began kissing the arch, the ankle, and, lifting her leg, the back of her knee. Susanna lay back on the bed and groaned from this totally unexpected source of pleasure.

Rab gently repositioned her so that he had room to lie beside her.

Susanna turned to him as soon as he was in bed, and as her nude body molded against his, her heart began to hammer. When he kissed her, she breathed the scent of him. His hand trailed across her smooth skin, causing her to throb with anticipation, and she moaned in pleasure as her own hands began to explore his body. They kissed again, a kiss that went beyond passion to become one of exploration and wonder. It was a lovers' kiss, unique in all the world because it had a taste that was neither hers nor his, but theirs.

This time Susanna began the exploration, pushing her hand down across his hard, muscled body until she made the discovery of a steel-hard shaft that grew even longer as she grasped it, throbbing with a pulse of its own. Never had she touched a man there, and the exploration of it became an exercise of touch and measurement, not only enlightening, but exhilarating. She knew that she was causing him to grow and stiffen, that he was reacting to her, and that knowledge gave her a wondrous sense of power.

She felt Rab reach down to take her hand in his, but then he surprised her by pulling it away. She looked at him questioningly.

"You can't keep that up, my sweet, or this will end before we can get it started."

He chuckled when the expression in her eyes indicated that she wasn't sure she understood what he was talking about.

"Trust me."

His words were muffled because he spoke them even as his mouth covered hers in another kiss, which, while now familiar to her, was even sweeter because of their shared intimacy. He took some of her hair into his hand, then ran his fingers through it as he continued to kiss her lips and stroke her body.

Susanna was on fire. She knew that this time there would be no holding back, no interruption. This time she would experience something new, she would complete what had, until now, only been started. Without conscious awareness of what she was doing, she began to writhe on the bed, not only in anticipation, but in some ancient and primeval sign from woman to man that she was ready for him.

Rab moved over her then, and Susanna knew intuitively that this should not be, could not be, and would not be rushed. She felt him slide in through her moist cleft.

Then, suddenly, and quite unexpectedly, she felt a sharp pain, and she made a little sound.

"The pain will be over in but a moment, my love," Rab said reassuringly, and even as he was speaking the words, the pain disappeared, to be replaced by exquisite sensations that fulfilled every promise and expectation she had been denied earlier this afternoon in the meadow.

Rab was giving her what she desired and needed, but more than that, he was giving her what she wanted, but dared not ask for. His tongue was both gentle and rough, tentative and demanding, enticing and frightening, and she sought it eagerly, lost in the sensations that were overcoming her.

From the fireplace, Rab and Susanna could hear the snapping and popping of the burning logs. From outside they could hear the pine trees sighing in the wind, as well as the lapping of the water. It was as if nature's own music were being orchestrated just for them, in rhythm and note, tone and tint, to their own racing pulse.

As they continued to make love, all thought and awareness of anything beyond themselves ceased. There was only pleasure, the feel of his tongue against hers, the rake of her fingernails across his back, and the soft suppleness of her body, molded so completely against his hard frame.

Outside, they heard someone call out to another, but they were unaware of the presence of anyone else in this place. They were only two in their private world, caught up in the sensations that were spinning inexorably toward a conclusion not yet achieved.

Susanna felt the penetration, long and deep, probing into that part of her never before touched, and she marveled that her body had a part that she had not only never felt before, but was not even aware of. She rose to meet him, squeezing down on him, not wanting him to withdraw but savoring the anticipation of the next sensuality-laden stroke. As they continued, she began to feel, in addition to the pleasure of the moment, the power of her own sexuality. She lifted her legs, making a *V* of them, no longer the eager and inexperienced student, but a confident and capable woman, secure in her sexual power.

The strokes grew stronger, faster, and her own reaction to them, augmented by skills just learned, started a maelstrom of consciousness deep inside, like the low rumble of thunder rolling over distant mountains. But the sensations grew, heightened, then spun out of control, bursting through her like a simultaneous bolt of lightning and booming thunderclap.

She lost control, screaming out his name, not knowing or even caring if anyone outside, or in any of the other cabins, could hear her. Then, even as she was still experiencing that peak, she felt another, and another still, until they came so close together that it was like one large explosion that carried her to the stars.

Rab had been close many times, but each time he came close, he fought it off, sustaining the drive by sheer will, until he was certain that he had brought Susanna to her zenith. Then, feeling her explode around him, literally as her moist chamber throbbed and massaged his shaft, he knew he could hold off no longer, and he let go, groaning in ecstasy as he emptied himself into her. Then, totally satiated, he pulled himself out of her and lay beside her, cradling her head on his shoulder, his arm wrapped around her, feeling the gradually receding heat of her body.

After a long moment of quiet, Susanna asked, her voice quiet and tentative, "Rab?"

"I'm here." Rab recognized the trepidation in her voice, so he said nothing more, deciding to let her lead the conversation.

"I'm a little frightened."

"Don't be."

"What if I got . . ."

"What was your father's name?"

"What?" Susanna didn't understand this sudden change in the conversation, and she was somewhat discomfited by it. "His name was Byron."

Rab pulled her tightly against him. "Then, we'll name him Byron."

A wave of relief swept over her. He had just told her by that answer that he loved her.

As she sat next to the window on the train, Susanna smiled. She didn't really need a train to get her back to Virginia City; she could have floated back on a cloud. She had no hint of the motion sickness that had affected her yesterday, and she was even able to find beauty in the way the sun played upon the bare mountains. Why had she thought this area was so ugly? She knew the answer to her own question. She had found it ugly because the eyes that had beheld the rock piles, holes, crevices, and smoke-belching mills for the last few years were the eyes of a different woman. Today, she was looking at everything from a totally different perspective. Today, she was looking at the scenery through the eyes of a woman in love.

She thought of the last twenty-four hours and realized how easily such thoughts could bring back to the surface not only the memories of those pleasurable sensations, but their awakening. Right now, she wasn't just remembering them, she was actually experiencing them.

Susanna looked over toward Rab, who was on the seat beside her. He was napping, and she reached down to put her hand on his. This proprietary touch was intimate because she was putting herself into his sleep, as it were.

Susanna had never been happier in her life. Having lost her job, her long and somewhat strained relationship with the Kirkland family, even her foolish agreement to marry Jesse, meant nothing to her now. She was in love, and nothing could go wrong.

Margaret Worthington was wearing a fawn-colored, velvet silk dress, ribbons streaming from the several flounces that puffed behind. She could not have looked more out of place for Virginia City as she stepped out to the edge of the depot platform and looked down the track. "You are sure he will be back on today's train?"

"He'll be back today," David assured her. "The only reason he didn't come back yesterday was because there was a problem with the train that runs between Glenbrook and Carson City."

"I am so anxious to see him." Margaret touched her blond hair. "How do I look? Will I look all right to him?"

"You look beautiful, Margaret, as you always do."

Margaret had arrived in Virginia City yesterday morning, shortly after Rab had left. David didn't know how Rab would react to her "surprise" visit, but he was reasonably sure he wasn't going to be too happy about it.

"But I still don't know why you went to all the trouble of coming here. Don't you have a wedding to be planning?"

"You didn't think I would stay away after Lila told me that Rab was in danger, did you?"

"I shouldn't have sent that telegram to her," David said. "It's all over now. And your being by his side might even have made it worse."

"Nonsense. When Rab is in trouble or danger, by his side is exactly where I am supposed to be."

They heard a distant whistle, but because the train was on the other side of the tunnel, it couldn't yet be seen. Then it was close enough for them to hear the echoing of the chugging as it rolled through the tunnel, and finally it came clear, already slowing down for its approach to the station.

"Do you think he will be happy to see me?" Margaret asked, again touching her hair.

David didn't answer.

Inside the train, passengers were already standing up and reaching into the overhead rack to gather their belongings.

"One thing about an unexpected overnight stay," Rab said, "is that we don't have to worry about baggage."

"Which is good, because I can go straight to the lodging house and take a bath," Susanna said.

"Hmm, I need a bath, too," Rab teased. "Can I take one with you?"

"Ha. The tub is barely big enough for one person. I could just see both of us in there. We would really have to be close . . ." Susanna paused in midsentence, then blushed. "That is your point, isn't it?"

"Why, Susanna, you are blushing. After yesterday, I didn't think you had a blush left in you."

"Hush," Susanna said, softening the word with a smile.

The train came to a halt, and everyone started toward

the end of the car to exit, but Susanna stopped halfway there. "You go ahead and get off. I left something back at the seat. It'll just take a second."

"All right," Rab said, continuing toward the exit.

As soon as Rab stepped down from the train, Margaret rushed toward him and threw her arms around him.

"Darling!" she shouted, then she kissed him, full on the mouth.

Susanna had just appeared in the vestibule of the train car, carrying the wilted bouquet she had retrieved, when she witnessed the reunion between Rab and a strange woman.

"Margaret! What—what are you doing here?" Rab asked, pushing her away gently, but firmly.

"Oh, well, darling, when Lila told me that you were in danger, my heart just leapt to my throat I was so frightened. I just had to come here no matter what Daddy had to say. Besides, there are some things about our wedding that only you can decide."

"Your wedding?" Susanna asked in a choked voice. Dropping the wilted flowers onto the brick depot platform, Susanna stepped down from the train, then started running away as quickly as she could, her eyes burning with tears.

"Susanna, wait!" Rab called. "Wait! I can explain!"

Margaret watched the woman run off, then saw Rab start after her. He took only a few steps in pursuit, then stopped and watched until the woman he had called Susanna disappeared behind the depot. He stood there for a long moment, looking in the direction in which the woman had gone.

Margaret stared at Rab's back until he turned and came back to her. She had never seen such an expression of pain on any man's face as she saw on his.

"Rab. Rab, who was that woman?"

"It is the woman I love."

Margaret forced a laugh. "Oh, don't be silly. You may have had some dalliance with her, but surely you are experienced enough to know the difference between that and love."

"What are you doing here, Margaret? Why did you come?"

"Why, darling, I had to come. David sent Lila a telegram, telling her that an attempt had been made on your life. I couldn't remain in San Francisco knowing that you were in danger."

"Didn't he also say that the man who had made the attempt was in jail?"

"Yes, but there could be others. Anyway, I know that your business here is over and you were about to come home, so I just made the decision to come back with you. We have much to talk about."

"Yes, we do." The expression on Rab's face told her that he didn't mean plans for the wedding.

Rab walked away, and as he passed David, David said, "I'm sorry, Rab. I had no idea. I'm sorry."

Rab put his hand on David's shoulder and squeezed it lightly.

*   *   *

Later, much later that day, Mary Beth knocked on the door. "Susanna? Susanna, it's me, Mary Beth."

Susanna opened the door just far enough for Mary Beth to see her red-rimmed eyes. She was holding a tear-soaked handkerchief. "Is it him again?"

"Yes. This is the third time he's been here."

"I don't want to see him. And tell him, please, don't come back again."

"Are you sure that's what you want?"

Susanna closed the door without answering.

Mary Beth went back down the stairs and saw Rab pacing back and forth by the front door. He looked up, his face in agony.

"I'm sorry, Mr. Trudeau, but she doesn't want to talk to you."

"She's got to talk to me. She has to let me explain. She has the wrong idea."

"Did she see a woman kiss you and discuss plans for your wedding?"

"Yes."

"Then, how does she have the wrong idea?"

"She did see a woman kiss me, and she did hear her say *wedding*. But that's where she has it wrong, because I have no intention of marrying that woman."

"But you are engaged to her?"

"I was. I won't be engaged any longer. I am going to break it off. I don't love Margaret, I am in love with Susanna."

"You're going to break it off?"

"Yes."

"So now Susanna must not only deal with a broken heart, she also must deal with breaking up your engagement."

"I—listen, she doesn't understand, you don't understand. I don't love Margaret, I never did."

"I'm sorry, Mr. Trudeau, but I think perhaps you should leave now. As I told you, Susanna doesn't want to see you, and all of your explanations to me do no good at all."

Rab nodded. "I understand. Thank you, Mary Beth, for your trouble. Please, do one more thing for me. Please tell Susanna that no matter what she thinks, I love her."

"Good-bye, Mr. Trudeau."

Rab checked out of the McAuliffe House, then went over to the International. He saw David in the lobby.

"Did you see her?" David asked.

Rab shook his head. "She won't see me." He noticed David's luggage on the floor beside him.

"You're going back to San Francisco?"

"Margaret and I have tickets on tonight's train. I'm sorry we didn't go back yesterday, before all this happened."

"It doesn't matter."

"It's all my fault," David said. "I let Lila push you into this. I knew you didn't want to get married, but I didn't say anything."

"Don't blame yourself, David. I knew it, too, and I

didn't say a word." Rab sighed. "But I'm going to now. Regardless of what happens between Susanna and me, I have no intention of ever marrying Margaret."

"When are you going to tell her?"

"I think she probably has a pretty good idea now. But I'll be taking the train back with you."

"What about your horse?"

"I've already made arrangements for Rebel. He'll be coming on the next train."

Only three people were in the depot for the late train: Rab, David, and Margaret. David, wanting to give Rab and Margaret an opportunity to talk, moved down to the far end of the waiting room.

"I'm not angry with you, darling," Margaret said. "I know how men are. I know that men have—let us say— needs. You have been here for a long time. It's only natural for you to find someone to take care of those needs. Once we get back to San Francisco, and you are mingling with your own kind again, instead of the—the type of people you find here, why I'm sure everything will work out just fine."

Rab looked at Margaret, but didn't answer her.

"Oh, and just wait until you see what the caterer has planned. Caviar and cream cheese, green salad, cream of red-bell-pepper soup, then lemon sorbet before the main course. It's going to be veal scaloppini with small red potatoes, carved in the shape of mushrooms, and the groom's cake will be chocolate cake with raspberry sauce."

The building began to shake then. "Oh, here's our train," Margaret said brightly, either unaware or uncaring of Rab's feelings. "I'm so excited. We have so much to do when we get back to San Francisco. I can hardly wait."

Annie Biggs had accompanied Roland Montgomery to the depot. Montgomery, a lawyer from Denver, had been Annie's client earlier in the evening, and he had asked her to come see him off, promising that the carriage he had hired would take her back.

They were standing alongside the carriage as the train arrived.

"Well, my dear," Montgomery said, reaching out to take Annie's hand in his. He raised it to his lips and kissed it. "As usual, you have made my visit to this otherwise dull and dreary city most enjoyable."

"It is always nice to spend some time with you, Roland." Annie gave him a broad smile. It wasn't hard to smile at him; he was thoughtful and not demanding, often taking her to dinner before business. And he paid well.

"You will spend some time with me when next I return?"

"You can count on it," Annie said.

She remained by the carriage as he walked toward the train so she could give him a final wave.

That was when she saw Rab Trudeau walking toward the train with a beautiful and elegantly dressed woman. From the way she was clinging to him, this did not appear to be a casual encounter. Annie watched as they boarded.

Then through the windows into the lit car, she saw them taking the same seat.

Annie couldn't help but feel angry and a little betrayed. She had liked Trudeau, had liked the way he treated her at the dance. She had thought that he would be Susanna's way out of the marriage that Kirkland was forcing upon her.

Annie turned back toward the carriage, then climbed in unassisted while the driver remained on his seat.

"Back to the hotel, miss?" the driver asked.

"No. To Chaney House."

✳ 21 ✳

Silver Mine Fraud
Publisher and Mine Owners Charged
(By wire from the Territorial Enterprise)

A recent story published in the Virginia City Pioneer was in fact the downfall of James Loudin, longtime publisher of that same newspaper. The article, written by a novice reporter who, no doubt, had little idea of the consequences of the story being penned, outlined in great detail the nefarious dealings not only of Loudin, but also of Messrs. Sam Van Cleve, William Burdick, and John Sheehan, owners of the now defunct North Star Mine.

That story resulted in the suspension of publication of the Pioneer newspaper, and its future is uncertain. Loudin has let it be known that the newspaper is for sale as he will need the funds thus generated to hire a lawyer to plead his case. It should be noted here that buying the

Pioneer would be a most foolish investment, as it has never equaled in quality, or distribution, the Enterprise. It is not believed by those who make it their business to pontificate on such matters that the Pioneer would long survive a new owner.

According to the novice reporter, who by the article became unemployed, the publisher of the Pioneer, working in collusion with the mine owners, undertook to print a series of articles containing spurious information about the mines, the purpose being to manipulate the price of stock.

Mr. Rab Trudeau, who this paper has learned is the majority owner of the Silver Falcon, suspected foul play with the reporting on the status of his mine. To investigate that, he appeared in Washoe and Storey Counties passing himself off not as a mine owner, but as a detective. Van Cleve, Burdick, and Sheehan, in an effort to keep Trudeau from discovering their corruption, hired the well-known regulator Asa Teague to murder Trudeau.

Teague's attempt failed when Mr. Trudeau, a man of known courage, strength, and physical prowess, overcame Teague while he was in the act and delivered the brigand to jail. Teague, in a plea bargain, has sought to lighten his own sentence by testifying against the aforementioned perpetrators of fraud, who are now in jail.

Mr. Trudeau has returned to San Francisco.

Rab was in the office of Sunset Enterprises. A two-day growth of beard and sunken eyes gave evidence that he had neither slept nor eaten in the last forty-eight hours, subsisting entirely on coffee laced with brandy. Forty-eight hours since Susanna, hurt and angry, had run from him. Forty-eight hours, and a lifetime ago.

He read the article with mixed emotions, pride in that it was Susanna who wrote the story that brought the corruption to a halt, and sadness because he had lost her. Had he lost her forever?

That he didn't know.

The article had called him a man of courage. What a lie that was. If he had been a man of courage, he would have told Margaret on the night she announced plans for their wedding that he didn't love her, and that he didn't want to marry without love.

And it wasn't just then. Even on the train ride back, he failed to tell her.

He had ridden in silence while she babbled on and on about the wedding:

"Of course, we aren't the only ones getting married next month. There are several other weddings planned in our social set, but none, not one, will be as grand as ours."

"Margaret, I don't want to get married."

"Oh, don't be silly. I've heard about this and read about this. Many people start having second thoughts as the wedding approaches. It is called pre-wedding nerves. It's only natural, darling."

"I don't want to get married."

"Well, I won't worry about it now, and I'm not even going to try and convince you that you're being silly. The articles I have read say that is something you should never do. You will get over it soon enough."

"Margaret, listen to me."

"Hush, darling." Margaret placed her finger across his lips. "This isn't something we should discuss on a train in front of strangers. I told you, it's only natural that you would be nervous."

Rab did not pursue it any further while they were on the train, but he was determined to make her understand, once and for all, the next time he saw her.

"Mr. Trudeau?" It was the purser for Sunset Shipping Lines.

"Yes, Mr. Sinclair?"

"I hate to bother you, sir, but Miss Worthington is here. Shall I let her in?"

Rab sighed. "Yes, show her in."

Rab stood to greet Margaret as she rushed in, giving him a perfunctory kiss on the lips. She had been shopping and was carrying three boxes with her.

"Am I disturbing you, darling? Oh, my, you look awful. When is the last time you shaved? Or changed clothes? You aren't among the uncivilized anymore."

The tone of her voice showed that she either didn't understand or wouldn't accept that their situation had changed.

Rab held his hand toward the sofa. "Sit, Margaret. We need to talk."

"Yes, we do. I have so much to tell you. Oh, wait until you see what I bought today. I found three hats, all so beautiful that I couldn't make up my mind which one I wanted, so I bought all three of them." She started to open one of the boxes.

"Margaret," Rab said more sternly. "We have to talk."

"All right, dear."

"I meant what I said on the train. There will be no wedding."

"But why?"

"It's about love. I've always envied what David and Lila had. I never thought it would happen to me—I knew it couldn't happen with us. I don't love you, Margaret."

"Oh, pooh, what is love, anyway?"

"I don't blame you for not knowing. I didn't know either, until I met Susanna. I have been happier on that mountain over the last six weeks than I have ever been in my life. I love Susanna. I don't know whether she will have me or not, but I know that I will never love another woman the way I love her."

"You mean you were serious? That—tart that I saw in Virginia City was more than just a fling?"

"She is much more. There will be no wedding between us, Margaret."

The smile left Margaret's face to be replaced not by tears, but by anger. Her eyes squinted, and she pulled her mouth into a snarl, then she threw one of the hatboxes at him.

"You can't just throw me away like an old shoe," she screeched.

"I'm sorry. Margaret, believe me, I never had any intention of breaking your heart. It's just . . ."

"Breaking my heart?" Margaret laughed, a high trilling cackle without mirth. "You arrogant bastard! Do you think my heart is broken? It's not a broken heart I must deal with. Do you have any idea how humiliating this will be to me?"

"That's what this breakup is to you? Humiliating?"

"Yes, humiliating. All of San Francisco society was expecting us to wed. It would have been more than a marriage, actually. It would have been a merger. Now I will have to send my regrets to everyone who has received an invitation, the governor, both senators, the mayor."

"Margaret, are you saying that you never loved me?"

"Oh, you silly goose. What does love have to do with marriage among people of our station?"

"I see."

"If you think I'm going to go away like some wilted violet, you are wrong. Everybody in San Francisco thinks you're such a prince. Wait until I get through with you."

"What will it take, Margaret?"

"What do you mean?"

Rab opened the drawer to his desk and pulled out his book of bank drafts and a pen. He dipped the pen into the inkwell and held it poised over a blank draft.

Margaret smiled broadly. "I think we can come to some accommodation."

*   *   *

Shortly after Margaret left, there was a light knock on the door; then it opened slightly, and David stuck his head in.

"Rab?"

"Yes, come on in." Rab pulled open the bottom drawer of his desk and took out a bottle of brandy and two glasses. "Have a drink with me?"

"I don't know." David looked at Rab with a worried expression.

Rab chuckled, poured two fingers into each glass, then stood up and walked back to the sink, where he emptied the rest of the liquor.

"Don't worry, David. I'm not going to lose myself in a bottle."

"I wasn't really worried."

"Really?"

David smiled. "Well, not too much." He held the glass out toward Rab, and Rab returned the salute.

David drank the liquor, then set the empty glass down. "I saw Margaret leave." The expression on his face put forth the unasked question.

"Yes, Margaret. We have come to an agreement." Rab glanced at the open book of bank drafts.

"I see," David said with an understanding nod. "Oh, Lila sends her love, and her apology, and begs your forgiveness."

"What? Lila is apologizing to me? Shouldn't that be the other way around? I know that I upset her when I broke off the engagement."

"I think she finally understands how it was, how you felt trapped into the marriage. She said, and these are her exact words, 'Thank God he didn't go through with it.'"

"You are married to a fine woman, David."

"I think so. So, now the question is, when are you going back?"

"I don't know. I think Susanna might need a little time."

"Don't give her too much time. Something like this needs to be perfectly balanced."

"I know. And right now I feel like a tightrope walker wearing a blindfold."

It was three full days before Susanna left her room. She didn't eat a bite the first day; the second day Mary Beth brought her a biscuit and a cup of hot tea and talked her into taking that. On the third day Annie brought her a bowl of soup.

Finally, on the fourth day, Susanna came downstairs. Annie and Mary Beth were playing a game of whist in the parlor.

Mary Beth saw her first. "Susanna. Oh, I'm so glad you came down. Are you hungry? Can I get you something to eat?"

"I'll wait until Harriet serves lunch."

"I guess you know you are a heroine," Annie said. "The *Enterprise* ran a story. Loudin and the North Star owners are all in jail."

"Poor Mr. Loudin," Susanna said. "I can't help but feel sorry for him."

"Well, I would say he isn't worth feeling sorry for," Annie said, "but at least if you are feeling sorry for him, maybe you will quit feeling sorry for yourself."

"Oh, Annie," Susanna said. "You remember, I asked you once how do you know if you are in love? Once I fell in love with Rab, I didn't have to question it. I just knew that it was so."

"That's too bad. I'm afraid Mr. Trudeau turned out to be a scoundrel after all," Annie said.

"He came here to see you several times before he left," Mary Beth said. "He told me to tell you that he loved you. He said that he didn't love that woman, that he had never loved her, and he wasn't going to marry her."

"That may be so," Annie said. "But I saw the way that woman was hanging on him when they got on the train."

"What are you going to do now?" Mary Beth asked.

"I don't have any choice. I'm going to ask Mr. Kirkland if I can work for him."

"You could always try to get on at the *Enterprise*," Annie suggested. "Mr. Elliott went there."

Susanna shook her head. "No. I know you won't understand this—I'm not sure that I do. But, after all this, I really don't care to work at a newspaper again."

"Are you feeling any better, Susanna?" Mary Beth asked.

"I don't know if I will ever feel any better."

"Honey, you aren't the first woman who has had to deal with a broken heart," Annie said. "And it is for sure and certain that you won't be the last."

"Oh." Mary Beth walked over to the hall table and picked up a packet of papers. "You have a letter, and three telegrams."

"I don't even want to see them," Susanna said, waving them away.

Mary Beth put them back on the table. "I'll just leave them here."

On the fifth day Susanna went to work for Gus Kirkland, though it was hardly worth it, for the amount of money he was paying her barely allowed her to stay at the lodging house.

It wasn't hard to catch on to the work; she had done it before, as Kirkland had employed Jesse, Alice, and Susanna while they were growing up. *Employed* wasn't quite the word for it, because then she had worked for him without pay. He had not singled her out, though, because at the time Jesse and Alice had also worked for free.

When she returned to work, she was surprised to see that Jesse was there as well.

"I don't have any choice," Jesse told her. "I lost all my money in bad investments."

"Oh, Jesse, I told you not to invest in North Star."

"It wasn't just North Star. I was speculating in all of them and none too wisely. I should have listened to you."

Susanna did the work almost by rote, never smiling, not even at the customers. Because neither Gus nor Minnie knew about her affair with Rab, they attributed her melancholy to her having been fired from the newspaper, and Gus expressed some reservations about letting her work because he felt that she might be running customers away.

She had told no one in the family the real reason for her depression, but she knew she was going to have to tell Jesse. It took her a while to summon the courage, but after she had been there a week, she followed Jesse down to the stockroom when he went to take an inventory of men's boots.

The stockroom was under the store in the back, and because it was dug into the side of the mountain, it almost gave the illusion of being a cave. It was dark and dreary, and neither Susanna nor Alice had ever been comfortable going there alone.

"Jesse?"

"What are you doing down here? I thought you didn't like this place."

"I wanted to ask you something. But I wanted to ask it in private."

Jesse looked around the stockroom and smiled. "You can't get much more private than this."

"I want to ask you to marry me."

"What?" Jesse replied with a gasp. "You want me to marry you?" He was shocked by her proposal.

"Yes. Mr. Kirkland has asked me to marry you, and I agreed."

"Oh, I see." Jesse stared at her for a moment. "And that's it? The only reason you want to marry me is just because Pop asked you to?"

"Not entirely." Susanna took a deep breath. "There is another reason."

"Oh?"

"You know the man that was here for a while, the one everybody thought was a detective?"

"Yeah, Rab Trudeau. Turns out he owns the Silver Falcon," Jesse said, thinking he was giving her new information.

"Yes."

"What about him?"

Tears began to slide down Susanna's cheeks. "I—I may be carrying his baby."

Jesse stared at her for a long moment, not in condemnation, nor anger, nor even jealousy. She actually thought that she saw compassion in his expression.

"Do you love him, Susanna?"

"That doesn't matter."

"Do you love him?"

"I—I thought I did. That was before I learned what a scoundrel he is."

"So he has gone back to San Francisco without so much as another word, has he?"

"Yes. I mean no. He has sent a letter every day. And I've received at least a dozen telegrams from him."

"What does he have to say?"

"I don't know. I haven't read any of them."

"Why not?"

"There is another woman, a woman he is engaged to. She came here to see him."

Jesse took a handkerchief from his pocket and handed it to her. "Wipe your tears, little one."

"Thank you." She took the handkerchief and held it to her eyes.

"Do you love me, Susanna?"

"I have always loved you, Jesse. But—"

"I know. I've always loved you, too, in the same way. I've always considered you a sister no matter what Pop and Mom said. But if you need me to marry you, I will. And if you are carrying another man's baby, we'll keep it our secret."

"Oh, Jesse," she said, the tears springing anew. She embraced Jesse, who pulled her to him.

She felt an overwhelming warmth of love for him— sisterly love.

"Let's tell no one until after it's over."

"Not even Pop and Mom? Not even Alice?"

"Nobody."

"We'll have to have a witness."

"I'll ask Annie to be our witness."

Jesse chuckled. "Annie. Yeah, I like that."

"Honey, are you sure this is what you want to do?" Annie asked when Susanna told her what she had planned.

"I'm positive."

"I don't know, I think you should think about this for a while."

"I thought you were the one who was so down on Rab. You saw him at the depot with that woman."

"Yes. But I've also read his telegrams." She held her hand out before Susanna could say anything. "I know,

I know, it's not right to read other people's mail or their telegrams. But I believe he really loves you, Susanna. You should at least hear him out."

"It's too late for that. I have asked Jesse to marry me and he has agreed. And Jesse knows all about Rab. Now, will you be my witness or not?"

"Of course I will. If that's really what you want."

"It's what I want."

"You're going to marry Jesse?" Mary Beth asked.

"Mary Beth! You were listening?" Annie challenged.

"Yes, I'm sorry. Susanna, you are making a big mistake."

"It's my mistake to make."

The train was less than five miles from Virginia City, but it had slowed considerably as it started climbing the steep grade that ended on Mount Davidson.

Rab was sitting next to the window looking down at the side of the track. It seemed to him that they were going so slowly that he could see each small ballast pebble as they passed. He found himself, almost involuntarily, pushing against the seat in front of him as if in that way he could help the train up the grade.

He got up from his seat and walked up to the vestibule in the front of the car; then, holding on to the assist rail, he leaned out to look forward along the side of the train. He could see each car all the way up to the engine, and as the track made a curve to the right, he could see the big driver wheels wreathed in steam from the drive cylinder, and he could hear the chugging sound rolling back to him. He had to fight against the urge to leap down from the train and start running.

Annie went with Susanna to the house of Judge Vernon Head, where the marriage was to be performed. Jesse was waiting for them, sitting alone in the swing on the front porch.

At one time, Judge Head's house had been one of the finest residences in Virginia City. A big house, it had a wraparound porch, cupolas, gables, dormer windows, and four chimneys. A widower now, Judge Head had let his house run down in the years since his wife had died. It was now badly in need of a paint job, and some of the windows were broken and boarded over.

"Are you sure you want to do this? You don't have to, you know," Jesse said as he rose from the swing.

"Let's go in," Susanna said.

"All right," Jesse said, then knocked on the front door.

A long, formal table was in the dining room, but it was piled high with papers, evidence that it had not been used for its original purpose for many years.

After Jesse told him what they wanted, Judge Head began shuffling the papers around, mumbling to himself, "I know I have some here." Then, with a triumphant grunt, he found what he was looking for. "Here it is. A marriage license."

Pushing some of the papers aside, he sat down and began laboriously filling out the form.

When the train came into the depot, Rab leaped down from the car before it had even stopped rolling. He ran toward a parked carriage for hire and jumped into the backseat.

"Chaney House!" he shouted. "Hurry!"

The driver snapped the reins, and the team moved out at a trot. Because the lodging house was downhill from the depot, the carriage moved at a brisk pace.

At Chaney House, Mary Beth was sitting in the parlor, quietly weeping.

"If it is what she wants, we have no right to interfere," Harriet said.

"It's not what she wants, Mama, you know that as well as I do. She doesn't love Jesse. Not like that, anyway. She loves Rab Trudeau."

"One of the lessons we all must learn, darling, is that we don't always get what we want."

There was a knock at the door, and Mary Beth stood, but her mother held out her hand.

"I'll get it. Unless you want to answer it with tears in your eyes."

Mary Beth sat back down, lost in the disquieting thoughts of her closest friend getting herself into a loveless marriage. She heard voices at the front door, indistinct, but something about the male voice got her attention. Getting up, she moved into the foyer. It was Rab.

"Mary Beth, where is she?" Rab asked anxiously.

"Do you have a carriage?" Mary Beth asked.

"Yes."

"Come on! Maybe it isn't too late!" Mary Beth rushed past him, and Rab, knowing there would be no time for questions, hurried after her.

"Hurry!" Mary Beth shouted as she climbed into the carriage. "The corner of Howard and Taylor as fast as you can get there."

"That's all uphill," the driver protested. "I'm not sure I can make my horses run all the way."

"Can you make them run for a hundred dollars?" Rab asked.

"Mister, for a hundred dollars, they will sprout wings and fly."

"Ward? Your last name is Ward? But you have gone by the name Kirkland ever since you've been in this town," Judge Head said.

"She's not my sister, Judge," Jesse said. "My family took her in when she was a little girl. Her last name is Ward."

"All right, then, let's get started. Who is the witness?"

"I am, Judge," Annie said.

A look of recognition passed between Annie and Judge Head. The judge had been a widower for a long time. He cleared his throat. "All right. Mr. Kirkland, Miss Ward, if you'd stand there in the doorway, we'll get started."

Susanna and Jesse moved into the doorway between the dining room and the parlor. Judge Head cleaned his glasses, then put them on.

"I've got a book of marriage ceremonies here somewhere," the judge said as he rifled through more papers on the table. "Ah, here it is. Now we're ready."

He stood before them. "Now, Mr. Kirkland, Miss Kirkland, we are gathered here—"

"Miss Ward," Jesse corrected.

"Miss Ward. We are gathered here—"

"No!" a man's voice shouted as the front door burst open. "Susanna, you can't marry him! I love you and you love me. You know that!"

"Here, what is this?" Judge Head asked. "What do you mean bursting in here like this?"

Jesse looked over at Susanna and, seeing the expression on her face, held up his hand. "Judge, hold it up for a moment, would you?"

"What is going on?"

"Give us a minute."

Jesse looked at Susanna, then over at Rab. The expressions on both their faces told him everything he needed to know.

"It's not too late, Susanna," Jesse said.

"But I, Jesse, you . . ."

Jesse kissed Susanna on her forehead; then, with a smile, he walked over to the table where the marriage license lay. Picking up a pen, he drew a line through *Jesse Kirkland* and then wrote in *Rab Trudeau* above it.

"What are you doing?" Judge Head asked.

"My sister loves this man. And I love her too much to see her make a mistake. They are the ones you are going to marry."

"Your sister?" Judge Head sputtered.

"You wouldn't understand."

"Will you marry me, Susanna?" Rab asked.

Susanna stared at him as if unable to believe that he was actually here.

Rab stepped up to her and took her hands in his. "I love you, Susanna. I love only you, and I want to spend the rest of my life with you."

Susanna smiled. "Would you take me to Pago Pago?"

Rab laughed in unbridled happiness. "My own sweet Susanna." He took her in his arms and kissed her.

Epilogue

The *Cajun Queen*, a seven-hundred-ton bark, lay along-side the Vallejo Street Wharf. Mr. and Mrs. Rab Trudeau were standing next to the gangplank, saying good-bye to David, Lila, and their children. Lila was holding little Davey.

"I've made arrangements with Randolph," David said. "He will have a ship meet you on the other side of the Isthmus. That should take almost a month off your voyage."

"Thanks," Rab said.

"I think it's wonderful that you are going to reconcile with your father so he could meet Susanna," Lila said. "I know he is going to love her as much as we do. I just wish that we were coming as well."

"I wish you were, too," Susanna said. "I've never been to New Orleans, and I am so looking forward to meeting Rab's family." She reached for the baby, and Lila handed him to her. "I'm going to miss this handsome little tyke." She hugged him to her.

"Oh, I nearly forgot." David reached into his attaché case. "This just came; it is the first copy of the *Pioneer* since you bought it. And there is a note for you, Susanna." David handed her the note.

> *Dear Susanna,*
>
> *So, you run off and get married, leaving me to pick up the pieces of the mess you made with the newspaper, did you? Well, not to worry, Annie has proven to be a big help, and we'll do just fine. Congratulations, and do stop in to see us if you ever come back this way.*
>
> *B. D. Elliott*
> *Editor, Virginia City Pioneer*

Half an hour later, the *Cajun Queen* was sailing through the Golden Gate, with Rab and Susanna at the stern, watching the city of San Francisco recede behind them. A frothy, white wake marked the passage of the ship.

"Nervous?" he asked.

"A little."

"You needn't be. We have a fair wind behind us."

"I wasn't talking about the ship," Susanna said.

Rab put his arm around her and pulled her closer to him. "Neither was I."

Fantasy.
Temptation.
Adventure.

**Visit PocketAfterDark.com,
an all-new website just for Urban
Fantasy and Romance Readers!**

• Exclusive access to the hottest
urban fantasy and romance titles!

• Read and share reviews on
the latest books!

• Live chats with your favorite
romance authors!

• Vote in online polls!

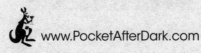

www.PocketAfterDark.com

26119

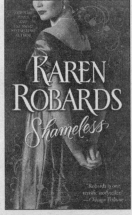
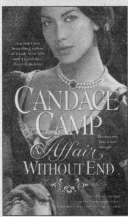
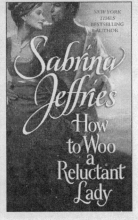